One Hot
CHASE

Other Books by Anna Durand

One Hot Chance (Hot Brits, Book One)
One Hot Roomie (Hot Brits, Book Two)
One Hot Crush (Hot Brits, Book Three)
The Dixon Brothers Trilogy (Hot Brits, Books 1-3)
One Hot Escape (Hot Brits, Book Four)
One Hot Rumor (Hot Brits, Book Five)
One Hot Christmas (Hot Brits, Book Six)
One Hot Scandal (Hot Brits, Book Seven)
One Hot Deal (Hot Brits, Book Eight)
One Hot Favor (Hot Brits, Book Nine)
One Hot Bash (Hot Brits, Book Ten)
One Hot Moment (Hot Brits, Book Eleven)
Natural Obsession (Au Naturel Nights, Book One)
Natural Deception (Au Naturel Nights, Book Two)
Natural Passion (Au Naturel Trilogy, Book One)
Natural Impulse (Au Naturel Trilogy, Book Two)
Natural Satisfaction (Au Naturel Trilogy, Book Three)
Lachlan in a Kilt (The Ballachulish Trilogy, Book One)
Aidan in a Kilt (The Ballachulish Trilogy, Book Two)
Rory in a Kilt (The Ballachulish Trilogy, Book Three)
The American Wives Club (A Hot Brits/Hot Scots/Au Naturel Crossover)
Brit vs. Scot (A Hot Brits/Hot Scots/Au Naturel Crossover)
A Novel Secret (A Hot Brits/Hot Scots/Au Naturel Crossover) (
Dangerous in a Kilt (Hot Scots, Book One)
Wicked in a Kilt (Hot Scots, Book Two)
Scandalous in a Kilt (Hot Scots, Book Three)
The MacTaggart Brothers Trilogy (Hot Scots, Books 1-3)
Gift-Wrapped in a Kilt (Hot Scots, Book Four)
Notorious in a Kilt (Hot Scots, Book Five)
Insatiable in a Kilt (Hot Scots, Book Six)
Lethal in a Kilt (Hot Scots, Book Seven)
Irresistible in a Kilt (Hot Scots, Book Eight)
Devastating in a Kilt (Hot Scots, Book Nine)
Spellbound in a Kilt (Hot Scots, Book Ten)
Relentless in a Kilt (Hot Scots, Book Eleven)
Incendiary in a Kilt (Hot Scots, Book Twelve)
Wild in a Kilt (Hot Scots, Book Thirteen)
Unstoppable in a Kilt (Hot Scots, Book Fourteen)
The Notorious Dr. MacT (A Hot Scots Prequel)
The British Bastard (A Hot Scots Prequel)
The Complete Echo Power Trilogy
The Janusite Trilogy (Undercover Elementals, Books 1-3)
Obsidian Hunger (Undercover Elementals, Book Four)
Unbidden Hunger (Undercover Elementals, Book Five)
The Thirteenth Fae (Undercover Elementals, Book Six)
Cyneric (Undercover Elementals, Book 7)
Janus (Undercover Elementals, Book 8)

One Hot CHASE

Hot Brits, Book Twelve

ANNA DURAND

JACOBSVILLE BOOKS JB MARIETTA, OHIO`

ONE HOT CHASE

ISBN: 978-1-958144-66-4 (paperback)
ISBN: 978-1-958144-67-1 (ebook)
ISBN: 978-1-958144-68-8 (retail audiobook)
ISBN: 978-1-958144-69-5 (library audio)

Manufactured in the United States.

Jacobsville Books
www.JacobsvilleBooks.com

Publisher's Cataloging-in-Publication Data
provided by Five Rainbows Cataloging Services

Names: Durand, Anna.
Title: One hot chase / Anna Durand.
Description: Marietta, OH : Jacobsville Books, 2024. | Series: Hot Brits, bk. 12.
Identifiers: ISBN 978-1-958144-66-4 (paperback) | ISBN 978-1-958144-67-1 (ebook) | ISBN 978-1-958144-68-8 (retail audiobook) | 978-1-958144-69-5 (library audio)
Subjects: LCSH: Man-woman relationships--Fiction. | Love-hate relationships--Fiction. | British--Fiction. | Americans--Fiction. | Romance fiction. | BISAC: FICTION / Romance / Contemporary. | FICTION / Romance / Romantic Comedy. | FICTION / Romance / International. | GSAFD: Love stories. | Humorous fiction.
Classification: LCC PS3604.U724 O25 2024 (print) | LCC PS3604.U724 (ebook) | DDC 813/.6--dc23.

Prologue

Sabrina

Picking out a wedding gown is no easy task. It's like trying to find the elusive Moby Dick in an ocean of chiffon and lace. But this gown isn't even for me. I'm hunting for the perfect dress for my sister. She's about to marry the sweet, sexy British man of her dreams.

I watch while Tabitha tries on yet another wedding dress, turning this way and that in front of a full-length mirror while biting her bottom lip. I love my sister, but she's kind of turning into a bridezilla. Okay, Tabby isn't that crazed about her upcoming nuptials. But she has tried on fourteen gowns in the last twenty minutes. Time for a sisterly intervention.

"Tabby, why don't you just close your eyes and grab a dress at random?"

My sister gapes at me. "Is that supposed to be a joke? It's not funny. This is the one and only time I'll ever get married."

"Yeah, I know. Sorry. I don't mean to be obnoxious. You finally found the right guy, and I'm so happy for you and Spencer. If you want to try on fifty more dresses, that's fine with me."

Tabby drags me into a suffocating hug. "Thank you, Bree. You're the best sister."

I'm the only sister she has, but saying so might trigger another suffocating hug. This time, I might not survive getting smothered. Maybe I lack enthusiasm for dress shopping because the only man I ever married turned out to be a skunk in men's clothing. Peter Levine was not my Prince Charming, though I'd thought he might be. I have the worst taste in men. Knowing that hasn't spared me from heartache.

Tabitha bows her head and sighs pitifully. "I can't try on any more gowns. It's hopeless."

I sling an arm around her shoulders, tugging her close. "No more doom and gloom talk. You found your Prince Charming, a guy who adores you and would do anything to make you happy. Not only is Spencer British and hot, but he's also completely devoted to you. So, turn that frown upside down. We'll find the right dress."

Tabitha kisses my cheek. "Don't know what I'd do without you, Bree."

"Why don't I go hunt through the racks to find something different? You should sit down and relax. Okay?"

She nods.

I walk out of the changing room and march down every aisle, even ducking inside empty changing rooms in case someone abandoned the perfect dress in there. Just when I think I should give up, I finally see it. The Dress. Not just any wedding gown, mind you, but the absolutely perfect one that was made for Tabitha. A sense of exhilaration energizes me as I nab the Moby Dick of wedding dresses.

Then I hoist it above my head and grin. "This is the one, Tabby."

My sister's eyes widen as she takes in the gown I've selected for her. It's a sleek, off-the-shoulder number with delicate lace detailing and a subtle shimmer that enhances Tabby's creamy complexion. I can already picture how it'll hug her curves and make Spencer's jaw drop when he sees her walking down the aisle.

"Oh, Bree," she breathes, reaching out to touch the fabric. "It's...it's perfect."

I beam, feeling a rush of sisterly pride. "I told you we'd find it. Now, let's get you into this beauty."

As I help Tabby slip into the dress, I can't help but feel a pang of...something. Not quite jealousy, but a wistfulness that catches me off guard. I push it aside, focusing on zipping her up and adjusting the bodice.

"Okay, turn around and look." I step back to give Tabitha a full view of herself in the mirror. The moment she sees her reflection, her eyes well up with tears. She turns slowly, taking in every angle, her fingers tracing the intricate lace patterns.

"It's...it's everything I dreamed of," she whispers, her voice thick with emotion.

I feel a lump form in my throat. Despite my earlier impatience, seeing my sister so radiant and happy makes my heart swell. "You look absolutely stunning, Tabby. Spencer won't know what hit him."

My sister laughs, a sound of pure joy that echoes through the fitting room. She turns to me, her eyes sparkling. "Thank you, Bree. I don't know how you do it, but you always know exactly what I need."

I shrug, trying to play it cool even as I feel a wave of emotion washing over me. "What can I say? It's a gift."

My sister pulls me into another hug, more gently this time. "You're going to find your happily ever after too, you know. Someone who deserves you."

"Let's focus on your fairy tale, not my non-existent love life," I say breezily, deflecting the issue with a forced chuckle. "Now, spin around again. I want to make sure this dress is as perfect from the back as it is from the front."

As Tabitha twirls amid the soft swish of fabric, I catch a glimpse of myself in the mirror. My messy bun has come half undone, wisps of strawberry blonde hair framing my face. I quickly tuck the loose strands behind my ears, trying to regain my composure. But as I watch Tabby beaming at her reflection, I feel a surge of emotions bubbling up inside me.

"You know, Tabby," I say, my voice softer than I intended, "I always thought you'd be the first one to get married. I might have walked down the aisle before you did, but you found your Prince Charming first. My failed marriage doesn't count. Funny how life throws you curveballs, huh?"

My sister's eyes meet mine in the mirror, her expression softening. "Oh, Bree..."

I wave my hand dismissively, forcing a laugh. "No, no, don't go all sappy on me now. I'm just thinking out loud. Besides, who needs a man when you've got a fabulous career as an insurance underwriter? It's every girl's secret ambition."

Naturally, my sister doesn't miss the self-deprecating sarcasm in my voice. Tabby turns to face me, her hands on her hips. "Sabrina Remington, don't you dare start that self-pity routine. You're brilliant, beautiful, and have so much to offer. Just because things didn't work out with Peter doesn't mean you're doomed to a life of loneliness and actuarial tables."

I roll my eyes, but can't help smiling at her fierce defense. "Okay, okay. I promise not to wallow in self-pity...at least not until after your wedding. Deal?"

Tabitha narrows her eyes at me. "That's not exactly the enthusiasm I was hoping for, but I'll take it. Now, help me out of this thing so we can go celebrate finding The One."

As I carefully unzip the gown, I can't resist asking, "By 'The One,' do you mean the dress or Spencer?"

Tabby laughs, her eyes twinkling. "Both, of course. Though right now, I'm dying to see my honey."

Once the alterations are done, and everything is paid for, we head for our favorite restaurant to celebrate. After that,

Tabby wants to go home to Spencer, and I don't blame her for that. She's happier than I've ever seen her.

Will I ever find my perfect catch? I'll find out soon enough. I'm flying to England tomorrow to begin my search. Somehow, I just know I'll find my PC, no matter how long the search takes.

Chapter One

Sabrina

Just call me Sabrina Remington, man hunter. I have all the tools of the trade—determination, sex appeal, and brains. My designer dress catches the attention of every passerby, but so far, I haven't spotted any potential targets in my search for a British hottie here in London. How difficult can it be? If my sister could snag her PC, I can do it too. That would be my Perfect Catch, not a personal computer or Prince Charming. Fairy tales and circuitry won't get me what I want. It's time to fry those circuits and get real about love.

I swore I'd never date again. But I don't want to be the only Remington girl who isn't hitched. That's pathetic.

As I step out of the taxi that brought me to my destination, I give the driver a generous tip. He kept me entertained with his jokes during the ride from Heathrow airport to the luxurious Savoy Hotel in the heart of London. The name alone exudes sophistication, doesn't it? *Savoy.* My almost brother-in-law, Spencer Halfenaked, used his connections to secure me a suite at one of the most exclusive hotels in the city. He's a great guy, and he makes my sister Tabitha so happy. Spencer's friend, the British billionaire Diana Hahn, arranged for me to stay in one of the swankiest suites at the Savoy.

But I digress.

As I make my way toward the building's entrance, I tilt my head back to admire the large, illuminated letters above me that spell out the name: S-A-V-O-Y. *Wow.* I'm actually here. A grin spreads across my face as I take in the moment. Finally, after all these years, I've left America and arrived at my destination. And it all begins here, at the Savoy.

I try my best to keep my jaw from dropping to the floor as I step into the foyer. *Holy cow.* This is by far the fanciest hotel I have ever laid eyes on, even compared to the ones I've seen on television. Growing up in Asheville, North Carolina, I never had much exposure to luxury or glamour. Londoners probably think this hotel is nothing special. As I come to a halt in the center of the grand foyer, I spin around slowly to take in every detail. That includes gorgeous harlequin tiles on the floor and a sparkling chandelier suspended above me.

When I'd said goodbye to my sister Tabitha at the Asheville airport, I'd asked her how much the hotel cost. It took some prodding, but I eventually got her to confess just how expensive the Savoy really is.

Four thousand dollars a night, that's how much. *Four thousand.*

Damn, I have amazing family and friends.

I approach the front desk, where a friendly-looking clerk welcomes me with a warm smile. He efficiently checks me in and gives me a key card, then gestures toward a bellhop who takes command of my luggage. We ride the elevator up to my floor and straight to the one-bedroom River View Suite, which offers a stunning panorama of the Thames. I tip the bellhop generously, thanks to the spending money donated by my family and friends. They support my wild ideas about man-hunting. Not sure why they're willing to finance my plan. I suppose they realize I'm on a mission and nothing can stop me from searching for my PC.

As soon as the bellhop leaves, I begin to explore my environment. The entryway and bathroom both feature stunning harlequin tiles, but ooh, the living room offers lavish wood floors. And wow, I've never seen such a huge TV before. There's even a cozy fireplace and a comfy sofa for cuddling up with my as-yet-unnamed honey.

Finally, I tear myself away from the fireplace and rush over to the big picture window to get a closer look, nearly stumbling over the small table and chairs placed only a few inches away from the glass. An exclamation of "shit!" bursts out of me, but I cannot be stopped. I plaster my hands and face to the window.

And I start talking to myself. It's a bad habit of mine. "Ooh! Oh, my god! That huge Ferris wheel is the London Eye."

Spencer described the giant wheel to me, and I can't wait to take a spin on it during my UK adventure. He also promised that I'd have a great view of Westminster Bridge from my suite, which I can now see in the distance. I can also see another bridge, but I can't recall its unusual name. And though Big Ben isn't within sight, I know it's nearby.

Once I'm done gawking, I turn around—and yelp.

My heart races briefly. I hadn't noticed the big mirror hanging on the wall beside the TV. It's possible I'm a little too excited about my ritzy vacation. A quick perusal of the rest of my digs convinces me that I've died and gone to heaven.

Once I've washed away the travel grime in my luxurious shower, I spiff myself up for the evening. Tonight, I won't need to leave the hotel. I'm heading straight for the Savoy's Beaufort Bar.

The moment I step into the room, I know this is where I'll find my first target. It sets the perfect mood for my hunt. With dim lighting and stylish chairs, plus a DJ spinning steamy tunes, I feel the warmth of anticipation blossoming within me. And as I browse the menu, I discover a variety of indulgent options like caviar, oysters, grilled chicken with spicy dressing, and tempting desserts. I settle on a cocktail first, selecting a Halo Highball made with whisky as well as carbonated strawberry and pink peppercorn wine water. Not sure what that is, but it sounds yummy.

Sipping my drink, I browse the room for a potential target. But most of the men who walk into the bar arrive with a woman on their arm. *Come on, there must be one hot single guy in this hotel.*

I take a slow sip of my cocktail, letting the flavors mingle on my tongue as I survey the bar. And there he is—my quarry. A tall, gorgeous man in a three-piece gray suit saunters into the room, his movements smooth and confident. He pauses for a moment, scanning the crowd before he begins to make his way toward me. As he comes closer, I can't resist admiring the way his suit hugs his muscular frame, accentuating the broadness of his shoulders and the narrowness of his waist. His dark brown hair is cropped short, just long enough for me to run my fingers through it. His crisp white shirt is open at the collar, revealing a hint of the tanned skin beneath.

When he finally reaches my table, our eyes meet and a jolt of electricity shoots through me. His slow, knowing smile shifts my pulse into overdrive and gives me a tingly feeling that spreads downward to settle between my thighs. I take a deep breath, inhaling the scent of his cologne, a mix of sandalwood and musk that makes my head spin. As I gaze into his deep blue eyes, I know this guy must be the one I've waited for.

He pushes one hand into his pocket, cocking his hip just enough to accentuate the bulge of his dick. "Darling, please tell me you're alone tonight."

A rush of warmth steals my breath away. That deep voice and his British accent could make me weak in the knees, if I weren't already sitting down. "Yes, I'm by myself. Would you care to join me?"

"I'd love nothing more."

He waits patiently while I adjust my position to make room for him on the bench. Then he settles onto the cushioned seat beside me and wraps an arm around my shoulders. "You, my sweet, are the most delectable creature I've ever met. You're American, aren't you? I noticed your accent when you spoke."

"Yes, I'm American. And you are British."

"Ah, but I'm so much more than merely British." His mouth kinks into a sly smile, and he winks. "Think of me as your erotic tour guide, the only man who can make all your most scandalous fantasies come true tonight."

My inner muscles clench, as if in anticipation of the delights he promises to deliver. I know this guy might be full of it, but I don't give a damn as long as I come like a rocket blasting off into outer space.

A one-night stand? I've never done that before. But I've had enough of always playing by the rules and getting burned.

I gaze directly into the shimmering pools of his blue eyes. "Yes, please, I want that."

"You won't regret it, darling." He leans in closer, and the heady scent of his cologne turns me on even more. "First, a kiss."

He leans in closer until his breaths whisper over our lips, almost touching. Now I can see the faint creases around his blue eyes and the darker rims that surround them. I can't believe I'm actually doing this. When he lightly presses his lips to mine, my jaw slackens and a soft sigh whispers out of me as my lids drift closed.

Suddenly, the intoxicating scent of him fades away.

He clucks his tongue. "Oh, no, pet, that won't do."

My eyes fly open. "What?"

The guy wrinkles his nose, and his lip curls. "Did you have any garlic this evening?"

I pull my head back. "Excuse me?"

He straightens and puckers his lips. "If you mean to seduce someone, at least have the decency to brush your teeth first. Halitosis is not a turn-on."

For a few seconds, I'm confused by his statement. Bad breath? I made sure to brush my teeth before coming to this bar. But I won't bother explaining myself to this jerk. He hasn't earned the right to criticize my personal hygiene.

"I haven't eaten anything yet," I quickly inform him, as if it's any of his business. "You are the rudest man I've ever met."

The jerk studies me for a moment, as if he's trying to assess my intelligence or…something. "Never mind that, pet. I'll overlook your halitosis this time. But for the benefit of your future lovers, remember to use mouthwash too."

"You jackass. I do not have bad breath."

The obnoxious man scoots closer until our thighs brush against each other. "Don't worry, darling, I'll still fuck you."

"No, you will not. I despise you. Out of all the jerks I've ever met, you win the prize for being the most insufferable."

Maybe that isn't entirely true. No one could surpass my ex-husband for the title of Rat Fink of the Century.

The stranger sitting beside me hooks his finger under my chin and kisses my cheek so delicately that my pulse accelerates. I can't deny he smells deliciously good. As he skims his lips up to my jawline, my nipples begin to tingle. It must be the scent of his cologne making me feel this way. I'd bet that in everyday life *he* smells like garlic—and stinky sweat socks.

He murmurs into my ear, "Let's order a drink first."

"I already have a cocktail."

He glances at my glass, waving at it dismissively. "No, no, no, my sweet, that won't do. Rose-colored cocktails are for cocks who never get any tail. We need a real drink." He flags down a waiter, who quickly makes his way to our table. "Bring us a bottle of Grey Goose vodka."

"I apologize, sir, but we only serve cocktails."

Undeterred, he pulls out three fifty-pound notes. "Then bring us the entire bottle. Keep the change."

The waiter's eyes flare wide briefly, then he nods and hurries off to fetch the vodka.

Yeah, I'm taken aback by the man's generous tip too.

But then the sexy jerk nuzzles my neck, sending waves of desire pulsating through my body. I melt into his embrace. If only he didn't smell so irresistibly yummy...

The waiter returns quickly, placing a bottle of vodka and two tumblers on the table. They young man hesitates, as if he wants to ask whether we want him to open the bottle, but ultimately decides against it. He scurries off to attend to other customers.

My mysterious companion slides his hand down my thigh and slips it under my dress. As his long fingers gently caress my mound, I inhale sharply and squirm on the bench. He moves his hand inside my panties to cup me intimately, making me gasp again. With one hand still covering my mound, he deftly opens the vodka bottle and pours a generous amount into each tumbler.

Then he hands me a glass. "Vodka should be savored in small sips to let the flavor and the fiery sensation gradually take hold and suffuse your senses."

"Uh, sure," I reply, struggling to regain control of my wits while his hand still rests on my intimate areas and the soft, alluring tone of his voice is driving me out of my mind.

"Take a sip, love."

I wrap my fingers around the glass and lift it to my mouth. The aroma of cream and pepper with a hint of whisky teases my senses. As I tilt the glass back and let the liquid glide over my tongue, I taste notes of freshly baked bread, creamy sweetness, honey, and a touch of citrus. The intense combination of flavors and aromas awakens all my senses and every part of my body. But I can't solely blame the vodka for that. The man whose hand is inside my panties deserves some credit too.

He sips from his own glass and moans with pleasure before nibbling on my earlobe. "Now, darling, it's time for you to come, right here in this booth."

Chapter Two

Declan

This woman is driving me mad. The sweet scent of her, the softness of her skin, that beautiful face, and her sensual body make it impossible for me to resist my lust for her any longer. Should I shag her right here in this bar? Probably not, but I couldn't care less about what's proper or socially acceptable. For too long, I've followed the rules and tried to behave like a respectable gentleman. But I'm done with that rubbish.

What has playing by the rules ever gotten me? Nowhere I wanted to be, that's for sure.

My hand is still nestled inside this woman's knickers, and yet I have no idea what her name is. It's better this way. She can't accuse me of any sort of wrongdoing if she has no idea who I am. Never have I engaged in such a scandalous act with a stranger, right here in a posh bar at a luxury hotel, where anyone might catch us in the act.

The most breathtaking woman I've ever seen aims her surprised gaze at me at me. "You aren't really going to do this, are you? Not here in a public place."

"Of course I'll do it." To prove my point, I trace the outline of her lips with my finger. The sensation of her slick flesh against my palm makes me even randier than I was a moment ago. But she doesn't seem to notice my heightened state of arousal. "Now, darling, I'm going to kiss you while I pleasure you with my fingers."

Her breaths accelerate, becoming rapid gasps as her chest rises and falls heavily. She takes a swig from her glass of vodka which causes her to cough.

"Try not to spew all over me, darling. Unless we're naked, and I'm spraying my cum all over your lovely body."

"I-I can't do this. Not here."

"We should enjoy a kiss first, then. Afterward, you can decide whether you want to admit that I've made you so randy that you would let the waiter fuck you on this table while I watch."

I seal my lips over hers before she has a chance to protest. The strawberry blonde goddess remains frozen for a brief moment, then surrenders with a soft moan as she melts against me.

This woman has pushed me to the brink of madness, igniting a wild desire within me driven by sheer primal hunger. Never before have I behaved so recklessly. I might not be the most honorable bloke, but even I have my limits. Yet with her, I've thrown away all the rules I crafted for myself.

As I push my tongue between her lips, a deep groan rumbles out of me, and I revel in the velvety texture of her flesh. The goddess exhales a moan while I begin to pet and stroke her drenched folds, exploring every millimeter of her mouth. The air around us becomes infused with her sweet essence, making my cock twitch as if it's impatient to feel her wetness wrapped around it.

Bloody hell, I'm raring to go too.

I savor the feel of her soft, velvety tongue entwined with mine whilst she releases another soft moan. I trace my fingers along her delicate folds, determined to explore every inch of her mouth and taste her in every way possible even while my hand grows slicker and coats my fingers. Our private space has become redolent with the intoxicating aroma of her arousal. My own desire is swelling too along with my cock. I can't wait any longer. I need to be inside her now.

But I won't do that until we are alone in my suite.

She clings to my coat lapels, dragging me closer until our chests are pressed together. With one hand, I cradle her nape and tilt it back slightly, exposing the sensitive skin of her throat. How does she taste so incredible? It's more than just the vodka we've been drinking. I can't explain the intense attraction I feel for this mysterious woman.

I brush my thumb over her clit.

She jerks and gasps.

I flick my thumb repeatedly until she freezes, caught in the throes of her climax. Her cries are stifled by my lips on hers, and I go on teasing her nub until she finally melts into me. As I peel my lips away, she gazes up at me dreamily. I can't be that good.

Her sweet smile warms me. "Wow, that vodka is amazing."

"It wasn't the alcohol that made you lose control, pet. It was me."

She raises her brows. "You're taking all the credit?"

"Of course I am. Now, let's go to my suite and shag until we can't even utter a single word or move a muscle."

She nibbles on her lip. "Shouldn't we at least know each other's names first?"

I huff. "Bloody hell, woman. How can you be so finicky? You allowed a stranger to touch you intimately and give you an earth-shattering orgasm."

"Oh, please. I never said it was *that* good."

I gently hook a finger beneath her chin. "Yes, you did, pet. The look in your eyes and the way your breaths grew heavier proves that I am indeed the best you've ever had."

Her lips purse. "We haven't even done the deed yet."

"But we will—soon—and you'll praise my prowess."

"You are the most obnoxious, arrogant jerk I've ever encountered." She crosses her arms over her chest, which lifts those luscious tits. "Don't get any ideas about taking me back to your room or going anywhere with me, you arrogant lout."

I quickly finish my drink, downing it in one gulp. "How can you be so prudish after what I did for you a moment ago? A woman who wears a dress as revealing as yours should have no trouble shedding the rest of her inhibitions."

She puckers her mouth again, but this time, she also snaps her spine straight. "Are you implying I'm promiscuous floozy? You're the one who shoved his hand inside my panties. Guess that makes you a gigolo."

For reasons I can't fathom, I need this woman to come back to my suite with me. Never before have I craved any woman this much—until tonight. "Perhaps we shouldn't talk, darling, if you're going to be so…particular."

"Oh, you cretin. I will never—"

I cut off her outraged response by covering her mouth with mine. Every time she calls me an insulting name, it only makes me hunger for her even more. "I can't wait for you to give in and admit how badly you want me. Why don't we skip ahead and go to my suite now?"

She stares at me for a moment, then takes a sip of her vodka before slamming the glass down on the table. "Fine, let's do it."

My body tenses up in sheer shock. Did the prima donna really just agree to come with me to my room? It's about bloody time. As that realization sinks in, I become a touch disoriented from the shock. But the sensation doesn't last long. "You should lead the way, though. Can't have anyone accusing me of indecent exposure. My flaming erection is your fault, after all."

She rolls her eyes at my cocky comment. "You really think you're God's gift, don't you?"

"Absolutely." I slide out of the booth and offer her my hand. "Shall we go now?"

She accepts my hand, sliding out of the booth.

As I suggested, she walks ahead of me to shield my obvious erection. I keep an arm around her waist as if I'm simply a considerate gent escorting a lady. As we leave the Beaufort Bar, the hall appears empty, so I walk alongside the mysterious woman. Her strawberry blonde hair falls over one side of her face, and she tucks it behind her ear. Who is this goddess? I've told myself more than once that I don't care about names, but now my curiosity is getting the better of me again.

I hold the lift doors open as she sashays inside. Fortunately, we are the only ones in the car. As soon as the doors close, I press her against the wall and trap her wrists with my own. Then I kiss her. Passionately. Sensually. Our kiss becomes so intense that it feels as if we're making love right here in the lift.

As soon as the doors open again, I take her hand and virtually drag her out of the elevator and down the hallway to my suite's door. My hand trembles faintly as I try to insert the key card into the lock. I fumble with it, dropping it once before finally managing to accomplish the task. But even then, I struggle to turn the key.

The woman I desperately need to shag bites her lip, releasing it slowly as she snatches the key card from my hand. The cheeky woman unlocks the door herself, then pushes it open with a playful grin. "Jackasses first."

I clear my throat and brush past her into the suite.

As she shuts the door, she gazes down at the floor. "Ooh, more harlequin tiles. I love that. It feels very...British."

I grunt in response and take her hand, leading her into the spacious living room that boasts a lovely view of the city skyline. But I can't focus on that right now. Halfway across the room, I halt abruptly.

"Something wrong?" she asks. "You seem confused."

"Don't be ridiculous."

The fetching American leans around me to get a better look at the hallway. "That must be the bedroom."

"It is, but we won't be fucking there. It's too ordinary."

She tries to hold back a laugh, but it splutters out of her anyway. "You don't talk like anyone else I know."

"And I am eternally grateful for that. Why should I want to be like everyone else? It's rubbish."

She spins around in a circle, her eyes widening with every step. "This room is incredible."

"It's not just any room. This is the Royal Suite."

She dismisses my statement with a flap of her hand. "Whatever. Like anybody cares about that."

I swiftly remove my suit jacket and toss it onto one of two large, plush sofas that flank the living area. "Take off your clothes now, darling."

She smirks. "I'll let you act like a jackass while we're getting it on. Afterward, it'll be a different story."

"Please only speak if you're screaming 'yes, you're amazing' or 'please make me come so hard I'll think I've died and gone to heaven.' Understood?"

The silly chit bursts out laughing.

And I growl, "Take off your clothes immediately."

While I wage a battle against my own clothing, desperately struggling to shed all of it, she simply unties two straps and lets the garment tumble to the floor in a heap of fabric. I trip twice while struggling to remove my shoes and stumble into a small table, smacking my knee into the hard edge. "Bloody hell!"

"Are you all right?"

"Yes, I'm fine." I gesture toward the wall. "Sit your arse on that couch, the one facing the window."

"Which one? There are two."

I wave my arm again as I peel my socks off. "The one directly in front of that white column."

Suddenly, I remember something vital. I need a condom. My trousers are on the floor, so I quickly grab them and search through my pockets until I find a foil packet. Thank heavens. The pressure in my groin has become almost unbearable. After covering my cock, I return to the woman.

She obediently sashays over to the window and settles her delectable arse on the sofa.

But that's not where I want her. So, I saunter toward the couch and motion for her to turn around and face me. "No, pet, I commanded you to face the window. Then get on your knees with your hands on the sill."

The cheeky chit turns round and wriggles her arse.

I climb onto the small couch, spreading my thighs and grasping her hips. The moment I plunge my length inside her, a sigh of relief rushes out of me as if I were a schoolboy who just shagged a girl for the first time. But I can't think about that or anything else. All my attention is focused on the slick heat of her body as it surrounds my cock. Animalistic grunts and growls emerge from me as I thrust deeply into her velvety channel, completely lost in the moment. The wet sucking sounds of our bodies merging fills the room.

She tosses her head to the side, flinging her hair away from her face. "Harder, please, let's make the couch bounce."

A grunt is all I can muster in response.

The bloody woman tightens her inner muscles around me.

I gasp. And then I lose control, pounding into her with such force the couch thumps and bounces and scrapes across the wood floor. The scent of her cream wafts around me, driving me ever closer to the edge. I grip the windowsill with both hands, framing her body as I pummel her harder and faster whilst she screams and begs for more. When I feel her body tense up, I know she's about to explode.

The sheen of sweat glistens on her skin as she throws her head back and cries out, "Yes, yes, you caveman, don't stop, you rock!"

She seems incapable of forming words anymore, too consumed by the pleasure of her climax.

I can't hold back any longer, and I thrust twice more before my body freezes and my release erupts inside her luscious body. I've never experienced such an intense climax before. This woman has completely shattered my self-control. For a moment, we both remain still. Then I release my grip on the windowsill and carefully ease myself off the couch so I can help her dismount as well. Her legs seem shaky, but her expression is pure contentment.

She molds her body to mine, trailing her hands up and down my chest. "I'm hungry, caveman, feed me. And after that, we need to do it again."

"I couldn't agree more."

We order room service and take turns feeding each other before we shag again, three more times before the night is over. Thankfully, I always carry extra condoms in my trouser pocket. We fall asleep together on the bed. But when I wake up in the morning, I'm stunned by what I find.

The woman is gone.

Do I feel used? Perhaps. But it was just a one-night stand. Wasn't it?

That's what I wanted. And it's what I got. But now, I can't stop thinking about the goddess who captivated me last night. So, I ring the front desk. "Hello, this is Declan Wilde in the Royal Suite. Did you happen to see a stunning strawberry blonde in the hotel this morning? I need to know which room she's in."

"Yes, sir, I did see her. But we can't disclose personal information about our guests."

I'll have to come up with a believable story, then. This will hardly be my first time lying. "She left her purse in my suite. I would like to return it to her personally."

"I don't know…"

"You know who I am. Surely, you realize you can trust me."

The bloke hesitates for a moment. "My apologies, sir. Of course, I'll give you the lady's contact information."

"Thank you…what is your name?"

"Daniel, sir."

"A pleasure to meet you, Daniel."

I quickly get dressed and head down to the lobby where Daniel hands me a slip of paper with the mystery woman's number written on it. I immediately hail a taxi, determined to find her, for reasons I can't fathom. I took a suite at the Savoy to escape from my everyday life and…figure out what I want. The strawberry blonde beauty who stole a piece of my soul has turned my world upside down. How did a hot shag become a life-altering experience?

Somehow, some way, I will find the goddess and learn her name. She will be mine.

Chapter Three

Sabrina

As dawn approached, I had stealthily sneaked out of the Royal Suite. My heart was racing as I hurried to my own digs, packing all my belongings into my bags while plotting my escape. From whom? The man who had taken my body over and over again, giving me the most incredible sexual experiences I'd ever had. The first time had been mind blowing and filthy as well as brief. But I begged him for more, and surprisingly, he obliged. The way he made love to me after that quickie…It left me feeling so confused that I had to run away.

But sneaking out in the middle of the night was a cowardly move on my part.

Ugh, what do I do now? My family and friends had funded this vacation for me. Will they be able to get their money back since I left after only one night? Although I have no desire to see that man again, I can't help but feel guilty for running away like this. Now, I'm at a loss for what to do next. Spending some time alone to think seems like my best option.

Um, where should I go? I'm a tourist in a strange city.

I hurry down to the lobby and ask the desk clerk, Daniel, to call a taxi for me. Once I'm in the car, I ask the driver to recommend some of London's best sights along the river. After all, I am still a tourist and might as well make the most of my trip before I…do something else. There's no way I'm going back home to Asheville with my tail between my legs. And returning to the Savoy is out of the question. What if that man is still there?

The driver drops me off near a statue of Cleopatra on the Victoria Embankment, adjacent to the River Thames. According to my driver, it's one of the must-see attractions for tourists. After giving it a quick glance, I find a bench in a nearby park and sit down. The river isn't as picturesque as I had imagined it to be. Maybe I picked a bad spot.

Suddenly, a shadow looms over me.

Oh, great. The last thing I need right now is company. All I want is some time alone with my thoughts.

"Sabrina, darling, there you are."

I recognize that voice and instinctively turn to face the man who spoke. "Are you stalking me?"

He laughs. "No, pet, I wouldn't do anything so mundane."

I jump up from the bench and spin toward him. "Then how did you find me? And how do you know my name?"

He shrugs one shoulder. "With determination and a dash of skullduggery, a chap can accomplish anything."

I have no idea what any of that means. Despite my best efforts not to, I can't help admiring his physique, though I saw him naked last night. Today he's wearing a light blue shirt with two buttons undone (of course), khaki pants, a sleek brown leather jacket, and suede sneakers. I'm pretty sure the whole outfit is designer, and therefore way above my clothing budget. The dress I wore last night had blown a good chunk of my vacation budget.

But damn, the jerk looks good enough to lick—and nibble.

I feel downright frumpy in comparison, with my jeans, peasant top, and discount-store sneakers. I love these shoes, but I'm sure this conceited ape will turn his nose up at them.

As I swivel to face him, I cross my arms over my chest. "So, you admit to stalking me."

"Once again, it was not stalking," he insists, cocking his hip as he hooks his thumb inside his waistband. "This is a public park, after all."

I clutch my purse tightly, as if I'm afraid he might try to snatch it from me. But I don't actually think he would. "How did you even find me?"

He smirks. "I have my ways."

I shake my head in disbelief. "We had separate hotel rooms, and I never gave you my room number. That means you stalked me." I narrow my gaze, but he simply chuckles. "Tell me how you found me, or I will scream."

"No need for that. I'll gladly explain," he says smoothly. "I persuaded the desk clerk, Daniel, to give me your personal information. Then I tracked down the taxi driver, Roger, who told me he'd dropped you at the statue of Cleopatra."

I set my hands on my hips and glower at him. "You are unbelievable."

"Thank you for the compliment, pet. Perhaps my methods were a bit dramatic, but I couldn't let you walk away after one night."

Holy shit. This jerk is a master manipulator. Even I'm starting to believe his lies.

As he stands there, oozing charm and seductive appeal, I try to reach into my purse without drawing his attention. I have a small bottle of perfume. Maybe if I sprayed that in his eyes, it would give me enough time to run away.

He tilts his head slightly, still smiling. "Don't you want to know who I am, Sabrina?"

I glance around, hoping someone might wander by so I can shout for help. Luckily, a police officer is ambling down the path toward us. I turn back to the attractive but evil man in front of me. "No thanks. I don't need to know your name."

Bolting down the paved path, I frantically wave my arms in the air. "Help! Officer, please help!"

The policeman immediately starts running toward me and we meet halfway.

"What's wrong, miss?" the young cop asks. "Did someone nick your wallet?"

I point back toward the way I came. "That man over there, he followed me all the way from the Savoy Hotel to this trail. Please arrest him."

"What's your name, miss?"

"Sabrina Remington."

"I'm Constable Mansfield, and I'll gladly handle that tosser for you." He gazes past me intently. "That man seems to be approaching quickly. No worries."

The constable jogs down the path toward the obnoxious man, stopping in front of him. They exchange a few words before both bursting into laughter. Constable Mansfield then rejoins me with the man in tow.

The reptile has the audacity to smirk at me. "Sabrina and I just had a little disagreement and she ran off without me."

Ohh, I want to deck him so badly. But I resist the urge and instead glare at the constable. "I am not with this jerk. He's been harassing me."

"You must be mistaken, miss." Constable Mansfield gestures toward the evil man. "You're one lucky lady. Not many women get the chance to date a celebrity."

"What are you talking about? Who is this guy?"

"Guy?" The constable chuckles. "This is Declan Wilde."

"And I should I know who that is…why?"

The constable gives me an incredulous look. "He's Declan Wilde."

I throw my hands up. "So what?"

The jerk pats the officer's arm. "It's all right, mate. You know how women can be when they feel ignored. Go ahead, I'll take care of this. No harm done."

And the officer casually walks away down the path.

I slowly step back, keeping a safe distance between us. "Who the hell are you? A mobster? Cops bow down to you, desk clerks and taxi drivers worship you. It's insane. I've never even heard of Declan Wilde."

"Well, maybe you should look me up on your mobile phone." He casually strolls over to another bench and plops down onto it, stretching his arms across the back. "Go ahead, take your time."

I fume for about three seconds, then reluctantly pull out my phone and open the web browser, typing in his name. Oh no, he's actually famous. This is just perfect. No matter how much he stalks me, nobody will care because he's part of the famous Wilde family dynasty that's been around for ten generations. I didn't make that up. It's written in the headline of the very first article that pops up. Declan is described as a "multifaceted playboy-millionaire" and is one of the most well-known people in all of London if not the entire UK.

My shoulders slump as I shove my phone back into my purse. I plop down on the bench a few feet away from Declan. "This is just great. The slimeball who charmed me last night is just another womanizer. Ugh, my luck couldn't be worse."

"Relax, pet, this is your lucky day." His cocky smile returns. "You've caught the biggest fish in the dating world—me, Declan Wilde."

"Then I'm throwing you back into the sea." I lift my chin. "Besides, I'm a vegetarian."

Declan chuckles. "Is that why you devoured an eight-ounce steak last night?"

"You brainwashed me." But yeah, I do love steak. This hunky bag of human slime doesn't need to know that.

"So, you only eat meat when Declan Wilde shags you?"

I growl—seriously, I do. "You're evil."

"Sabrina darling, you're adorable when you get angry. So fiery and irresistible."

"I hope you burn in hell for eternity."

I spin around on my heels and march down the path, adamantly refusing to look behind me and see if that jerk is following. I veer onto the grass, cutting across it in an attempt to shake Declan off my trail. When I reach another, parallel pathway, I pause to plan my next move. Luckily, my phone has a maps feature, so I use it to plot my escape. I follow Carting Lane since it seems like the best option since I didn't rent a car. Since I had planned on staying at the Savoy and using taxis for transportation, I don't have many other options. But now that I've checked out of the hotel, going back there isn't an option either.

My route takes me through a narrow street, or maybe it's just a pedestrian walkway, until it finally leads me to The Strand, which apparently is what this road is called—just "The Strand," not Strand Street. At least, that's what it says on my map. Now that I'm here, I have no idea where to go next.

Scanning the area, I notice the Adelphi Theater across the street. That's interesting, but it doesn't help me navigate this unfamiliar place.

A taxi approaches, so I wave to get the driver's attention.

"Don't leave without me, darling. I'm an excellent tour guide."

Oh no, not him again. Hearing Declan's voice confirms my suspicions. He has been following me. But I decide to play along and act like I can't hear him. As soon as the taxi stops, I jump in and shut the door.

Meanwhile, Declan just stands there on the sidewalk, wearing that cocky grin.

"Where to, miss?" asks the driver before turning to look at me with a smile. "Oh, it's you again. Didn't catch your name last time."

"Sabrina Remington," I reply, tapping my foot nervously. I want to tell Roger to hurry up and drive away from here, but I don't want to be rude.

"I'm Roger Jones. Nice to officially meet you. Where do you want to go this time, lovey?"

"Not sure. Do you have any recommendations? I'm on vacation here in the UK."

"How about Trafalgar Square? It's not too far from here."

"Perfect."

As Roger starts the taxi rolling, I try my hardest to avoid looking at Declan out the window. My eyes seem to have a mind of their own and force me to glance at him, the annoyingly cheerful jerk who's been following me.

"Are you and Declan Wilde dating?" Roger asks curiously.

"No, absolutely not. I just met him yesterday, and he's been nothing but rude to me."

"What? I can't believe that."

Great. It seems like even Roger is a fan of Declan, just like that constable. Instead of getting into a debate about his supposed charm, I take a different approach go for politeness. "Do you know Declan personally? I don't. Everyone seems to love him, though."

"Yeah, everyone does. He's a good man. One of the best."

"What does he do for a living?"

Roger continues driving with one hand on the wheel while he turns to face me. "Declan Wilde isn't your average playboy. He's actually one of the most generous philanthropists in England. And he's a successful digital entrepreneur too."

"I've never heard of that. What does a digital entrepreneur do?"

"Lots of things." Roger navigates around a corner, then explains. "Sir Declan's company discovers podcasters and helps them find their niche. But he also gives struggling online storefronts a boost with grants. He nurtures social media influencers too, and he also finds and hires computer wizards who've lost their jobs. And that's just the tip of the iceberg. He only takes a minimal salary for himself."

What?! That's's what I want to shout, but I stop myself out of politeness. The jackass is also a do-gooder? It's hard for me to wrap my head around this new information. "What kind of playboy is Declan?"

"He loves women, but he always treats them with respect. 'Playboy' isn't really the right word for him. Declan Wilde isn't like anyone else."

No kidding. Have I completely misjudged him? No, he was stalking me. And it seems like he plans to keep on doing that.

On the way to Trafalgar Square, Roger and I talk about everything except for Declan. The driver is delighted when I mention that my sister is marrying a British man.

"Will she move here?" Roger asks. "I assume your parents are in the States."

"Yeah, they own a lovely antique shop in Asheville, North Carolina. But Tabitha won't be relocating to England. She works with her fiancé, Spencer, at a company in Arlington, Virginia."

"He won't get to see his family much, eh?"

"Oh, he can visit them anytime he wants and vice versa. Spencer has friends who are super rich, including two billionaires."

Roger grins at me. "Are you having me on? Billionaires?"

"It's true. Diana Hahn, formerly Diana Sangster, married an American man and they live here in London. Then there's Evan MacTaggart, who mostly lives in Utah with his American wife but also visits Scotland from time to time."

He chuckles. "No wonder you were staying at the Savoy. Did your mates pay for your holiday?"

"Yep." Should I tell Roger about my mission? He's so nice, and maybe he could help. "Okay, this might sound crazy, but I'm actually in England to find my PC."

"Somebody stole your computer?"

"No, no. I mean my Perfect Catch, aka my PC."

"Oh, I see. Declan would be perfect for a sweet girl like you."

How do I tell Roger how much of a jerk Declan really is without hurting his feelings? It's clear that he's a big fan of that asshat. But can I really blame him? Declan can be charming when he wants to be, like when he seduced me last night. Maybe I should try the diplomatic approach. "Actually, Declan isn't really my type. No offense to him. I just have certain criteria for my PC and he doesn't quite fit the mold."

"Fair enough." Roger slows down as we approach our destination. "Where should I drop you off, lovey?"

"Hmm, as close as possible to the cool statues and museums, if you don't mind."

"Sounds good," he says as we navigate a traffic circle and reach our destination. "Here you go, Sabrina. On your right is the Equestrian Statue of King Charles the First. And on your left, you'll see all the famous Trafalgar Square monuments."

"Thank you so much, Roger." I hand him some money, making sure to give him a generous tip for his kindness and great conversation during the ride. "I really enjoyed talking with you."

"The pleasure was all mine, Sabrina." He hands me his business card. "Give me a ring if you need another ride."

I lean over to give him a quick kiss on the cheek. "You're the best."

Roger smiles as he drives away, and I walk toward the big statue in front of me.

At least Declan isn't here to ruin my fun.

Chapter Four

Declan

Sabrina Remington once again ran away from me. I tried to keep up, but by the time I reached the street, she had already jumped into a taxi and disappeared. If only I had driven my own car to the Savoy, I might have been able to follow her. My desperate need to keep track of Sabrina has led me to behave like a complete fool. But the most embarrassing thing I did this morning was sprinting down The Strand until Sabrina's taxi was out of sight. At least she didn't see me sprinting after her, so my pride is somewhat intact.

After flagging down my own taxi, I return to the Savoy and my suite. I order breakfast and lounge on one of the oversized couches while I wait, stretching out and propping my hands under my head as I gaze up at the ceiling. No one who knows me would believe I could act this way. Yet here I am, behaving just the way Sabrina accuses me of doing—acting like a bloody moron.

My mobile rings with a familiar tone.

I dig it out of my pocket with a groan. Though I'd rather not speak to the caller, I know I must answer. "Hello, Julian, how are you this morning?"

"Don't give me that nonchalant greeting, Declan. You were caught doing something…unbecoming of the Wilde family's golden boy."

"Me? The golden boy?" I chuckle. "Did Mum put you up to this? Or was it Dad? No, it's probably Darcy. Our sister loves to meddle in my life."

"If you didn't give everyone the impression that you're a notorious playboy, then maybe Darcy wouldn't harass you."

Oh, bollocks. "Where precisely did she see us in the hotel?"

"In the corridor outside your suite."

I didn't even notice Darcy there. I was too focused on seducing Sabrina Remington. My cock was in control, not my brain. "How upset is Darcy?"

Julian chuckles. "Upset? She's over the moon about it. You haven't dated anyone in so long that our parents will probably throw a huge bash to mark this rare event."

"If only I could strangle you through the phone, I would."

"You have a mobile phone. Airwaves are hard to control."

"Aren't you so clever, Julian. I'm laughing so hard that I might pass out from exhaustion." I drop my head into my hand and let out another sigh. "I highly doubt Darcy was shocked by what she saw. She's thirty-one years old, after all, not a quivering virgin. Did she also happen to see me leaving the Savoy?"

"No, Darcy didn't mention anything about that. Why do you ask?"

"I don't disclose the details of my liaisons."

Julian stifles a laugh, proof that he finds this situation amusing. "When was the last time you were with a woman, Declan? Before last night, that is."

"Leave it alone. I have other matters to attend to." Such as tracking down an American woman who despises me. "Cheers, Julian."

And I end the call before he can say anything else.

I need to know why Sabrina scurried away in the middle of the night. That's all. I don't give a flying toss whether she wants to date me or shag me or anything else. Honestly, I couldn't care less about that. All I want is to understand why she bolted, so I won't feel like a failure who can't even keep a woman for one night.

Yes, absolutely, that's the only reason I need to find her.

A knock at my door signals the arrival of my long-awaited meal. My stomach growls because I'm half-starved from the wait. It's only been ten minutes, but it feels like an eternity. I quickly make my way to the door and swing it open. A young-looking man, probably in his twenties, brings in a tray of food for me. I give him a generous tip as he leaves with a smile on his face and a bounce in his step.

I devour the food as if I haven't eaten in years, my hunger fueled by memories of a passionate night with a strawberry blonde. But now that my stomach is satisfied, I need to satisfy another craving.

Finding Sabrina will be a challenge. I had good luck bribing the hotel staff and a taxi driver last time, but she has since checked out. I'll need to come up with a new plan. How many American women named Sabrina Remington could there possibly be in London? If I can track down the driver, Roger, maybe he can provide some clues.

To accomplish this task, I must invoke all my most devious powers of trickery.

I make my way down to the lobby to speak with Daniel, the desk clerk.

He greets me with a warm smile. "Good afternoon, Mr. Wilde. How may I assist you?"

"I was wondering if you've met Sabrina Remington."

"Of course. She's lovely."

Time to put my devious plan into action. I lean against the front desk and lower my voice to a softer tone. "Well, here's my dilemma, Daniel. As I mentioned before, Sabrina is my girlfriend, but we had an argument last night. That's why she left in such a hurry. I need to track her down, but she took a taxi and I have no idea where she might have gone"—Yes, I'm pulling out my entire arsenal of lies and trickery—"However, Roger often drops off passengers here at the hotel. Do you happen to have his contact information? I'm desperate to find my beloved. She's unfamiliar with this city."

Daniel hesitates for a moment before responding cautiously. "Um, I know I helped you out once, but I'm not really allowed to give out personal information concerning taxi drivers…"

"Please, Daniel, this once could you break the rules? I'm hardly a serial killer. Couldn't you just slip me Roger's number this once?" I hold my palms together in a pleading gesture. "I'm terribly worried about Sabrina."

Daniel hesitates briefly, tapping his finger on the desk, then nods. "I'll get that number for you, Mr. Wilde. Just give me a moment."

Blimey. Even I'm impressed with how effortlessly I executed this little con. I must be more skilled at deception than I realized.

Daniel hands me a slip of paper. "Here's the number."

"You are a lifesaver."

After spewing so many untruths, I wander into the entryway to wait for both Roger and Daniel. The cabbie arrives first. Daniel points him toward me, and Roger grins as he approaches.

"It's you again, mate," he says. "Heard you lost your girl. I dropped her off at Trafalgar Square, by the statue of the king, about eighteen minutes ago. She might still be there."

"Thank you, Roger. You are a treasure."

"No need to butter me up, sir."

"Perhaps not, but I do owe you a tip for passing the information on to me." I hand him several pound notes. "For a job well done."

"Thanks. You're all right, sir."

"Please, call me Declan."

Just as Roger exits the hotel, I notice my car pulling up outside. I don't recognize the driver, but I suspect Julian is responsible for this gift. I barely give the valet time to open the door before I jump into the vehicle, tires screeching as I speed off onto The Strand. I might be driving a little too fast. If I get pulled over, it doesn't matter. The fine will be insignificant to me. Wealth does have its perks.

When I arrive at Trafalgar Square, I decide to park my car in a garage, which is not something I typically do. But desperate times call for unconventional measures, right? Not sure that's how the saying goes. I make my way to the statue of King Charles the First, hoping to find Sabrina there. But I don't see her. So, I jog across the street to Nelson's Column but still have no luck and continue past the fountains with no sign of her there either. In just twenty minutes, she couldn't have gone very far from where Roger had left me. Frustrated, I turn in a circle trying to think of where an American woman might go to see the sights.

That's when I notice the National Gallery. Would Sabrina enjoy something like that? I have no clue, but I might as well check just in case. After searching every corner of the museum, I come up empty handed. She's gone, and it feels like I've lost her all over again. Exhausted and sweaty, I exit the National Gallery and slump against the building, bowing my head in defeat.

A whistle pierces the air, then a man's voice shouts, "Oy! Come over here. A pretty little bird like you should be legally required to put on a striptease."

"You should be so lucky, moron."

I recognize that voice. It's Sabrina.

My heart races as I jump up and scan the crowd for her. I have to find Sabrina before she disappears. And then I spot her—or rather, the top of her strawberry blonde head. She's standing near Nelson's Column, looking up at it in awe. I start running toward her. As I get closer, I see who was harassing her. It's a group of young men who barely look old enough to buy a pint in a pub.

As I approach Sabrina, she seems to be focused on something, or someone, else. I stand behind her and throw a fierce glare toward the group of young tossers. The moment they realize who I am, their faces turn pale and they scurry away.

Sabrina turns to toward me with a displeased expression. "Declan? I told you to leave me alone."

"Yes, you did. But I have a better idea."

"I don't care. Stalking is not an attractive trait." She waves a dismissive hand at me. "Go away, shoo. For good this time."

"I'm not a mosquito, darling." I wrap my arm around her waist and pull her close. "Let's have some fun. We can go to my car. It's parked in a nearby garage."

She blows out an exasperated breath. "Do I need to hit you over the head with a baseball bat? For the last time, leave me alone."

"No need for violence, pet. But it's telling that you've done everything but ring for the police."

"I already did that. Your good buddy Constable Mansfield vetoed the idea. You probably brainwashed him."

Perhaps I feel a smidgen of guilt over that incident, which probably explains what I say next. "I apologize for my previous behavior. But I did not brainwash anyone. I might have, ah, fed Constable Mansfield a porky or two, that's all."

"You gave him a pig?"

I strenuously resist the urge to laugh. "No, pet, I told him a lie. He believes you are my girlfriend and that you ran away because we had an argument. I rushed after you to make amends."

She shakes her head. "And you think that confession will make me forgive you for hounding me. You're a jackass and a loon."

I stare at her for a moment, then drop to one knee, clasping my hands in a pleading gesture. "Please forgive me, Sabrina. It was a retched thing to do, and I apologize wholeheartedly. Don't blame the constable. This was all my fault."

She studies me as if I'm a strange specimen she found in a laboratory. Whether she believes my apology or not, it's true. I do regret my behavior.

I give up and rise to my feet, brushing off my coat. "Let's not lie to each other, pet. You want me, and we both know it." I slant closer to breathe in her alluring scent. How is it possible for her to smell this delectable all the time? It's almost criminal. "Tell me why you ran away last night and again this morning."

"Because you're an insufferable cretin."

I tilt her chin up with my finger, forcing her to meet my gaze. "Let's be honest. Have you ever experienced a more intense orgasm than the ones I gave you?"

She flattens her lips.

"If you refuse to answer, darling, then I'll have no choice but to ravish you with a passionate kiss right here in this public place."

"Why are you so evil?" she hisses through gritted teeth. "Fine, you're the hottest guy I've ever slept with. Is that what you wanted to hear?"

"Why did you skulk out of my suite?"

She stares at me as if she wants to uncover all my secrets. "I'll answer your question if you tell me why you've been following me like a hawk."

That sounds like a dangerous proposition. But danger turns me on. "I accept your offer."

"Why have you been stalking me so relentlessly?"

"Because we had mind-blowing sex last night, multiple times, and I fell under your spell." I gently tuck a strand of hair behind her ear. "Now it's your turn to explain."

"Okay. I sneaked out of your room in the morning because"—She shuts her eyes tightly—"I'd never experienced anything so intense and erotic before. It unsettled me."

"I accept your explanation. Now, will you cease and desist telling everyone that I'm stalking you?"

She squints at me briefly before releasing a gusty sigh. "All right, I'll stop doing that. But I don't want to see you again. I'm leaving London."

"Where are you going?"

"None of your damn business."

Why does her insolent behavior make me so fucking randy? It's baffling. But our verbal sparring always has that effect on me. Never in my life have I behaved so recklessly and, if I'm being honest, foolishly. Surely it has nothing to do with... No, impossible.

Sabrina walks away, and I can't resist watching her hips as they sway in the most stimulating manner. My trousers have grown tight. Even as she disappears behind Nelson Column's, I stay rooted in place. My feet seem to have become glued to the ground, refusing to move even a fraction of an inch. Why am I so fixated on Sabrina? She's just a random woman I shagged last night. Yet there's something about her that keeps me coming back for more.

"Are you really that infatuated with a column, mate? Or are you having a stroke?"

I swerve my head to stare at the bloke who uttered those words. "Excuse me? I don't appreciate strangers discussing the state of my health."

"Relax, Declan. I'm not interested in your health. I have a job to do."

"I'm not concerned with your job."

The bloke chuckles again and playfully punches my arm. "Your mother sent me. She wants to know why you were at the Savoy. Since I'm an old friend of Julian's, and a former constable, I offered to find out where you'd gone."

"How could my family know I was at the Savoy?"

The bloke shrugs. "Your sister grassed on you."

Oh, bollocks.

Chapter Five

Sabrina

I flag down another taxi and hop in, asking the driver to take me to a specific address that my sister had mentioned before. I didn't have time to call Roger for help. I needed to get away from Declan as quickly as possible. Panicking might not be the smartest option right now, but my mind is spinning out of control.

Why does Declan affect me so deeply? Maybe I do know why, but I'm not ready to admit it yet.

The driver drops me off exactly where I wanted to go, and I give the driver a generous tip before dashing up the steps of the unfamiliar house in front of me. As I reach for the doorbell, I wonder if they'll think I'm crazy. But I remind myself to be brave and just do it.

So, I press the doorbell.

A few moments later, the door opens to reveal a handsome guy with a welcoming grin. "Hey, Sabrina, come on in. Diana and Pippa are in the living room. We're all excited to get to know you. Follow me."

Derek Hahn is a fellow American, but his wife Diana is a British billionaire. As I walk into the house, I suddenly realize who Pippa is. Diana's brother passed away years ago, leaving his daughter under Diana's care, and later she adopted the girl. So, Pippa is both Diana's daughter and her niece. It's all rather complicated.

We enter what seems to be a sitting room or something of that sort. Most Americans don't have fancy names for their rooms, at least not anyone I know. Diana and Pippy are sitting on a luxurious sofa, smiling as they see me.

Pippa hurries over to me and wraps her arms around my waist in a firm hug. "I'm so happy to finally meet you, Sabrina. We've been hearing all about you and Tabitha. Can't wait to see her at the wedding. I already know Spencer and his brother Kendall."

"I'm happy to meet you too, Pippa. Spencer mentioned that you're the smartest young lady in all of England."

The girl blushes, then she dashes back to Diana.

Derek motions toward a high-back chair. "Why don't you have a seat, Sabrina?"

"Thank you." I sink into the comfortable chair Derek pointed out for me. It has plush cushioning that feels wonderful. "But please call me Bree. That's what my friends and family call me, and I'm sure we'll become good friends."

Derek takes a seat beside the two women in his life, casually draping an arm over the back of the sofa. The sound of a baby crying echoes from elsewhere in the house.

Diana turns toward her daughter. "Pippa, dear, would you be a love and look after your little sister for me?"

The teenager rolls her eyes. "What you mean is 'Pippa, get lost so the adults can talk in private.' Right?"

"Exactly," Derek chimes in with a wink. "Go on, kiddo."

Pippa obediently makes her way down the hall. As she disappears from sight, she calls out, "But I'm not a child!"

"Yes, you are," both Derek and Diana shout in response.

Sitting opposite two strangers, I can't help feeling slightly uncomfortable. They seem like nice people, and I'm sure we'll become friends eventually. But right now, it feels like there's a pebble in my chair, though I realize there isn't one. A minute ago, I confidently declared that we would all be great friends. Now, I'm not so sure.

Derek moves closer to his wife, and they both aim pleasant smiles at me. "Can I do something for you, Bree? A desperate phone call, asking for urgent help, is my kind of problem."

I raise my brows. "What exactly is your specialty?"

"I'm a bodyguard. In fact, I own the company—H&M Protective Services. The 'M' stands for Marshall, who used to be my boss before he retired and sold the business to me."

I sit up straighter, leaning forward. "You're a bodyguard? That's terrific. Can you protect me from a rude jerk who's been harassing me?"

"Absolutely. That falls right inside my wheelhouse."

My shoulders slump. "That sounds perfect, but I doubt I can afford your services."

Diana aims a motherly smile at me. "Don't worry, love. There will be no charge. If Spencer Halfenaked recommended you, that's all we need to know."

"Oh. That's great." Do I sound like a moron or what? *Sheesh.*

Derek studies me for a moment. "Tell us about the jerk who's been following you around."

"He's been trailing me since—Well, that part doesn't matter." I almost let it slip about my wild night with Declan. Being stalked is exhausting. "This guy seems to have connections everywhere, and they're all willing to help him harass me. He even convinced a hotel clerk to give him my room number and a taxi driver to tell him that I went to Trafalgar Square. That's how he found me again."

"Do you know the stalker's name?"

"Yes, unfortunately. He goes by Declan Wilde, but who knows if that's his real name."

Diana shifts in her seat, suddenly looking at me as if I've just revealed that I was abducted by aliens. "Did you say Declan Wilde?"

"Yes."

Diana and Derek exchange puzzled glances, then she cautiously asks, "Are you absolutely certain that was his name?"

"I'm positive. He told me so himself."

She stares at me with disbelief for a moment before relaxing back into her chair. "I'm sorry, love, but that can't be right. Sir Declan Wilde is one of England's most esteemed philanthropists as well as a successful businessman. He was awarded a knighthood for his charitable endeavors."

"Awarded a what?" I can't believe what I'm hearing. Declan is evil. "That creep is no knight in shining armor."

"Knighthood is strictly ceremonial. Declan doesn't carry a sword or wear armor."

Derek's brows furrow as he glances at his wife. "Baby, I think there must be something else going on here. Sir Declan must have a reason for his actions. But I trust Bree's account. Why don't I pay Sir Declan a visit myself? Then I can decide if any further action needs to be taken."

I perk up. "You would do that for me?"

"Of course I would. If it turns out Declan has a secret life as a stalker, I'll expose him so hard he won't know what hit him."

Diana smiles lovingly at her husband. "My love, you are the sweetest man in the world."

He leans in close and whispers, "Don't go spreading that rumor around. I have a reputation to maintain."

She playfully pats his cheek. "No need to worry. Bree won't tell a soul. Will you, pet?"

"Nope. My lips are sealed. But I'm still in shock about that jack—I mean, Sir Declan's behavior." Every time Diana uses the word pet, I feel weird about it. Why? Because Declan also likes to call me that, though with very different intentions.

Derek jumps out of his seat. "You lovely ladies can stay here. I'll go have a chat with Declan."

I leap up too. "I'm coming with you."

"No, Bree, that's not a good idea."

"But he's been stalking me. And what if he uses hypnosis on you? He's the devil."

Derek is desperately trying not to burst into laughter, and I can't blame him. Even I think I sound like a lunatic. But Derek is too kind to say so.

Instead, he places a comforting hand on my shoulder and gives me an empathetic smile. "I get that you're upset by Declan's behavior. But if you can trust me, we'll get this all sorted out, I promise. Does that sound good?"

"Yes, thank you. I swear I'm not normally like this."

As he leads me away, he tells Diana, "We won't be long, baby. Don't worry."

"I never worry, Derek. You know that."

He winks at her. "Sorry. I almost forgot you're tough as nails."

In the hallway, Derek shrugs into a jacket that looks designer to me. I bet his wife bought that for him. Derek doesn't strike me as the type to splurge on high-end fashion. Instead of leading me through the front entrance, he steers me toward the back of the house and out into the crowded parking lot behind it. The London neighborhood features upscale houses packed closely together. Despite the tight quarters, it's undeniably beautiful here.

Derek uses his key fob to unlock the passenger door of his luxury car. Then he offers me his hand to help me inside.

Sir Declan never offered to do that for me, but then again, I ran away before he had the chance to be chivalrous. Not that I believe for even a nanosecond that he would've done that.

As we ride in style in a super-expensive Jaguar sedan, I take in the scenery as we leave central London behind and pass through opulent neighborhoods where the richest people in

London live. I crane my neck to get a glimpse of the lavish mansions and extravagant cars as we zoom down the streets.

"Where are we headed?" I ask, sinking back into my seat.

"Straight to Declan's flat in Knightsbridge," Derek replies, glancing at me out of the corner of his eye. "A flat is what they call an apartment here."

"Yeah, I know. Spencer told me all about England and his British friends."

Derek deftly navigates around a corner, using only one hand. "I heard they might throw a wild party for Tabitha and Spencer's wedding."

"Tabby and Spence would rather keep it simple."

Derek turns onto a narrow street. "We're almost there. Are you ready to face Declan?"

"I don't want a confrontation. I just want him to stop stalking me."

"Understood."

Luckily, Derek finds a parking spot near Declan's apartment building, so we won't have far to walk. I'm worn out from arguing with that jerk. The building itself is stunning, a mix of modern and traditional design. We climb a few steps to reach the entrance, then ride an elevator—a lift, as Brits call it—to get up to Declan's fancy bachelor pad. Derek presses the doorbell.

Seconds later, the door swings open, and Declan greets me with a smirk. "Now who's stalking whom, darling? I imagine you brought your mate as a witness to my alleged depravity."

"Careful," Derek warns, his gaze flinty. "You don't want to tick off a bodyguard. Sabrina is under my protection until I determine whether or not you can be trusted. My wife knows you and vouches for your character, but I need to see the proof for myself."

Declan's brows shoot up. "Your wife? Who the bloody hell are you?"

"I'm Derek Hahn. Diana Sangster is my wife, though she goes by Diana Hahn these days."

"Oh. Well, that explains a few things. Diana has been a strong supporter of my charitable endeavors, but I didn't know she had finally tied the knot."

I can't resist jumping into the conversation. "How could you not know that Diana got married? I thought she was famous in London."

Declan studies me with interest. "Sorry, I don't keep up with gossip these days. Lost my appetite for it." He shoots a quick glance at Derek, then smirks again. "Will your bodyguard be following you around permanently? Or is this strictly a 'let the bodyguard try to frighten Declan' sort of visit?"

"I can't imagine you would ever be afraid."

His eyes widen briefly. Then he crosses his arms over his chest and releases a heavy sigh. "I promise not to stalk, bother, or otherwise annoy Sabrina Remington unless she does so first. Now, may we have a private conversation without a chaperone? I will allow you to restrain me if that will make you feel better."

I can't tell if he's serious or if he's mocking me. But for some strange reason, I want to talk to Declan alone. So, I turn to Derek and say, "Thank you for all your help. I can handle Declan on my own now."

Derek nods crisply, then gives Declan's hand a strong shake. My bodyguard warns him not to make me cry, or else he'll come back just to beat up Sir Declan. Derek turns to leave the apartment, and the door clicks shut behind him.

Now I am alone with the jackass.

I allow my gaze to wander over his entire body, though I know I shouldn't. He might get the wrong idea if he notices me checking him out. My appraisal begins at his feet as I take in his fancy leather shoes and crisp white socks. Slowly, my attention travels upwards. I admire his designer clothes that he seems to always wear. His pants tightly hug his thighs, which I know are strong and powerful thanks to our liaison last night. Then my gaze move on to his muscular biceps and broad shoulders.

Damn, he's hot.

Every time we'd met, he'd left the top two buttons of his shirt undone, no matter what he was wearing. The glimpse of dark hair poking out reminds me of last night when I was kissing and nuzzling his chest. He smelled so good that I wanted more. But Declan is an alpha male, for sure, and he took command of our sexual encounters.

Our first "shag," as Brits would call it, had been wild, frenetic, and incredible. But the other times we got it on last night were…something else. Hot, yes, but also sweet and slow.

"Are you done ogling me, pet? If you keep licking your lips that way, I might have to fuck you right here on the floor."

Chapter Six

Declan

I am certainly not the cleverest man in the world, or even in London. Anyone with a functioning brain would concur with that suggestion. I'm a ruddy fool. If Sabrina continues to rub her lips together as if she means to devour me, I might just have to take her right here on the floor. Only an idiot would even think about doing that. Sabrina should do a runner again and go straight to the nearest police station. I'll admit to any accusation she makes against me.

Sabrina looks up at me and bites her lip, slowly releasing it. "Do you really mean that?"

"What? Afraid I can't remember anything I said in the last sixty seconds." No, my mind insists on replaying the way she bit down on her lip only to let it slide free gradually.

"You suggested something very naughty."

"Ah, yes, that." I move closer, leaving only a foot or so between us. "Would you like me to follow through on that promise?"

She glances down at my groin and licks her lips before returning her attention to my face. "Oh, yes, I want that—Sir Declan."

My title has never really appealed to me. But when she says it in that seductive tone...I'm no longer certain that I'll be able to resist doing what I suggested earlier.

"I love saying the words Commander of the British Empire." She sidles closer. "That's the sexiest title I've ever heard, Sir Declan."

"Please don't call me that. It sounds ridiculous."

"Which part bothers you? 'Sir' or 'Commander of the British Empire'?"

"All of it." Now that we're together again, and she seems determined to seduce me, I suddenly feel that I shouldn't give in to her unspoken offer. "Go back to your friends, darling. I'm no good for you or any woman."

"Bullshit." She lays her hands on my chest. "Please take me right here on the carpet, Your Knightliness."

"My full title is Commander of the British Empire, not Your Knightliness." Why did I invoke my title? I dislike it. But Sabrina drives me mad with lust for her.

The seductress presses her body to mine, writhing in a deliberate attempt to arouse me. Bloody hell, it's working. "Your full title is even sexier."

I can barely catch my breath, and my chest heaves as she grinds herself into my groin. My cock is thickening with every passing second. But I finally manage to gasp, "Are you sure you want to do this on the floor? My bedroom has a plush mattress and silk sheets."

The strangest, most intoxicating woman I've ever met kneels in front of me and begins to undo the button on my trousers. "We'll get to the bedroom later."

"Sabrina—"

"Call me Bree. Since I'm about to go down on you, I really think you should use my nickname."

"Whatever you say, darling." That flurry of syllables flew out of my mouth in a rush . "Have you been drinking?"

She tilts her head back, aiming a mischievous grin at me. "Just relax and let me taste you, Sir Declan."

"I wish you would stop calling me that."

She gives me a curious look. "You weren't this reserved on the night you gave me a mind-blowing orgasm in the Beaufort Bar."

Memories of that night flood my mind, particularly the expression on her face when she came in my hand. That had been the most intoxicating thing I'd ever seen. Why am I trying to talk her out of giving me head? If she wants to consume me, it would be impolite to reject her offer.

I gently caress her cheek with one hand. "Please suck me off, Bree."

She flashes me another mischievous grin. Then Sabrina Remington drags my trousers and underwear down to my ankles. The enchanting woman stares at my erect penis as if it were a succulent steak that she can't wait to devour. She skims her hands up and down my thighs while my cock grows harder and the crown reddens. Only when a droplet of cum forms at the top does she move her hands up to my groin, massaging my inner thighs and spurring me to let out a long sigh of relief.

I push my hands into her hair and do something I never imagined I would ever do. I plead for mercy. "Please, Bree, go easy on me. I'm not as young as I used to be. You might give me a heart attack if you keep teasing me like this."

Her wicked grin returns as she seals her lips around my bollocks. The tip of her nose brushes against my cock, and I gasp in surprise. When the succubus pulls away, she licks her lips once more. "I already love the taste of you. But I seriously doubt you're so feeble that what I'm doing would actually give you a heart attack. My guess is you're in your late thirties."

"I'm thirty-seven. You're quite perceptive to guess my age so closely."

"Don't you want to know my age?"

"I might be a bloody stupid arse, but even I'm not foolish enough to do that."

"My age doesn't bother me. I'm thirty-four, in case you were curious."

With both hands, I massage her scalp, relishing the softness of her hair brushing against my skin. "I'm curious about every-thing when it comes to you, pet. Absolutely everything."

She takes me into her mouth again, making eager noises as she feasts on my cock with slow and deliberate movements. The torturous pace makes my heart beat faster.

"Fuck, Bree, you are incredible at giving head."

Her lips curl into a smile even while she goes on pleasur-ing me with her mouth. When she swirls her tongue round the head of my cock, I suck in a sharp breath and surrender to her every desire. This woman has accused me of being wicked and a stalker, but now she's on her knees giving me the best blowjob I've ever had. My, how quickly things have changed.

As she fondles my balls, she licks and suckles me with in-creasing vigor.

My heart pounds louder and faster, almost as if someone were pounding on a door. I pause, listening closely. Is some-one knocking? Or am I imagining that? I push Sabrina away gently. "Do you hear that banging sound?"

"Mm-hm." She gazes up at me, seductively dragging her tongue over her lips. Her voice has become huskier too. "Please tell me that's not your door."

"Unfortunately, it is. Someone needs me."

"Yeah, *I* need you—in my mouth."

"I want that too." I hurriedly pull up my trousers and strug-gle to zip them up. "But first, I need to punch the wanker who interrupted us."

Bree sighs and slumps against the couch.

I race to the door and yank it open, careful to reveal only half of my body since my erection is now hard as granite. But I'm shocked to see my brother standing there. "What are you doing here?"

"I heard you were meeting that crazy woman who thinks you're stalking her. Was it a good idea to be alone with her?"

"This is not the time, Julian."

He leans sideways, trying to peek around me because he's an annoying arse. "What's the big secret, Decky?"

"You know I hate it when you call me that, *Julie*."

My brother simply laughs. "Do you think I care? Can't wait to tell Darcy and Leo about this. The great Declan Wilde, firstborn in the most prestigious family in London, having a secret affair with an American girl." He edges closer and winds up bumping into me. "Sorry, Decky. You can't keep this under wraps forever. Come on, don't you want to get it off your chest?"

Sabrina appears beside me. I hadn't even noticed when she approached. All my attention had been centered on my pesky brother.

Her curiosity clearly gets the best of her, and she asks, "Who is this guy? He kind of looks like you, but not exactly."

Julian's grin widens. "I'm Decky's younger brother. Our sister Darcy is third in line after me, and our brother Leo is fourth."

"Wow, four siblings? I only have one—my sister Tabitha. I'm Sabrina, by the way."

My brother tries to wedge himself between me and Sabrina, but I quickly step in front of her. "Get out of the way, Julian, or you'll be kissing the door in about four seconds. One, two, three—"

"Okay, okay, calm down, Declan. It was lovely meeting you, Sabrina. You should come to Wildewick Hall sometime."

"Wildewick Hall?" Sabrina's eyes light up with curiosity. "That sounds like something out of a Jane Austen novel."

I groan inwardly. The last thing I need is Julian inviting Sabrina to our ancestral home where she might meet our parents. "It's nothing special, really. Just an old, drafty mansion."

"Oh, don't listen to him," Julian interjects, his grin widening. "Wildewick Hall is a marvel. Centuries old, with secret passages, a hedge maze, and gardens that would make even the most jaded botanist weep with joy. We even have our own lake with a flock of swans."

Sabrina's eyes glitter with excitement. "Swans? Ooh, I'd love to see them."

I shoot Julian a warning glare, but he ignores me, focusing on Sabrina's obvious enthusiasm.

"Well then, consider yourself officially invited," Julian says with an outrageous flourish. "We're having a garden party next weekend. You simply must come."

Sabrina claps her hands together, practically bouncing on her toes. "A garden party? That sounds amazing!"

I clear my throat, trying to regain control of the situation, though that feels like a hopeless task. "Bree, darling, I'm not sure that's the best idea. My family can be a bit... overwhelming."

She turns to me, her green eyes sparkling with mischief. "Oh come on, Sir Declan. Are you afraid I can't handle your stuffy British family?"

"The Wildes are not stuffy. But that isn't the issue. It's just..."

She lifts her brows. "Just what?"

I don't want you anywhere near my family. That's what I wanted to tell her, but it would sound elitist. Sabrina has no idea about my romantic past. I doubt she would have any interest in sleeping with me if she did know.

I place a hand on my brother's chest and give him a gentle shove. "Bugger off, Julian. Go back to your wife and baby."

He raises his hands. "All right. Goodbye Sabrina. Goodbye, Decky."

At last Julian leaves, and I shut the door, turning around to face the woman who just moments ago had my cock in her mouth.

Her gaze narrows a touch. "So, are you going to tell me why you don't want me at the garden party? Is it because I'm not sophisticated enough for your family?"

I knife a hand through my hair, and my tone turns growly, though I hadn't intended to sound that way. "I am not that conceited. It's just...my family can be a bit much. Especially when it comes to discussions of my love life. I'd rather not talk about it right now. Besides, we barely know each other."

"Okay, no problem." Sabrina saunters over to the sofa and settles onto it, spreading her arms out as if she's inviting me to join her. "Now, where were we before your brother so rudely interrupted?"

I swallow hard as my gaze trails down her luscious body. "I believe you were about to give me a heart attack."

The sound of her melodic laughter, so sweet and yet sensual too, sends warm shivers down my spine. "Oh please, Sir Declan. I'm sure a big, strong knight like you can handle little old me."

I groan at the repeated use of my title. "Bree, I asked you not to call me 'Sir.' "

My feet move without my permission, and I seem to have no control over my body anymore. Before I realize what's happened, I'm standing directly in front of her. I tip my head down slightly to stare into her shimmering green eyes.

With her body mere inches from mine, she lays her hand on the cushion beside her and pets the velvety fabric in a distinctly erotic manner. "But your title suits you so well. Brave, noble Sir Declan, always ready to rescue a damsel in distress."

"Is that what you are? A damsel in distress?" My voice has dropped to an even lower, huskier register. "A few hours ago you called me evil."

"And then I offered to suck you off. I've seen another side of you, thanks to your brother's visit." She shrugs one shoulder. "Now you seem human."

"You are a very confusing woman."

"Call it a woman's prerogative." Bree stretches one leg out, nestling it between my knees, and then walks her toes upward until the largest one teases my cock. "I want you, Declan. Right now. I don't care what you do to me as long as I go off like a nuclear bomb. Better make me scream too. But first, I'm going to devour you."

"On the couch?"

"Mm-hm." She pets the cushion again. "Sit down, please."

What else can I do? My heart is racing, my pulse thunders in my ears, and I'm certain my cock will explode at any moment. So, I drop onto the cushion beside her.

Sabrina kneels at my feet and pushes between my thighs. Her fingers deftly undo my trousers once more, and I lift my hips to help her slide them down. Her eyes widen as she takes in the sight of my fully erect cock.

"My, my, Sir Declan," she purrs, "you certainly are...well-equipped."

I groan, both from the anticipation and her use of my title again. "Bree, please..."

She licks her lips, her gaze locked on my throbbing erection. "What are you begging for? Tell me exactly what you want."

"I want your mouth on me," I growl, my patience wearing thin. "Now."

A wicked grin spreads across her face. "As you wish, Your Knightliness."

Before I can protest that ridiculous phony title, she takes me into her mouth, and all coherent thought flies out the window.

Chapter Seven

Sabrina

I take my time stroking his length, making sure to build up the intensity until he's ready to explode like a super-volcano. His chest rises and falls rapidly, and his cheeks are flushed with pink. A droplet of moisture glistens on the tip of his crown, tempting me to lap up the salty goodness. But I'll hold back for now. Instead, I stop stroking him but keep my fingers wrapped around his shaft while I use my other hand to cup his balls. He moans as I massage them, virtually begging for more.

Damn, I don't know how much longer I can hold out. Despite my hunger for his cock, I want to stoke his need even higher to heighten his pleasure. So, I let go of his erection and dance my fingers along his inner thigh.

Declan's deep groan sends shivers through me and ignites a powerful ache in my clit. As I trace delicate circles on his inner thigh, inching closer to where I know he wants me the most. His muscles tense under my touch.

"Sabrina," he growls, his voice husky with need. "You're driving me mad."

I flash him a wicked grin. "That's exactly the idea."

My resistance crumbles, and I lower my head until my nose touches his thigh. My tongue lightly grazes the sensitive skin, causing him to jerk his hips in response. Pulling back slightly, I whisper cool air over the damp trail my tongue has left behind.

He thrashes his head, seeming half entranced, his eyes rolling back in his head. Inch by inch, I dance my fingers up his body, ghosting them over his straining erection, teasing it until he lets out a sharp gasp. Then I return to cupping his balls again, pulling one into my mouth to suckle it like I'm starved and his manly parts are the only food I can consume. Damn, he tastes incredible—and I haven't even gotten to the yummiest part of his body.

Declan clenches the sofa cushions tightly with both hands. "You must be a succubus sent to torment me."

I release his sac from my mouth and lick my lips. "Mmm, but you love every second of it."

"You have no idea how much, pet, no idea at all." The blazing fire in his eyes proves his hunger for me is real and intense, and he loves what I'm doing for him.

But am I done teasing? Not even close.

As I trail open-mouthed kisses along his length, I also flick my tongue intermittently, leaving him on the brink of ecstasy, never quite getting what he wants. His fingers grip my hair, urging me to keep going. The look on his face proves to me just how badly he needs the release I'm denying him.

I maintain eye contact as I paint open-mouth kisses on his shaft and slowly lick my way up to the top, swirling my tongue around the tip and savoring the flavor of pre-cum on my tongue. The salty-sweet flavor explodes on my taste buds. I can feel myself tightening in anticipation of what comes next—me, of course. Declan's breath hitches, and I can feel his abs clenching as he fights for control. My nipples have become hard pebbles, and they're so sensitive that even the slightest touch makes my clit throb.

Now I'm taking him fully into my mouth, inch by delicious inch, until the head of his cock hits the back of my throat. His guttural groans vibrate through me as my cheeks hollow out and I suck hard. My head bobs up and down while I work him with one hand, increasing the intensity of my sucking, knowing that he must be about to erupt. But I'm not done yet. With a wet 'pop' I release him from my mouth, earning a sharp gasp from Declan.

"Sabrina, please," he begs, his voice ragged with need.

I'm breathing harder too, and my cream has soaked my panties. Never have I ever been this hot for a man. Maybe I should worry about that, but I'll think about it later. Now, I need to drive him to the brink of madness before I finally let him erupt. So, I trail my fingers up his taut abdomen, reveling in the firmness of his muscles and the way his dick twitches when my hair grazes his belly.

"Please what, Declan?" I tease, my lips brushing against his ear.

"Suck me off before I lose my sodding mind."

I suppose I've tortured him enough, and besides, I'm desperate to devour him. "It's time, Sir Declan. Are you ready?"

"Fucking do it already."

"Whatever you need, baby." I rip my shirt open, sending buttons flying, then tear open my bra that opens in front. I toss the garments aside. "Lie on your back. I've got a surprise for you that I guarantee you'll love."

I shed my bra and shirt, then shimmy down his body until my face lies directly above his engorged cock. The term man candy takes on a new meaning here with this man.

Declan growls, low and primal, before slinging his arms around me to pin me to his chest. Then he flips us around in one swift motion. Now he's on his back, pinned beneath me, and I'm straddling his muscular body. His blue eyes smolder with a fierce lust.

Lowering my head, I take him into my mouth once more, this time with a newfound urgency. My tongue swirls around his stiff dick as I bob up and down, savoring every inch of him. Declan's hands tangle in my hair, guiding my movements as he thrusts his hips upward.

I can't stop myself from moaning yet again as the vibrations make him shudder beneath me. My hands roam over his chiseled abs, tracing every defined muscle. I can feel the tension building in his body, his breathing becoming more ragged with each passing second.

"Fuck, Bree, you're bloody amazing."

His words spur me on, and I increase my pace, hollowing my cheeks as I suck harder and harder. I can taste more of his pre-cum on my tongue, salty and intoxicating. Declan's hips buck wildly, his control slipping away with every passing moment. I can feel him tensing, teetering on the edge of bliss.

"Bree, love, I'm close. So bloody close." Declan's fingers tighten in my hair as his breathing grows ragged. "Oh god, Bree. I'm about to—"

He doesn't finish the sentence as his release hits him in a tidal wave of pleasure. I feel him pulsing against my tongue as he spills into my mouth with a guttural groan that echoes through the room. I swallow eagerly, lapping up every drop as his hips buck beneath me one last time. His fingers tangle tighter in my hair as he rides out the waves of his climax.

When the last tremors subside, I pull my mouth free and lick the last bits of his cum from my lips. I allow myself a moment to appreciate the undeniable beauty of his naked chest dappled with pink. Declan lies sprawled on the bed, chest heaving, a thin sheen of sweat glistening on his skin. His eyes are closed, lips parted as he struggles to regain his breath.

A surge of pride ripples through me. I did that to him. I reduced this gorgeous, cocky man to a quivering lump.

"Bloody hell, woman," he finally manages, cracking one eye open to look at me. "Were you trying to kill me?"

I grin, tracing lazy patterns on his chest. "If I was, I wouldn't have let you come yet. I'd have tortured you for hours just to see the look on your face."

His grin is somewhat lopsided. "I need to reciprocate, darling."

"That's unnecessary."

"Like hell it isn't."

Declan reaches for me, his strong hands grasping my hips. In one fluid motion, he flips us over so I'm on my back, pinned beneath his muscular body. His blue eyes blaze with renewed hunger as he gazes down at me.

"My turn," he growls, his accent thicker with desire. "I intend to lap up every molecule of your cream, which will surely be the most delicious food I've ever tasted. The scent of you is maddeningly enticing. I simply must eat you up."

Declan trails hot, wet, open-mouthed kisses along my neck, pausing to suck gently at my pulse point. I can't help the breathy moan that escapes my lips as electricity shoots through my body. His stubble grazes my sensitive skin, making me shiver.

"Declan," I gasp as he moves lower, peppering kisses across my collarbone.

His hands glide up my sides to my breasts as his thumbs graze the undersides. I arch into his touch, desperate for more contact. He chuckles against my skin, the vibration sending another wave of pleasure through me.

"Patience, love," he murmurs, his heated breath whispering over my flushed skin. "I intend to savor every inch of you."

His mouth descends to my breast, his tongue swirling around my nipple before he takes it between his lips. Convulsive gasps tumble from lips, and I arch my back as he alternates between gentle suction and teasing flicks of his tongue. His free hand kneads my other breast, his thumb brushing over the sensitive peak.

"Declan, please," I whimper, my hips rolling against him instinctively.

He releases my nipple with a soft pop, looking up at me with a wicked gleam in his eyes. "Please what, darling? Tell me what you want."

"I want... I need..." The words catch in my throat as his hand trails down my stomach and he dances his fingers along the waistband of my panties. My skin tingles everywhere he touches me, and I'm practically vibrating with need.

"Use your words, love," Declan purrs, his voice low and seductive. "Tell me exactly what you want me to do to you."

I swallow hard, my cheeks flushing even more. "I want your mouth on me. Please, Declan. I need you to taste me."

"Anything for you, my sweet."

Declan hooks his fingers under the elastic of my panties and slowly, torturously, pulls them down my legs. The cool air hits my heated core, making me shiver. He tosses the scrap of lace aside and settles between my thighs, his warm breath fanning over my sensitive flesh.

"Christ, you're gorgeous," he murmurs. "The most beautiful creature I've ever laid my hands on. Your hair is like silk, your lips are just plump enough to arouse a man's hunger, and the touch of your skin makes me crazed for you."

I gasp as Declan's tongue glides over my heated flesh, teasing my folds with feather-light strokes. My hips buck involuntarily, desperate for more pressure, but his strong hands hold me in place.

"Patience, love," he murmurs against my skin.

He continues his torturous exploration, alternating between long, slow licks and quick flicks of his tongue. When he finally circles my clit, I cry out while tangling my fingers in his hair.

"Oh god, Declan," I moan. "Please don't stop."

He hums in response, the vibrations adding another layer of sensation. His talented tongue dances over my most sensitive areas, building the pressure low in my belly. Just when I think I can't take anymore, he slides two fingers inside me, curling them to hit that perfect spot, and I arch off the bed with a cry of ecstasy. The dual sensation of his fingers pumping in and out while his tongue works magic on my clit is almost too much to bear. My thighs tremble as the pressure builds like a coiled spring ready to snap.

"That's it, love," Declan murmurs against my flesh. "Let go for me. I want to feel you come undone."

His words, combined with a particularly skillful flick of his tongue, send me careening over the edge. My back bows as waves of pleasure crash over me, Declan's name falling from my lips in a breathless chant. He doesn't let up until I'm a dazed, incoherent mess.

When the last aftershocks subside, Declan plants a soft kiss on the tender underside of my throat. "You are a goddess in the throes, Bree. I should bow down at your feet to worship you."

"Now you're going a little overboard, don't you think? I love the compliments, and especially the mind-blowing orgasm, but you deserve all the credit for that."

He wags a finger at me. "No, no, love. Your pleasure inspired me."

I laugh, feeling light and giddy in the afterglow. "Well, if that's the case, I'd be happy to inspire you again sometime."

His eyes darken with renewed hunger. "Sometime? How about right now?"

I expect him to dive in again since his mouth still hovers millimeters from my sex. But instead, he sweeps me up in his arms and carries me into the bedroom. It's huge, opulent, and gorgeous. The bed looks like a California king. Declan is a large man, but not unusually tall. He must simply like having a big bed.

He discards my blouse and my bra. Both are ruined, but I don't give a hoot about that. He keeps hold of me while he thrusts the covers aside. Then he drops me onto the mattress, where I bounce and squeak in surprise. "You will come again, here on my bed, while I show you all the tricks I know for pleasuring a woman. How does that sound?"

Before I can respond, he's kissing me again, deeply and passionately. I can taste myself on his lips, and it sends a fresh wave of arousal through me. His hand slides down my body, cupping my still-sensitive core.

"Declan," I gasp against his lips. "I don't know if I can—"

"Trust me, Bree," he murmurs, his fingers working their magic on my folds. "You can, and you will burst like a firework for me."

And just like that, I'm putty in his hands again. His touch is electric, reigniting the fire in my veins and deep inside my sex. As I arch into him, craving the climax I know he can give me, I feel his big palms covering my tits. The sensation ignites an erotic tingle between my thighs. I need him inside me, need it so badly that I can hardly breathe. I feel his dick firming up and lengthening while I writhe like a snake beneath him, releasing hungry little noises.

This man knows exactly how to turn me on, like no one else ever has.

Declan places soft, wet kisses on my belly as he slides his body onto mine and moves upward ever so slowly. When he reaches my breasts, he cups them so he can lick, suckle, and ultimately devour them in a manner I've never experienced before.

But he's not done yet.

Chapter Eight

Declan

Sabrina's body has become a sensual canvas, blank and ready for me to paint her pleasure on her skin. That might be the most ridiculous thought I've ever had. But I don't think I'll share that line with her. She would most likely think I'm barmy. And because of Sabrina, I have gone half mad—with lust for her. Yet it's more than sexual hunger I feel right now. I want to get to know Sabrina Remington.

I might have a better chance of doing that if I hadn't stalked her this morning.

No, it wasn't stalking.

Then what was it, you moron?

Rather than answering my own question, I return all my attention to Sabrina's lush body. She writhes as I go on suckling her tits, and the highly aroused look on her face ensures that I'll soon grow hard enough to shag her again. But when she spreads her thighs and bends her knees, I can't resist the invitation she's just given me. I fumble with the nightstand drawer, finally opening it enough that I can grab a condom packet and rip it open. As I kiss her deeply, holding myself up with one arm, I miraculously manage to roll the condom onto my erection.

Now it's time to claim her body—slowly. I mean to milk every last drop of her lust and consume it until I'm drunk with her pleasure. I grip the pillow at either side of her head, giving up her mouth, and thrust inside her channel. The scent of her cream inundates my senses, and my pulse accelerates while I begin a leisurely pace of pushing inside her and pulling out again and again.

Sabrina gasps, her fingernails digging into my shoulders as her eyes flutter closed, her lips parted in a silent moan of ecstasy. I can't look away from her face, captivated by every subtle shift of expression as I move within her.

"Declan," she breathes, and my name on her lips is the sweetest sound I've ever heard.

I increase my pace gradually, reveling in the way her body responds. Her hips rise to meet each thrust, creating a perfect rhythm between us. I dip my head to trail kisses along her jaw, down her neck, tasting the salt of her skin. "Look at me, Sabrina."

Her eyes open, those mesmerizing green orbs locking onto mine. The intensity I see there nearly unravels me. Sabrina's gaze is a mix of vulnerability and desire, and I feel something shift inside me. This isn't just about physical pleasure anymore. There's a connection forming between us, something I can't quite name but desperately want to explore despite having known her for less than two days.

"You're beautiful," I whisper, my voice husky with emotion.

A hint of a smile plays on her lips. "You're not so bad yourself, Sir Hot Stuff."

I chuckle, loving how she can inject humor into even our most intimate moments. It's part of what draws me to her— that sharp wit, that playful spark. I slow my movements, savoring every sensation while I continue pushing in and pulling out. Her juices dribble onto my bollocks. She arches her back, lifting her tits, moaning hungrily as I press those succulent globes to my chest. As she glides her hands up my back, she traces invisible patterns on my skin, leaving trails of invisible fire in their wake.

"Declan," she gasps, "I need..."

"What do you need, love?"

"More," Sabrina breathes, her tone both a demand and a plea. "I need more of you."

I'm only too happy to oblige. I increase my pace, driving into her with renewed vigor. While I drive into her with more force, the room fills with the sounds of our heavy breathing and the rhythmic creaking of the bed. The aroma of her desire for me wafts around us. She wraps her legs around my waist, pulling me deeper, and I groan at the exquisite sensation.

"Like this?" I ask, my voice strained with the effort of maintaining control. I can't hold out for much longer.

"God, yes," she gasps as she throws her head back.

I can feel her trembling beneath me as her inner walls pulsate around my cock. She's close—fuck, I am too—and I'm determined to push her over the edge first. So, I slide one hand between our bodies to find her clit, and I massage that sensitive bundle of nerves with my thumb.

Sabrina's eyes fly open, a look of surprise and pleasure crossing her face. "Oh! Declan, yes, make me come."

I rise onto my straight arms and pound into her.

The bed thumps and creaks and scraped across the wood floor amid her desperate cries and my snarling shouts. The moment she comes, I give in and pummel her twice more as waves of electric shocks barrel down my spine and directly into my cock. I unleash everything I have until I'm completely done.

Reluctantly, I pull out of her body. I'm still struggling to breathe normally, but I manage to get rid of the condom before I lie down beside her.

Sabrina's chest is still heaving. Her cheeks are rosy red too.

I stroke her arm delicately with my fingertips. "Have I done you in, pet?"

Sabrina turns her head to face me, a playful glint in her eyes despite her breathlessness. "Done me in? Hardly. I'm no wilting flower."

"Yes, I'm keenly aware of that fact."

She props herself up on one elbow, her strawberry blonde hair falling in messy waves around her shoulders. "Mm, thank you so much for that. You are phenomenal in bed—and on the sofa."

Not sure I appreciate her gratitude. It sounds dismayingly like she's dismissing me. Does she think I'm a gigolo? I force a chuckle, trying to mask the unexpected sting of her words. "Well, I aim to please. But this wasn't just a casual fling for me."

Sabrina's eyebrows arch slightly, a flicker of something—surprise? uncertainty?—crossing her face. "Oh? And what exactly is this then, Sir Declan? You're the one who seduced me in a bar and refused to tell me your name."

"Yes, but I, ah, changed my mind before we left the Beaufort Bar." I pause, realizing I've stepped onto precarious ground. We've known each other for barely two days, yet I feel a connection I can't easily dismiss. "I'm not entirely sure what this is, but I'd like to find out. If you're amenable, that is."

She tilts her head, studying me with those captivating green eyes. "Declan, I..." She bites her lower lip, abruptly seeming anxious and almost vulnerable. "I'm not great at this whole relationship thing. I've been burned before and can't go down that road again."

"But you're searching for your perfect catch, aren't you?"

"Well, um, yeah. That was the idea."

I reach out and tuck a stray lock of hair behind her ear, letting my fingers linger on her cheek. "I'm not asking for a relationship, Sabrina. Not yet, anyway. I'm just saying I'd like to get to know you better. Maybe take you out on a proper date?"

Sabrina hesitates for longer than I'd like. But then she leans into my touch, a small smile playing at the corners of her mouth. "A proper date, huh? What did you have in mind?"

"Well, we could start with dinner. There's this little Italian place I know in Covent Garden. Fantastic pasta, even better wine." I grin, tracing my thumb along her jawline. "And if you're feeling adventurous, we could take a moonlit stroll along the Thames at night to see the Illuminated River. It's an art installation that lights up some of the most iconic structures."

"That does sound nice."

But she seems uncertain. What on earth did her ex do to make her so skittish? I suppose my behavior didn't help matters. I need to figure out how to ease her worries. But first, I must take care of another need.

"Ah, give me a moment, love. Nature calls."

Her brows knit together.

I rush into the bathroom. Once I've relieved my immediate needs, I take the time to spruce myself up a bit with cologne and a breath mint. And for reasons I cannot explain, I hesitate as I reach for the doorknob. If Sabrina is about to tell me to bugger off…No, I shouldn't think that. I straighten my shoulders and lift my chin, then saunter out into the bedroom.

Sabrina is gone. So are her clothes.

"Bollocks!" I hiss as I race into the living room. "Sabrina, wait!"

I've caught her at the door. She's wearing the blouse and bra she'd torn apart earlier, though she seems to have tucked them in somehow as a stopgap measure.

Sabrina freezes, her hand on the doorknob. She turns slowly, her eyes wide. "Declan, I…"

Mustering all my willpower, I take a step closer, careful not to crowd her. "Please, don't go. Not like this."

She bites her lip, glancing between me and the door. "I'm sorry, I just…I panicked. This is all happening so fast."

"I know," I say softly. "And I understand if you need space. But running away isn't the answer. Talk to me, Bree."

She takes a deep breath, her shoulders sagging slightly. "It's just...I'm not used to this. To feeling so...exposed. Not just physically, but emotionally. It scares me."

Her fear is visible and palpable, like an unsettling aroma in the air. She wants to flee. She had intended to do that, believing I was still in the bathroom. What can I do? I have only one option.

So, I reach out, gently taking her hand in mine. "If you feel you need a bit of space, I understand. But you don't need to run away. I have an alternate suggestion."

"Like what?"

"You can run, go wherever you like. But I am going to chase you."

Her brows fly upward, then her jaw drops. She seems incapable of speaking.

"You wanted to hunt for your perfect catch," I remind her as I shuffle a few inches closer. "You can still do that. Hordes of men would clamor to win your heart. All I'm asking is that you let me chase after you as well, and that you permit me to use whatever means necessary in accomplishing my quest."

"Why in the world would you do that?"

"Because you are worth it, darling."

Sabrina's eyes widen, a mix of surprise and something softer flickering across her face. For a moment, she seems at a loss for words, her usual quick wit failing her.

"I... I don't know what to say," she finally manages, her voice barely above a whisper.

I take another small step closer, careful not to overwhelm her. "You don't have to say anything right now. Just...don't run. Not like this. Keep me posted on your general whereabouts. I'll do the same for you. Or we could use an app that will let us find each other's location. It can be turned off at any time."

"Well, I guess we could try that." She glances down at her makeshift blouse as a rueful smile tugs at her lips. "I suppose I'm not exactly dressed for a dramatic exit, am I?"

I chuckle as relief washes over me. "No, not quite. Though I must say, you make even torn clothing look fetching."

Sabrina gives a derisive snort, but I detect the hint of a blush on her cheeks. "Why would a wealthy, handsome Commander of the British Empire care so much about winning me over? I'm not worth it."

"I intend to prove you wrong on that count."

She pulls the door open further, about to leave.

"Wait, love." I snatch her shoes up off the floor and hold them out to her. "You'll want these, I assume."

"Oh. Yeah. Thank you."

She accepts the shoes, her fingers brushing against mine. The brief contact sends a jolt through my body, reminding me of our earlier intimacy. She slips the shoes on quickly, her eyes darting between me and the door. Finally, she gives me a tight smile. "I appreciate what you're trying to do, but I need some time to process all of this. It's...a lot."

I nod, trying to mask my disappointment. "I understand. Take all the time you need. But remember, I meant what I said. I'll be chasing you, Sabrina Remington."

A small smile plays at the corners of her mouth. "Well, Sir Hot Stuff, you better be prepared for a wild goose chase. I'm not easy to snare."

"I wouldn't have it any other way," I reply, returning her smile.

With one last lingering look, Sabrina slips out the door, leaving me alone with nothing but sofas and tables to console me. I lean against the doorframe, watching her hurry down the hallway toward the elevator. Just before she turns the corner, she glances back, our eyes meeting for a brief moment. Then she's gone.

I close the door and lean my forehead against the cool wood, letting out a long sigh. What the bloody hell just happened? In the span of two days, I've gone from a carefree bachelor to a man utterly bewitched by a woman who seems determined to keep me at arm's length.

Running a hand through my hair, I move back into the bedroom. The rumpled sheets and lingering scent of our lovemaking are a stark reminder of what transpired here. I begin tidying up, my mind racing with thoughts of Sabrina. Her fear of commitment is evident, but I will prove to her that I would never hurt her. From the moment I first saw Sabrina Remington, I knew I must have her. But now, I realize that need is for more than a fantastic shag. We have more in common than she knows, and soon, I will prove that to her.

As I finish straightening up the bedroom, my mind keeps forcing me to recall things I wish I could bury deep inside my psyche. The way her eyes sparkled when she laughed, how her body fit perfectly against mine, her vulnerability. I shake my head, trying to sweep away those thoughts. This isn't like me at all. I've never been one to pine after a woman, especially one I've known for such a short time.

But Sabrina is different. There's something about her that's gotten under my skin, and I can't shake it off.

I grab my phone, my finger hovering over her contact information. Should I text her? No, that would seem too desperate. She only just left my flat less than an hour ago. I need to give her the space she asked for, even if every fiber of my being wants to chase after her right now.

Instead, I pull up my travel itinerary. I'm supposed to fly to New York tomorrow, but suddenly, the idea of leaving London—leaving Sabrina—becomes utterly untenable. I ring my executive assistant to give the bad news that New York is off, and I'll be taking an indefinite leave of absence. No one on my staff needs to know the reason why. They won't question me about it. I am the CEO, after all. But I can't focus on work, hence the extended holiday.

I have just one project on my mind—finding Bree. The chase begins now.

Chapter Nine

Sabrina

Now that I've left Declan behind, I grab yet another taxi and head for Derek and Diana's house to retrieve my luggage. They invite me to stay for tea, but I decline that generous offer. Pippa is disappointed. I can't explain to my new friends why I have to get moving again. I'm letting Declan chase me, and there will probably be mind-blowing orgasms involved. So, yeah, I'll keep my plans to myself.

Where should I go? Someplace touristy but away from Declan's apartment or the Savoy Hotel. A quick look at the map on my phone gives me a great idea. I drop my bags off in a locker at a "left luggage" facility inside a train station. That way, I can access my stuff again whenever I want.

Finally, I'm on my way to my first destination.

The sun is setting, casting a warm glow over everything, just as I arrive at the open-air theater in Regent's Park. The place is bustling with people of all ages who have come to experience whatever play is on tap for tonight. I find a spot on the grass, surrounded by couples cuddling on blankets and families unpacking picnic baskets. I blend into the crowd, my eyes darting around for any sign of Declan. My heart races, partly from the thrill of the chase and partly from the lingering memory of my steamy time with Declan in his luxury apartment earlier.

As I settle in on the grass, I can't help but wonder if Declan will figure out where I've gone.

How could he? I didn't leave any clues for him.

As the actors take the stage, I feel a smile curving my lips. They're performing *A Midsummer Night's Dream*, one of my favorite Shakespeare plays. The fairy lights strung above the audience twinkle to life, creating a magical atmosphere that even the bard himself would approve of, I'm sure. I try to focus on the actors strutting across the stage, their voices carrying Shakespeare's words through the warm summer air. But my mind keeps drifting back to Declan. His deep blue eyes, that devilish smirk, the way his accent makes even the most mundane phrases feel like verbal foreplay.

As I let myself get lost in the magical world of star-crossed lovers and fairies, my smile broadens into a grin. My own midsummer night's adventure is about to unfold. But even as I laugh at Bottom's antics and sigh at the romantic entanglements, I wonder where Declan is. Has he given up? Or is he hot on my trail? Maybe I gave him the slip too well, and he has no idea where I've gone.

I'm so engrossed in the play that I almost miss the tall, muscular figure slipping into the crowd. My heart races as I spy a glimpse of a familiar head of dark hair. Though I can't see his mesmerizing blue eyes, I'd recognize that man anywhere. It's Declan. How did he find me so quickly?

I duck my head, using the woman in front of me as cover. My heart pounds as I watch Declan scan the crowd, his eyes searching. I hold my breath, torn between wanting him to spot me and hoping to remain hidden. The thrill of the chase courses through my veins, making my skin tingle with anticipation.

Declan moves closer, weaving through the sea of blankets and picnic baskets. My body sizzles just from the way he moves, all fluid grace and barely contained power. He's like a panther on the prowl, and I'm his willing prey.

Just as I think I've escaped his notice, our eyes lock. A slow, wicked grin spreads across his face. He's found me, and judging by the heat in his gaze, he's more than ready to claim his prize.

Declan makes his way toward me, never breaking eye contact. My heart races as he approaches, his tall frame cutting through the crowd with ease. He settles down beside me on the grass, close enough that I can feel the heat radiating off his body.

"Fancy meeting you here, darling," he murmurs. "Didn't peg you for a Shakespeare fan."

I try to keep my voice steady as I reply, "There's a lot you don't know about me, Mr. Wilde."

He leans in closer, his lips brushing against the shell of my ear. "I look forward to learning every...single...detail."

The way he emphasizes each word makes my insides melt. I struggle to maintain my composure, determined not to let him see how much he affects me.

"Well, you'll have to catch me first," I tease, my voice barely above a whisper.

Declan's eyes sparkle in the dim lighting, his voice deep and raspy with palpable hunger. "Oh, I think I've already caught you, love."

His hand brushes against mine, sending sparks racing up my skin. I can barely focus on the play anymore, too aware of his presence beside me. The actors' voices fade away as a bubble of silence descends around us. Declan leans in closer, his lips nearly grazing my ear.

"What do you say we find a more...private spot to continue this chase?"

My breath hitches in my throat. I nod, not trusting my voice. Declan stands, offering his hand to help me up. As I take it, he pulls me close, our bodies flush against each other for a moment before we move away.

We weave through the crowd, and Declan places a hand on the small of my back, guiding me away. We slip away from the open-air theater, following a winding path that leads deeper into the park. The sounds of the play fade behind us, replaced by the rustle of leaves and the distant laughter of other park-goers.

Declan leads me off the main path, into a secluded alcove hidden by a cluster of willow trees. Their drooping branches create a curtain around us, shielding us from prying eyes.

Then he presses me against the rough bark of a tree, his hands braced on either side of my head. "See? I've caught you, my sexy little fox."

I tilt my chin up defiantly, even as my pulse races. "Maybe I let you catch me."

His husky chuckle makes my nipples tighten. "Is that so? And what do you plan to do now?"

I'm breathing harder now, intoxicated by the scent of him. My voice becomes barely a whisper. "I...I'm not sure."

A crafty smile curls his lips. "Allow me to offer a suggestion, then."

Before I can respond, he crushes his mouth to mine. The kiss is hungry, passionate, filled with all the pent-up desire from our cat and mouse game. I melt into him, letting my fingers glide up his chest to tangle in his hair.

Declan growls low in his throat, pressing me harder against the tree. His hands roam over my body, exciting my ever nerve. I gasp as he nips at my lower lip. But when he thrusts his tongue deftly, forging deep to explore my mouth, I lose myself in the kiss. My body awakens to Declan's touch with an intensity that both thrills and terrifies me. His hands roam lower, anchoring my hips and tugging me flush against his burgeoning erection. I can feel every one of his muscles flex-ing against me.

"Bree," he whispers, his voice deeper and rougher. "God, you drive me crazy."

I pull back slightly, breathless from the power of his kiss. "Declan, we can't...not here."

He chuckles again, and the sound makes my clit throb. "Why not here? Afraid of getting arrested?"

The mischievous glint in his eyes makes my heart race. I'm tempted, so tempted, to throw caution to the wind and let him take me right here against this tree. But a small part of my brain—the part still clinging to reason—reminds me we're in a public park. Even the willow trees can't squelch the cries I know I'll make if he takes me right here, right now. My only option is to play it cool even while I'm aching for him.

So, I clear my throat and force myself to relax. "As fun as that sounds, I'd rather not give the local cops a show."

Declan's lips curve into a naughty grin. "Always the voice of reason, aren't you, love?" He dips his head lower, his lips grazing the shell of my ear. "But I'd wager I can make you forget all about being reasonable."

He draws my earlobe into his mouth and suckles it lightly.

I struggle to stifle a moan. My resolve is crumbling fast under his erotic onslaught. "Declan," I whisper, half warning, half plea.

Fortunately, he peels his lips away and sighs. But his voice has dropped to an even richer, deeper tone. "All right, darling. Your wish is my command. For now."

The promise in those words sends a shiver of anticipation through me. Declan steps back, creating a sliver of space between us, but keeps his hands on my hips. I immediately miss the heat of his body against mine.

"So, what's your next move, Miss Remington? Are you going to flee again, or are you ready to admit defeat?"

I arch an eyebrow, my competitive spirit flaring up despite my flushed cheeks and racing pulse. "Defeat? I don't think so, Sir Declan. This contest is far from over."

His eyes light up at the challenge. "Is that so? Well then, perhaps we should raise the stakes."

"What did you have in mind?"

Declan turns to the side, leaning against the tree, his focus exclusively on me. "If I can hunt you down again before midnight, you have to spend the entire night with me in my flat or at the Savoy, your choice."

A rush of heat floods my cheeks and spreads down to my sex, all because of Declan's proposition. A whole night alone with him, no interruptions, no chance of escape...The thought is both tantalizing and unsettling. "And if you don't catch me?"

"Then it's lady's choice. You may choose our next adventure, and it can be anywhere in the world. I'll take you there, darling."

The offer is tempting, almost too good to pass up. But the competitive part of me, the part that's been enjoying this cat and mouse game, isn't ready to concede just yet.

"Deal," I say, trying to keep my voice steady. "But you have to give me a ten-minute head start."

Declan traces a finger up and down my arm. "Five minutes."

"Ten minutes," I counter, trying to keep the breathlessness out of my voice. "Come on, Declan. You've got those long legs and insider knowledge of the city. Ten minutes is only fair."

"Always negotiating, aren't you?" He folds his arms over his chest and sighs. "All right, ten minutes it is. But don't think that extra time will save you, pet."

He steps backward, pushing away from the tree.

I take a deep breath, desperately trying to clear my head, still intoxicated by his nearness.

"The clock starts counting down right now," Declan declares. "Better run, little fox."

I don't need to be told twice. With one last challenging look over my shoulder, I dart out from beneath the willow trees and back onto the main path. My heart pounds as I weave through the park, my mind racing as fast as my feet. The cool night air whips against my flushed cheeks, a stark contrast to the heat

Declan's touch had ignited within me. I can still feel the ghost of his lips on mine and the scent of him lingering around me.

Where should I go? I need somewhere busy, crowded, where I can lose myself in the masses. Somewhere Declan might not think to look, at least not immediately. An idea strikes me, and I change course, heading for the nearest tube station.

As I descend into the underground, I'm hit by a wave of warm, stale air and the rumble of approaching trains. It's the perfect cover for me. I hop onto the first train that arrives, not caring where it's headed. As the doors shut behind me, I allow myself to briefly revel in the first leg of our game. Let's see how well Declan can track me through London.

I settle into a seat on the tube—what Americans like me call a subway—my heart is still racing from the encounter with Declan. As the train lurches forward, I pull out my phone to check the time. Eight minutes left before he starts his pursuit. I need a plan.

My mind whirls with possibilities as the train hurtles through the dark tunnels and passengers engage in conversation. I could jump off at the next stop and double back, or ride it to the end of the line. But Declan's probably familiar with the underground since he lives in London. I need to be unpredictable if I'm going to shake him off my tail.

At the next station, I make a split-second decision and dart off the train just as the doors are closing. Racing up the stairs, I take them two at a time and emerge onto a bustling street I don't recognize. Excitement zings through me.

While I blend into the crowd of late-night revelers and tourists, I allow the flow of people to carry me along like the current of a river. My gaze flits back and forth as I search for any sign of Declan's tall frame, his dark hair, or those gorgeous blue eyes. But I don't see anything. So far, so good. And I've just spotted my destination, a random place Declan might never think of.

I duck into a nearby pub. Inside, it's packed with people enjoying their Friday night. The warm glow of lights and the sounds of laughter spill out onto the street every time the doors open and swing shut again. I hesitate, unsure of where I should sit. It should be visible from the doorway. Don't want Declan to miss me in the throng of patrons.

I squeeze my way up to the bar, ordering a gin and tonic to calm my nerves. I'd prefer a glass of Grey Goose vodka, but a girl has to make do with what's available. As I sip my drink, I scan the room, half expecting to see Declan's smirking face appear at any moment.

But he's nowhere to be seen. I relax a little, letting the buzz of conversation and clinking glasses wash over me. Maybe I've actually given him the slip this time.

Just as I'm starting to feel smugly certain I've lost him, my phone buzzes with a text. My heart skips a beat. *Clever girl, using the tube. But you can't hide from me forever, darling. The hunt is still on.*

A frisson of anticipation races over my skin, mixed with a touch of nervousness. How did he figure out so quickly that I'd taken the tube? I down the rest of my drink, the gin burning pleasantly as it slides down my throat. Time to get moving again. The chase won't be as thrilling if he finds me so soon.

I slip out of the pub and back onto the bustling street. The night air feels cool against my cheeks, though my wool coat keeps the rest of me warm. When I glance at my phone, I realize it's been twenty minutes since I left Declan in the park. He could be anywhere by now.

On impulse, I hail a taxi.

"Where to, miss?" the driver asks as I slide into the backseat.

I hesitate for a moment, then grin. "Westminster, please. Drop me off at the best pub."

As we weave through the London traffic, I keep an eye out for any sign of Declan. I can't wait for our next adventure, and I have a fantastic idea for that.

Chapter Ten

Declan

Finding Bree is like trying to capture a particularly slippery fish with my bare hands. One moment, I thought I had her in my grasp, the next she'd flitted away, leaving only a ripple in the water. Who knew chasing after an American woman would become the most difficult task I'd ever undertake?

Where might a tourist go? She is a tourist, after all, though her holiday in London involves searching for a man. Or perhaps many men. Honestly, I don't know enough about her to understand her reasoning or her inner desires. I might be one of countless blokes who Sabrina has found and rejected.

I scan the bustling streets of Covent Garden, my eyes darting from one strawberry blonde head to another. None of them is her. I'd captured Bree the first time thanks to a method that would likely seem underhanded if I told Sabrina about it. That's why I didn't confess. Not yet. And I intend to use the same method every time until she figures out what I've done. Bree might be angry, or perhaps she'll appreciate my tactics. I never promised I would stick to fair play in this game.

The glow of pubs and restaurants and other after-dark establishments light my way. I check my mobile and follow the path prescribed by artificial intelligence or whatever it might be. I have no idea how digital maps work. I've just crossed the street when I see a familiar figure.

Ah, there she is. Well, almost. I'll need to actually enter the establishment to ascertain whether Bree is in there.

As I step inside the pub, the aroma of food wafts over me and makes my mouth water. I haven't eaten anything since I left my flat, too obsessed with hunting my bewitching prey. Though I have visited pubs many times, I've never tried this one before. The smoky lighting melds with the rich shades of the wood decor. As I scan the interior, my heart speeds up. Sabrina perches on a stool at the bar, looking as lovely and delectable as ever.

"Bree!" I call out, my voice barely audible over the cacophony of laughter, chatter, and a football match on the telly. I push through the crowd, muttering apologies as I go, and bump into one gent who scowls at me despite my immediate apology. The dim lighting makes it more difficult to seek out my quarry. The air is thick with the smell of fish and chips as well as a few other foods. I make my way to the bar, hoping to get a glimpse of Sabrina.

Then I see a familiar, shapely figure. It's *her.*

But she is not alone. Some tosser slouches on a stool beside her, chatting up the woman I shagged earlier today. Sabrina doesn't seem like the sort who would go to bed with one man, then seduce another at a pub.

Bree's head turns, and her green eyes flare wide as they lock onto mine. For a moment, I see a flicker of...something. Surprise? Guilt? Or maybe it's only the dim lighting playing tricks on me.

"Declan?" Her voice betrays a mix of confusion but also what I hope is a hint of pleasure.

I sidle up to the bar, positioning myself between Sabrina and the twat who's trying to seduce her.

She flashes me a brief scowl before returning her attention to the tosser.

"Just fancied a pint," I lie smoothly, ignoring the twinge of jealousy as I glance at her companion. "Didn't expect to find you here. Making new friends already?"

Her new mate shoots me a look that's equal parts curiosity and annoyance. He's tall, dark-haired, and admittedly attractive in a generic sort of way. Nothing special, if you ask me.

Sabrina's eyes dart between me and her new companion, and she seems to be enjoying this new game. But she can't make me jealous. Her lust for me is evident in her eyes. "Oh, you know me, Declan. I'm all about making friends."

Her voice drips with honey-sweet sarcasm.

"Yes, pet, I'm familiar with your penchant for collecting mates. You are quite the social butterfly, aren't you?"

She turns to her companion, placing a hand on his arm. "This is…um…"

"Crispin Webber," the bloke helpfully supplies, extending a hand.

I shake it, perhaps a bit more firmly than necessary.

Bree grins, twirling a lock of hair round and round her finger while her gaze remains glued to mine. "Crispin has been telling me all about the best spots in London for food and drinks."

I raise an eyebrow, fighting the urge to slug him in the gut. "I'm sure he does. Tell me, Crispin, what's your favorite chippy?"

He launches into a detailed explanation of some hole in the wall place I've never heard of. I nod along, feigning interest while watching Bree from the corner of my eye. She's fidgeting with her drink, noticeably uncomfortable with the situation she's found herself in. That looks like a gin and tonic. Based on how little of it she's consumed, I don't think she's all that interested in booze. But Crispin downs the last of his pint, ordering a second beer before the bartender has even taken away the first one.

I interrupt him mid-sentence. "Sounds lovely. I should try that pub sometime. Sabrina, would you fancy a dance?"

Her head snaps up, and her eyes go wide. "Dance? Here?"

I gesture to the small area near the back where a few couples are swaying to the music. "Why not? I'm sure Crispin won't mind if we take a friendly spin around the floor."

Her gaze flicks between me and Crispin. She bites her lower lip, a habit I've quickly come to relish as both endearing and so maddeningly stimulating that it makes my cock rouse. But right now, I'm contemplating all the ways I could render Crispin unconscious.

"Oh, I don't know, Declan," she says, her voice light but with an undercurrent of mischief. "I wouldn't want to leave Crispin here all alone."

The gent in question, bless his oblivious heart, waves a hand dismissively. "Don't worry about me. I'm perfectly content with my pint and the match." He nods toward the TV where a football game playing. "Chelsea is the best in the league."

I disagree with that statement, but I don't give a toss about the match. So, I extend my hand to Bree, not bothering to hide my triumphant smirk. "Shall we?"

She hesitates for only a few seconds before sliding off her stool. A red dress hugs her figure, accentuating every curve from her cleavage to her thighs. Where did she get that frock? It's not the same one she wore earlier.

Bree tentatively threads her fingers with mine. "All right, but just one dance."

I lead her to the small dance floor, my hand resting lightly on the curve of her spine. The music shifts to a slower tempo with a sensual beat as we find our spot among the other swaying couples. I pull her close, relishing the heat of her body.

"What are the odds I'd bump into you her?" I murmur. "Then again, perhaps you're following me."

Bree traces her tongue across her lips. The cherry red lipstick she wears makes me hunger to devour them. "I believe you're the one who's following me, Sir Declan. You were so desperate to catch me, after all. But I'm more interested in how you tracked me down."

I spin her out and then reel her back into my arms, buying myself a moment to think. "Pure coincidence, love. London's a small place when you know where to look."

She snorts, clearly less than convinced. "Right. And I suppose you just happened to choose this exact pub. This was the second pub I visited. I took three separate taxis to get here and jogged a block and a half. Yet you arrived only three minutes after I did."

"You started chatting up young Crispin only a few moments ago?"

"That's right. I rock the small talk."

She rocks everything, as far as I can tell. I'm beginning to think she's a closet genius, or perhaps an evil mastermind. No, I'm the dastardly villain in this story.

"You haven't answered my question," she purrs. "How did you—"

"That's a trade secret."

A playful smile curves Bree's lips. "Trade secret, huh? I didn't realize chasing after women was a profession."

I chuckle, pulling her closer as we sway to the music. "With you, it's a full-time job. But I prefer to think of it as...persistent admiration."

"Is that what you Brits call it?" Despite her annoyance, I can feel her body relaxing against me. "You know, most men would have taken the hint after being ditched once."

"Ah, but I'm not most men, am I?" I cup her arse with one hand, strictly because I love how it feels. "And I don't recall hearing you complain last night or this morning or this evening at Regent's Park."

"That was...a momentary lapse in judgment."

"Was it now? Seemed like several lapses to me. Delicious ones, at that."

Her fingers tighten on my shoulder, and there's a slight tremor in her voice. "You're incorrigible."

"Only when it comes to you, love." I spin her round again, making her frock flare out around her knees. When I pull her back, I make certain she's clutched even closer to me.

Sabrina clears her throat. "I, um, need to confess something to you Declan."

"Do you? Perhaps I should pull on a priest's vestments first."

"I'm serious."

A sigh blusters out of me. "Yes, I can see that you are. Why don't we grab that booth in the far corner? It will be more private."

She nods, glancing about nervously as I guide her to a secluded booth. We slide in, the buttery leather seats making only the barest of sounds. I notice how she fidgets with her hands, avoiding my gaze.

"Go on, love," I say, trying to keep my tone light despite the knot forming in my stomach. "What's this confession of yours?"

She takes a deep breath, finally meeting my gaze. "Declan, I...I'm leading you on, though I didn't mean to do that. Being a tease has never been my forte."

I sit back, arching an eyebrow. "Leading me on? That's quite an accusation to level at yourself, darling. Care to elaborate?"

She runs a hand through her hair, tousling the locks. "It's just...I'm not here for a holiday fling or some whirlwind romance. I came to London for a reason, and it's not to fall into bed with the first charming Brit I meet."

"But you did, and I'm honored that you chose me." I can't resist teasing her a bit. "After twenty-four hours in London, you've already enchanted several men."

"Several?" She snorts in an unladylike fashion, and even that turns me on. "You and Crispin are the only ones."

I cluck my tongue. "Don't forget Daniel and Roger. And of course, all the men you've bumped into whilst fleeing from me. I'd wager a hundred men or more have wished they could win your heart."

She rolls her eyes, but I notice the hint of a smile in that expression. "You know what I mean, Declan. My family and friends paid for this vacation so I could search for my perfect catch, not have naughty interludes in your flat and at a Regents Park."

I slant forward, my voice low and soft. "How can you be so certain that I'm not your PC? I've often been compared to Prince Charming." Before she can complain, I tell her, "Yes, I know the man you want is your perfect catch, not Prince Charming. But I could be both, couldn't I?"

Bree's eyes narrow with a mix of amusement and exasperation within them. "Oh, really? And what makes you so sure you're my perfect man, Mr. Wilde? For all you know, I could be looking for a quiet, bookish type who'd rather spend his evenings reading Proust than chasing women through London."

A boisterous laugh bursts out of me. "Darling, if that's what you're after, I'm afraid you've came to the wrong bar tonight. My last name is Wilde, after all."

She rolls her eyes again, but I spy the hint of a smile tugging at her lips. "You're impossible, do you know that?"

"Impossibly charming, you mean." I lean toward her. The scent of her perfume—something floral and intoxicating—washes over me. "Sabrina, I understand, I honestly do. You came here with a mission. But who's to say that mission can't evolve? Life has a funny way of throwing surprises at us when we least expect it."

She shakes her head. "Declan, I appreciate the sentiment, but *you* don't understand. This isn't just a silly whim. My family and friends pooled their resources to send me here. They're counting on me to find...well, to find someone specific."

"Someone specific? Do tell, love. Who is this mystery man you're after?"

Bree worries her lip in the most endearing way. "It's complicated. I'm not even sure he exists, to be honest. But I need to try."

I lean back, studying her face. "You said you needed to confess."

"Yeah, I guess it's about time for me to do that." She squeezes her eyes shut briefly, then aims those beautiful emerald eyes at me. "I'm terrified of what will happen if I find the right guy. You see, I was married for a year—until I found out that my husband was cheating on me. I caught him in the act, literally. After the required separation period, I finally got my divorce."

I feel a pang in my chest at her revelation. "Bloody hell, Bree. I'm so sorry."

She waves her hand dismissively, but I can see the pain etched in the lines around her eyes. "It was a long time ago. Well, not that long, I suppose. But I'm over it. Mostly."

"Oh, yes, clearly you are," I say dryly. "That's why you're on a wild-goose chase across London, looking for a man who may not even exist."

Her lips pucker tightly, and her nostrils flare. "It's not a wild goose chase. And he does exist. He must."

I raise an eyebrow. "Why, pray tell?"

She sighs, her shoulders slumping. "I guess I'm hunting for a ghost, for a man who can't possibly be real. Fairy tales are just that—stories we hope might magically transport us to another world where true love exists. If I search hard enough and long enough, maybe I will bump into the one man in the universe who won't ever let me down."

Disappointment ripples through me, though I do my best to hide it. Sabrina wants perfection. I'd assumed "perfect catch" was nothing more than a mantra. What a fool I've been. She told me from the start that she was seeking her PC. Sex with me had been nothing more than a pleasant interlude.

Bloody hell.

Chapter Eleven

Sabrina

Declan stares at me as if I'm a complete stranger who dragged him onto the dance floor for no reason. What about my confession has shocked him? I had a bad marriage. An awful one, actually. Maybe I had hoped for a little bit of sympathy, but that was a dumb idea. Of course Declan doesn't want to, um…date me. I don't want that either. No way. So what if sex with him was beyond incredible? So what if I really, really want to drag him into the restroom and beg him to screw me?

I will never do that again. The man I'm searching for is out there somewhere beyond this pub, probably beyond London and the whole UK.

Forget about Sir Declan. Right now. That's an order.

Giving myself stern orders doesn't seem like a sign of good mental health. Oh, who cares? It's time to say adios to Declan Wilde.

"Well, that's quite a revelation," Declan says as he studies me without blinking. "And I thought I was the one with a complicated past."

I shiver at his proximity. *Dammit, Sabrina, get a grip. He isn't that hot.* Who am I kidding? Of course he is.

"Oh, please," I scoff, trying to inject some levity into the situation. "I'm sure your past is far more interesting than mine. Probably filled with daring rescues and exotic locales."

He chuckles, a deep, rich sound that makes my toes curl. "You'd be surprised. But I'd much rather hear about your backstory. Tell me, what did you do when you found your husband shagging another woman?"

I hesitate, caught off guard by his genuine interest. This isn't how the conversation should go. I'm supposed to be saying goodbye, not spilling my guts to a virtual stranger. All I can do is stammer, feeling more exposed than ever, until I finally force myself to act like an adult. "I may have thrown his entire wardrobe out the window where it landed in the mud. I tossed his golf clubs too. Oh, and his precious collection of vintage whiskey got washed down the drain."

Declan's eyes widen. Then he busts out laughing. "Crikey, remind me never to cross you."

I start laughing too. "What can I say? I have a flair for the dramatic."

"I have no doubts you do." He wraps a lock of my hair around his finger, twirling it over and over. "Tell me, Sabrina Remington, what other talents are you hiding behind that feisty exterior?"

The way he says my name sends a shiver down my spine. This is dangerous territory, but I can't seem to stop myself from playing along. "Sorry, only my PC will know the answer to that question."

"If I beg, will you tell me?"

"Maybe. How badly do you want to know?"

"Desperately."

The intensity of his gaze makes my breath hitch. I need to change the subject before I do something stupid—like drag him into that bathroom after all.

"Well, for starters, I can tie a cherry stem with my tongue," I blurt out, immediately regretting my choice of words. *Way to keep things PG-rated, Sabrina.*

Declan's brows shoot up, his cocky smile widening into a full-blown grin. "Now that's a talent I'd love to see demonstrated."

"In your dreams. Better go hunt for another cherry-stem-twirling girl."

He moves even closer, his lips almost brushing my ear. "Oh, I can assure you, Ms. Remington, my fantasies are far more inventive."

A shiver runs through me at his words. This man is dangerous, in all the best and worst ways. "Well, aren't you full of surprises. I thought you British types were supposed to be all prim and proper."

Declan throws his head back and laughs, the sound rich and inviting. "Oh pet, you have so much to learn about us Brits. We're only proper in public. Behind closed doors...Now that's another story. But you know what I'm like after dark."

I need to get out of here before I do something reckless. But my feet seem to have become rooted to this spot, my body betraying my better judgment.

"Is that so?" I hear myself say, my voice husky for reasons I can't explain. "And here I thought all you guys did behind closed doors was drink tea and discuss the weather."

"You know that's not true, love. I've demonstrated that for you multiple times."

My heart races at the implication. This is spiraling out of control fast. I need to leave, to put some distance between us before I throw caution to the wind. But there's a part of me—a reckless, wild part—that wants to see just how far this can go.

Declan drags one finger down my breastbone. "I believe you're quite familiar with what I can be tempted to try."

"Hmm, yes." I pucker my lips and tap a finger on his nose. "You must not have been too excited about seeing again since it took you an hour to finally waltz into the pub. The first time you chased me, it didn't take so long. Must be losing interest."

"Never." He feigns offense. "You gave me no clues whatsoever. Naturally, I needed time to deduce your location."

But how does he keep finding me? It's a mystery I desperately want to solve, though I really shouldn't try. Inviting him to pursue me had been a lark, that's all.

Was it only a lark? Yes, absolutely.

Declan tenderly sweeps a lock of hair away from my cheek. "Let's go for a walk along the river. It's lovely in the evening."

That sounds an awful lot like a romantic thing. My pulse sped up when he made that suggestion, but not because I'm exhilarated by the offer. No, I'm…afraid. Of what he might say next. Of his tender expression. No, no, no, I won't go down the relationship road again. I traveled to London to find my perfect man, but now the idea frightens me.

Why couldn't Declan just keep acting like a jerk? I'm so damn confused.

"I need to visit the ladies' room," I tell him, snatching up my purse and coat.

"Somehow I shall survive until your return, my sweet."

A lump hardens in my throat, but I force a smile as I rush to the ladies' room. Instead of stopping there to relieve my needs, I slip out the side door and race down the sidewalk until I spot a taxi I can flag down.

"Where would you like to go, miss?" the very young driver asks.

"The Tower Bridge."

"Great choice. It's one of the most popular places for tourists. You know, the Tower Bridge has appeared in lots of movies."

"Uh-huh." I drum my shoe on the floor, waiting for this guy to shut up already and start the car moving.

Someone yanks the door open. "Not so fast, mate. You have another passenger."

Declan jumps into the car—smirking, naturally.

The driver glances back and forth between me and Declan, clearly confused. "Are you both going to the Tower Bridge?"

"No," I blurt out.

"Yes," Declan declares. He pulls me against him with one arm, then thrusts a few pound notes at the driver. "Let's get moving. My girl has been so eager to see the bridge. She simply got a bit overexcited and couldn't wait for me to pay the pub bill."

The jackass is back. All that sweet talk was garbage.

Declan kisses my cheek. "Relax, love, I'm here now."

I'm fuming as the taxi pulls away from the curb, my fingers itching to slap that smug grin off Declan's face. How dare he? I open my mouth to give him a piece of my mind, but he beats me to it.

"Now, now, darling," her murmurs, "let's not make a scene in front of our driver. The chap is only doing his job."

I glare at him, my voice a harsh whisper. "You have exactly five seconds to explain yourself before I grab your balls and twist them as hard as I can."

He clutches his heart. "You wound me, Sabrina. I thought we were having such a wonderful time."

"You call ambushing me and forcing your way into my taxi 'lovely'?"

He has the audacity to look offended. "My sweet, I merely accepted your gracious invitation."

"I never gave you any invitation," I seethe, trying to keep my voice low.

"Of course you did. You challenged me to chase you, and I'm simply following through."

I gape at him, momentarily stunned into silence. The nerve of this rat fink. Can't believe I sort of...liked him for about five minutes. Never again.

"That wasn't an invitation," I hiss. "That was...that was..."

"A dare?" Declan supplies helpfully, seeming far too pleased with himself.

My body wakes up at his mere presence, and I'm torn between anger and...something else I refuse to acknowledge. So, I mutter, "You're impossible."

"Impossibly charming, you mean," he quips, giving me a wink that sends an unwelcome flutter through my stomach.

"Stop telling me what you think I mean." I struggle to ignore the way my heart races at his proximity. "You're impossibly arrogant, that's what I meant to say."

"Arrogant? Perhaps. But you can't deny there's something between us, pet."

"The only thing between us right now is this seat," I retort, attempting to edge away from him. But the backseat is small, and I find myself pressed against the door.

"Then why are you blushing, Bree?"

I the heat in my cheeks intensifies. "I'm not blushing. It's just...kind of stuffy in here."

"Mmm, it is rather cozy," he agrees as he wriggles toward me. "But I doubt that's why your cheeks have turned a charming shade of rosy pink."

I swallow hard, desperately searching for a witty comeback. But my brain seems to have short-circuited, leaving me speechless as Declan's gaze holds mine captive.

"Cat got your tongue, Bree?"

"I...you..." My stammering only makes me sound more flustered. *Pull yourself together, woman.* Thankfully, the taxi comes to a stop, saving me from further embarrassment.

"Tower Bridge, folks," the driver announces cheerfully.

I practically leap out of the car, gulping in the cool night air like it's a glass of cold beer. Declan follows at a more leisurely pace, looking annoyingly composed.

"Well, here we are," he announces, gesturing grandly at the illuminated Tower Bridge before us. "Shall we take that walk I suggested?"

I cross my arms, glaring at him. "I didn't agree to any walk. I'm going home."

"Don't be so petulant, Sabrina. How about just a short stroll? The view is spectacular at night and very romantic."

I hesitate, torn between my desire to flee and my curiosity about what Declan might say or do next. Against my better judgment, I find myself agreeing. "Fine. One lap across the bridge and back. Then I'm leaving."

Declan's face lights up with a boyish grin that makes my heart skip a beat. "Brilliant!"

I wish he didn't look so adorably excited. That makes it hard for me to go on despising him.

He offers his arm, which I pointedly ignore as we begin walking. We're silent for a few moments as we take in the breathtaking panorama of the illuminated bridge and the glittering Thames below. I hate to admit it, but Declan was right. It is spectacular.

"So," says he, breaking the silence. "Are you going to tell me why you really ran out of that pub?"

I stiffen, caught off guard by his directness. "I told you, I needed the ladies' room."

His lips form a teasing curve. "You have no talent for lying, Sabrina. We both know you never intended to use the loo. What spooked you?"

I bite my lip, debating how much to reveal. "I...I don't do relationships. Not anymore. I told you that. But you veering dangerously close to relationship territory back there."

Declan is quiet for a moment, and I sneak a glance at him. His brow is furrowed, his expression thoughtful. "And that frightens you."

I bristle at his perceptiveness. "I'm not scared. I'm...cautious."

"Hmm." A hint of amusement tinges his voice. "Is that what you call bolting out of pubs and trying to escape in taxis?"

I shoot him a glare. "I don't see how it's any of your business. Gah, I wish I'd never told you about my marriage."

Declan stops walking, turning to face me. His expression is serious now, all traces of teasing gone. "It became my business when you challenged me to chase you, love. I don't take such invitations lightly."

"It was a moment of weakness. One I regret."

"Do you?" he asks softly, stepping closer. "Because I don't regret a single moment I've spent with you, Bree."

His words, and his use of my nickname, send a shiver down my spine. I take a step back, my shoulders hitting the railing of the bridge. "Declan, I—"

"Shh," he murmurs, closing the distance between us. His hand comes up to cup my cheek, his thumb tracing my jawline. "I know you're scared. I understand why. But I'm not your ex-husband, Sabrina. I won't hurt you."

I want to believe him. God, do I want to believe him. But the walls I've built around my heart are high and thick. My voice becomes barely a whisper. "You can't promise that."

"You're right," he agrees. "I can't promise I'll never hurt you. But I swear to you I have no intention of doing so."

"Then will you do me a favor?"

"Anything."

I fold my arms around myself. "Tell me about your worst relationship experience."

Chapter Twelve

Declan

She wants to know about my romantic past. I suppose I owe her that much, considering the painful memories she related to me. Her ex-husband sounds like a right bastard. The way she destroyed his wardrobe was brilliant, and it gave me more insight into the enigmatic woman I've kissed, shagged, and chased through the streets of London.

No, it was more than a shag. I made love to Sabrina Remington in my suite at the Savoy, then again in my flat. What does that mean? For now, I don't care.

So, I focus on the present—and the woman who has enthralled me. I peel her arms away from her midsection, clasping her hands. "Why don't we find a taxi and go back to my flat?"

Her gaze narrows. "To do what?"

"Fuck, of course."

She scowls at me. "You're trying to trick me into sleeping with you again. That's not the game, Declan. It isn't what we agreed to. You are supposed to chase me."

"I've caught you twice. Isn't that enough?"

The moment I spoke those words, I realized my mistake. But understanding came too late.

Sabrina lifts her chin, straps her arms over her chest, and puckers her lips. "Play the game or walk away. Your choice, jackass."

That word—jackass—actually stung this time. *How strange.*

I sigh, running a hand through my hair. "All right, all right. I'll play this your way, Sabrina. But don't think for a second I'm not aware of what you're doing."

She quirks an eyebrow, a challenge dancing in those emerald eyes. "Oh? And what exactly am I doing, Mr. Know-It-All?"

"You're scared," I say softly, taking a step closer. "Scared of what this might become if we let it."

For a moment, her façade cracks, and I see a flicker of vulnerability in her expression. But it's gone as quickly as it materialized.

"Scared?" She huffs, with a faint tremble in her voice. "Please. I eat fear for breakfast."

I decide to push a little further. "Then prove it. Have dinner with me tonight."

Sabrina's lips part as if she's about to speak. But she clamps them shut again instead. After a moment, she smiles with devious intent.

What is Bree plotting now?

"Okay," she says. "I'll have dinner with you and get naked with you too. On one condition."

"I accept your condition."

"But I haven't told you what it is yet."

With a careless shrug of my shoulder, I pretend as if I don't give a fuck about anything. And I step closer until we're nearly touching. "Doesn't matter. Whatever it is, I'm game."

A mixture of surprise and intrigue flickers across her face. She recovers quickly, though.

"Sure about that, Mr. Confident?" She trails a finger down my chest. "Here's the deal. You have to catch me. For real this time. But first, answer one question for me."

"Ask away, darling."

"How have you been able to find me so quickly? Twice I ran away, and you gave me a long head start. Do you have psychic powers, Mr. Wilde?"

"Ah, no, it's nothing like that."

"Then how—"

"Does it matter how?"

She lifts her brows. "I'll count to five, and if you haven't answered my question yet, I'm getting the heck out of here and the chase will be over."

I wipe a hand over my mouth, averting my gaze. "I, ah, played a dirty trick on you."

She leans back against the railing, eyeing me with skepticism. "Five, four, three—"

"Enough. I'll tell you." But I hesitate again before I finally spill the beans. "I sort of, ah, stole your mobile phone while you were in the bathroom in my flat and texted one of my employees. He talked me through how to insert a tracker that would allow me to follow your every movement."

Sabrina gawps at me. "You dirty, lying, conniving snake."

I've lost her, haven't I? And I deserve whatever scorn she heaps upon me. Blimey, if she screamed for a copper I wouldn't complain. In fact, I'd hold out my wrists and wait to be arrested.

But she doesn't even gasp. Instead, Bree gazes at me dispassionately for precisely three seconds according to my pounding pulse. Then she laughs.

My brows furrow. "You aren't incensed at my betrayal?"

She laughs again and playfully punches my chest. "Why would I be upset? This is a game, after all. The most fun I've ever had, to be honest. Why on earth would I quit now when it's just getting good?"

I suspect my expression mimics that of a cartoon character who just received a shock.

"Catch me if you can, Sir Hot Stuff."

Before I can react, she's darting away, her laughter trailing behind her as she disappears into the crowded London street where vendors peddle their wares. I stand here for a moment, stunned, before a grin spreads across my face.

"Bloody hell," I mutter, shaking my head and smiling. "You're on, Sabrina Remington."

I bolt after her, weaving through throngs of tourists and locals. The chase is on, and my heart races with exhilaration. Bree's strawberry blonde head bobs and weaves through the crowd, a beacon guiding me forward.

She darts left down a narrow alley, and I follow, my longer strides closing the gap between us. Just as I think I've got her, she spins around a corner, her laughter echoing off the brick walls.

"Come on, Declan!" she calls over her shoulder. "I thought you were supposed to be good at this!"

She never even demanded I remove the tracker from her mobile. And she let me get away with not telling her about my previous relationship.

I growl like a ruddy beast, picking up my pace as we burst out onto a bustling street, startling a group of pigeons into flight. Bree doesn't miss a beat, using the distraction to her advantage as she slips into a nearby shop. I pause outside, scanning the windows. It's a vintage clothing store with racks of colorful garments visible through the glass. *Clever girl,* I think, smirking. She's trying to lose me in a maze of fabrics and accessories. I push through the door, the little bell tinkling overhead. The shop is a riot of colors and textures, with narrow aisles winding between displays of dresses, hats, and scarves. I weave through the maze, keeping my eyes peeled for a flash of strawberry blonde hair.

"May I help you find something, sir?" an elderly shopkeeper asks, eyeing me suspiciously.

I flash her my most charming smile. "Just browsing, thank you. For my sister."

A giggle from somewhere in the back of the store draws my attention. I move swiftly, rounding a corner to find Bree trying on an enormous, feathered hat. She strikes a dramatic pose, batting her eyelashes at me.

"What do you think, Decky? Is it me?"

"Absolutely stunning. Though I think it might clash with your running shoes."

And I don't even mind that she used Julian's moronic nickname for me.

Bree fake pouts, tossing the hat aside. "Too bad. I was hoping to distract you with my fashion sense."

"Nice try." I step closer. "But I've got you now."

"Do you really?"

In one fluid motion, she ducks under my outstretched arm and darts past me, weaving through the racks of clothing. I spin round, giving chase once more. We dodge between mannequins and displays, earning a scandalized gasp from the shopkeeper as we race through her carefully curated collection.

"Sorry!" Bree calls over her shoulder, flashing an apologetic smile at the flustered woman.

I'm hot on Sabrina's heels as she bursts back out onto the street, the shop bell jangling wildly behind us. The chase resumes, our laughter mingling with the sounds of beeping cars and chattering voices. Bree leads me on a merry dance through winding alleys and bustling squares, always just out of reach.

As we round another corner, I spot an opportunity. There's a small park ahead, with a fountain at its center. Bree heads straight for it, clearly planning to use the open space to her advantage. But I've got other ideas.

I propel myself onward, moving faster, closing the gap between us. Just as we reach the edge of the fountain, I lunge forward to wrap my arms around Bree's waist. We tumble to the ground together, our momentum carrying us straight into the shallow water with a spectacular splash. Sputtering and laughing, we surface in a tangle of limbs. Bree's hair is plastered to her face, and water droplets cling to her eyelashes. She looks utterly ridiculous and completely breathtaking.

"Gotcha," I say, grinning triumphantly.

Though Sabrina tries to hide it, she's smiling too. "I suppose you did. Though I'm not sure dunking us both in a public fountain counts as a proper catch."

"Oh? And what would you consider to be an appropriate capture, Ms. Remington?"

She pretends to think about it, tapping her chin thoughtfully as water drips from her nose. "Well, Your Knightliness, I suppose a proper catch would involve less public indecency and more...private indecency."

I can't resist laughing. "I think that can be arranged."

Standing up, I offer her my hand. She accepts it, and I pull her to her feet. We're both soaked to the bone, clothes clinging to our bodies in a way that's sure to draw attention. But in this moment, I couldn't care less about the curious stares of passersby.

"Your place or mine?" I ask.

She pretends to consider, wringing water from her hair. "Hmm, well, considering we've thoroughly christened your flat already, why don't we try mine this time?"

"You checked out of your suite at the Savoy. Do you have a place of your own here in London?"

"Um...no."

I cluck my tongue, shaking my head. "Are you always this unprepared?"

My mobile rings.

"Bloody hell," I hiss as I swipe to accept the call, not even bothering to see who's trying to contact me. "What do you want?"

"You're in a foul mood. Did that girl throw you over?"

"Julian?"

"Who else would it be? Maybe you have amnesia, eh?"

I push Sabrina away and stumble backward, still trying to make sense of what I'm hearing. "Did you want something?"

"Yes. To find out if you'll be bringing Sabrina to our family dinner tonight."

Dinner? I have no idea what my brother is talking about. My cock had begun to swell the moment I pulled Sabrina into my arms and her soaked dress revealed her hard nipples. Nothing else can get through my brain right now. "What are you on about?"

"Dinner," my brothers says with sarcastic emphasis. "That's when human beings gather around a table to share various types of food."

"You're a cheeky sod. Do you know that?"

"Just answer my question and I'll say goodbye. Dinner at home, yea or nay?"

"Too busy tonight. Goodbye, Julian." I disconnect the call and struggle in vain to avoid noticing how translucent Bree's dress has become.

She quirks an eyebrow at me. "Family dinner, huh? Trying to hide me from the relatives already? Julian's the only one I've met, and that happened by accident."

I groan, running a hand through my wet hair. "I don't care to discuss my family right now. They have certain standards."

"Oh, I bet they aren't as uptight as you're making them sound," she teases, sidling up to me. "Besides, I thought you were supposed to be showing me a good time. What could be more entertaining than an awkward family dinner?"

I narrow my gaze on her. "You're enjoying this far too much."

She grins, unrepentant. "Guilty as charged. So, what do you say? Shall we give your family the shock of their lives by showing up soaking wet and disheveled?"

For a moment, I actually consider doing that. But no, I have a sodding reputation to uphold. Yes, and my outdoor adventures with Bree fit right in with my vaunted status. Maybe it's time I developed a bad reputation.

"You wanted to know about my past romantic entanglements," I say. "Well, there was only one serious relationship."

"What happened?"

"Eleanor and I dated for three years. I wanted to get married, and after two more months of thinking about it, she finally agreed." I rub my hand over my mouth, an unconscious delaying tactic that has become a habit lately, even before I met Sabrina. "But it didn't work out as planned."

Silence follows. An extended silence. Sabrina watches me with a neutral expression until she finally can't stand it any longer. "Are you going to explain the rest?"

I glance at her clothes. "You're shivering. Let's find someplace to get warm."

"Nice try, Declan." She gives me a stern look that she doesn't seem quite capable of pulling off. "Why won't you just tell me what happened between you and Eleanor?"

Because I know how it will sound, that's why. But I owe her the truth. So, I take a deep breath and meet her gaze.

"Eleanor left me at the altar," I say quietly. "Quite literally. I was standing there in my tuxedo, waiting for her to walk down the aisle, when her maid of honor came running in to tell me Eleanor had fled the church. Later, I learned she had run off with my best man."

Sabrina's eyes widen. "Oh, Declan. I'm so sorry."

I shrug, trying to appear nonchalant. "It was a long time ago. Water under the bridge and all that."

But Sabrina sees right through me. She steps closer, placing a gentle hand on my arm. "It still hurts though, doesn't it?"

I look away, unable to meet her knowing gaze. "Sometimes. But it's not the leaving that hurts the most. It's the not knowing why."

Sabrina's hand tightens on my arm, her eyes softening with understanding. "She never explained?"

I shake my head. "Not a word. Just vanished. I spent months trying to figure out what I'd done wrong, what I could have changed."

Bree clasps my hand. "It wasn't your fault. Sometimes people just...run."

Her words hit close to home, and I give her a pointed look. "Like you've been doing?"

She has the grace to look sheepish, but there's a spark of defiance in her eyes. "That's different. I'm not running away from you, not really. I'm running...toward something."

"And what might that be?"

"I'm not entirely sure," she admits softly. "But I think...I'm running toward the person I want to be. The one who isn't afraid to take risks, to let go, to..."

"To what?" I prompt, my voice barely above a whisper.

She takes a deep breath. "To fall in love again."

Chapter Thirteen

Sabrina

Holy cow, I can't believe I confessed all of that to Declan. I've never told anyone else about my innermost feelings. I feel like I've just stripped naked in front of a stranger. Well, not exactly a stranger anymore, I guess.

Declan's piercing gaze seems to drill deep into my soul. It's unnerving and exhilarating all at once.

"Has your brain frozen up, love?" he teases, that infuriating smirk playing at the corners of his mouth. "And here I thought you'd never run out of clever quips."

I roll my eyes, desperately grasping for my usual wit. "Oh please, I'm just giving you a moment to process all that information I just dropped on you. Wouldn't want to overwhelm that pretty little head of yours."

But my words lack their usual bite.

Declan's expression softens as he reaches out, his fingers barely grazing my cheek. The touch sends electricity coursing through me. "Sabrina, darling, you don't need to hide behind those walls anymore. Not with me."

I can't breathe or speak. His words have stunned me that deeply. I want to believe him, want to let myself fall into those impossibly blue eyes and never resurface. But I can't overhaul my mindset in a few minutes.

"Oh really?" I say with tartness in my tone. "And what makes you so special, Sir Declan? Your dashing good looks? Your ability to annoy me and then abruptly turn back into a charmer?"

He chuckles, but there's an intensity in his gaze that makes my throat thicken. "How about the fact that I see you, Sabrina Remington? The real you, not just the sassy exterior you show the world."

His thumb traces my jawline, and I can't resist leaning into his touch. "I see the woman who's afraid to love again but who yearns for it with every fiber of her being. The woman who hides her vulnerability behind quick wit and sharp retorts. The woman who's stronger than she realizes."

I swallow hard, my heart pounding. "Declan, I—"

"Shh," he whispers, leaning in closer. I can smell the faint scent of his cologne and see the sincerity in his gaze. "You don't have to say anything, love. Just...let yourself feel."

And then his lips descend on mine, tender yet insistent. For a moment, I'm frozen, overwhelmed by the implications of everything he said and the way he kisses me. But then something inside me breaks free, and give in, responding to his kiss with a hunger I didn't know I possessed. My fingers tangle in his dark, silky hair as I draw him closer. He wraps his arms around my waist as if he never wants to let me go, and I abandon myself to the sweet satisfaction he gives me. When we finally peel ourselves away from each other, we're both breathless and speechless.

Then it happens. His tender smile mutates into a snide smirk, and the spell breaks.

"What's wrong?" he asks. "You look rather...incensed. Like a bull trapped in a corral."

"I am a woman, not a bull."

"Ah, my mistake." His eyes twinkle with humor. "Perhaps a feisty little filly then?"

I squint at him, gusting a breath out through my nostrils. "Oh, you did not just go there, cowboy."

"Of course I did." His smirk deepens as he clearly enjoys my irritation. "What's the matter, Bree? Can't take a little teasing after such an intimate moment?"

Though I realize he's teasing me, it's still damn annoying. Maybe our new, deeper intimacy has knocked him off kilter too. I shuffle backward a few steps. "I can take plenty, Mr. Wilde. What I can't stomach is your sudden personality change. One minute you're all deep and understanding, the next you're back to being an insufferable skunk."

Declan's smirk falters briefly, a flicker of something—regret? vulnerability?—clouding his gaze. But it's gone as quickly as it appeared.

It's time for me to get away from him and draw some distance between us. "Goodbye, Declan Wilde. I'm moving on—and moving away from you."

"Yes, pet, go on and run away again. That's your forte, isn't it? Or perhaps you'll track down Crispin, the daft git who actually thought he had a chance with you."

All I can do is growl at him. Declan drives me insane. I don't care if he might be right, a little bit, once in a while. I'm done with the jackass. I swear I am.

"Are you giving up the quest for your PC?" he asks. "I suppose that's an appropriate moniker since you seem to think men are like personal computers that you swap out as you like."

I spin on my heel, fuming on the inside. How dare he? After everything I'd shared, after that kiss...

"You know what, Declan?" I spit out, whirling back to face him. "You're right. I am running away—from arrogant, emotionally stunted jerks like you who think they can play with people's feelings like it's some kind of game."

His smirk falters, and surprise flickers across his face. Good. I'm not done yet.

"For your information," I continue, jabbing a finger at his chest, "Crispin is twice the man you'll ever be. He may not have your looks or your charm, but at least he's genuine. At least he doesn't hide behind sarcasm to avoid intimate conversations."

Declan frowns. "Is that what you think? That I'm hiding?"

"Prove me wrong," I challenge, lifting my chin defiantly.

For a moment, we stand here, locked in a battle of wills. The air crackles with tension, and I'm acutely aware of how close we are, how I can smell the masculine scent of him.

Then he thrusts his hand out, grasping my wrist to drag me against him. I gasp, my free hand instinctively pressing against his chest to steady myself.

"You want something genuine, Sabrina?" he growls, his face inches from mine. "Here it is. I'm terrified of how you make me feel, of how easily you've slipped past every defense I've built."

Though I open my mouth, ready to lob another sarcasm arrow at him, I stop short of doing that. He sounds genuinely upset. Because of me? That's never happened before. But Declan has sneaked past my defenses too, and yeah, it's knocked me off kilter. I take a moment to compose myself before I reply. "Do you still want to chase me? Or would you rather go home? Go our separate ways?"

"We hardly know each other, pet. Ever since Eleanor left me, I've been careful about whom I take into my confidence. I've allowed the tabloids to portray me as a playboy, but that's far from the truth.." He bows his head, seeming to struggle with dueling emotions. Then he looks up at me. "But with you, I've let my guard down like never before. So, if you want to continue our chase, you can count me in."

I feel light-headed, as if I've been swept up inside a tornado and only now am I falling back to the ground. "I'm in, Declan, all the way."

His lips gradually curl upward into a devilishly steamy grin. "You won't regret it, Bree."

"Want to spice things up a bit?"

He flicks his tongue out, languidly sliding it across his lips. "Oh, yes, darling, I'd love that."

"Let's take the chase beyond the UK. I've always wanted to see Europe."

"Now is your chance, Bree. You will choose the locations, and I shall attempt to keep up with you." He brushes his fingertip over my bottom lip. "I will give you a two-hour head start. Use any means necessary to achieve your goal. That's what I'll be doing."

"This is the most erotic, exhilarating vacation ever. I'm already wet just thinking about what will happen when you find me again."

"Sabrina Remington, you are full of surprises." Declan hooks a thumb under my chin to place a soft kiss on my lips. "I can't wait to unravel more of your mysteries."

"Well, you'll have to find me first, Sir Declan."

"Challenge accepted, Miss Remington." He crushes me against his firm body for one more searing kiss before he releases me. "Your two hours start now. Make them count."

My heart racing, I grab my purse and dash out of the park, my mind already whirling with possibilities. As I hit the streets of London, I pull out my phone and start frantically searching for locations I might want to visit. My friends will provide anything I need to fund my journey, but I need to book a flight. Or do I?

When I find a cafe that isn't too busy, I call one of my new friends.

"Sabrina, how's it going?" Derek Hahn says. "Did you find your perfect guy yet?"

"Not quite. But I have some possibilities, and I could use a helping hand."

I hear a muffled voice, but I can't understand what the person said.

Derek chuckles. "Relax, Diana, I'll put you on speaker." Shuffling follows, then I hear Derek again. "Chill out, baby. She can hear you now."

"I do not need to chill out, love. Sabrina, what can we do to help?"

"Um…Let me borrow your jet? And the pilots?" She'll say no, for sure. It's a crazy ask.

"Of course, dear. Our jet is at your disposal for as long as you need it."

I jump up and down in my chair, but only the few patrons in the cafe can see that, thankfully. "That's amazing. Thank you so much. I'd kiss you both if I could. On the cheek, of course."

Two hours later, I'm settled into the plush leather seat of the Hahns' private jet, sipping champagne and plotting my next move. The thrill of the chase has my head spinning, and I can't help but grin as I imagine Declan's face when he realizes I've left the country—in a private jet.

"Where to, Miss Remington?" the pilot's voice crackles over the intercom. He has a pleasing British accent, but it's not as steamy as Declan's voice.

I pause, considering my options. Europe is a big place, and I want to make this as challenging for Declan as possible. My mind flashes back to last night and a conversation we had about his travels. Yeah, we actually talked a little bit. He mentioned a few places he'd never been.

"Never made it to Greece," he'd said with a wistful smile. "Always wanted to see the Parthenon."

Perfect.

"Athens, please," I tell the pilot. "And step on it. We've got a British gentleman to outrun."

"Happy to oblige, miss."

As the jet takes off, I settle back into my seat. This is it. The adventure I've been craving, the chance to break free from my carefully constructed walls and truly live. If I'm being honest with myself, the prospect of Declan pursuing me across Europe is more than a little exhilarating.

The flight to Athens is smooth, giving me plenty of time to plan my next moves. I research the area, mapping out potential hiding spots and escape routes. By the time we touch down at Athens International Airport, I have a rough itinerary sketched out in my mind.

The co-pilot informs me we'll be landing in twenty minutes.

Finally, I step off the plane and take a deep breath, feeling a mix of excitement and nerves as I gaze out the window at the sprawling city below. The ancient and modern structures of Athens blend together in a stunning panorama.

The second we land, I jump off the plane and into a waiting taxi. "Acropolis, please."

Jeez, I hope the driver understood what I wanted. I didn't have time for a crash course on the Greek language. Since he nods and pulls away from the curb, I assume he knows what I said.

While the street whizzes by in a blur of white buildings and vibrant life, I wonder where in the world Declan is now. Has he figured out I've left the country? Is he right behind me, or still searching London?

The driver drops me off at the base of the Acropolis, which consists of several temples. I pay the driver, giving him a generous tip, and make my way up the winding path. My eyes widen as I approach the Parthenon, a towering temple that once honored Athena, the goddess of war. I'd visited the Nashville Parthenon in Tennessee, an exact replica of the original but without all the missing bits. As I climb up the Acropolis hill, my pulse beats faster—not only because of the exercise I'm getting, but also because I'm so excited to finally see the original temple.

So what if most of it's been destroyed? The giant pillars are still intact.

For a while, I wander around the perimeter, taking pictures on my phone and marveling at the scenery. As I stand in awe before the ancient columns, a familiar voice cuts through the chatter of tourists around me.

"What a coincidence, meeting you here."

I freeze, abruptly breathless. Then I slowly turn to face Declan, who's leaning casually against a nearby column, looking infuriatingly handsome in a crisp white shirt and aviator sunglasses.

"How did you—" I sputter, unable to hide my shock.

Declan grins, pushing away the column to saunter toward me. "You aren't the only one with connections, darling. Though I must say, a private jet was a nice touch."

I try to regain my composure, but that's impossible to do with him standing there looking so scrumptious. "I'm impressed. But don't think this means you've won."

"Oh, I would never assume such a thing," he says, closing the distance between us. "The chase is half the fun, after all."

"If you think I'm going to make this easy for you—"

"Heavens, no. I expect nothing of the sort." He flashes me a grin and winks. "What's your next move? Will you dash off to another country? Or perhaps you'd like to explore Athens a bit more...together?"

I worry my lip, torn between the desire to run and the temptation to stay. Declan seems to sense my indecision and reaches out, only to retract his hand before he touches me. "You wanted me to follow you, pet, and so I did."

"Mm-hm." I must look baffled—because I am. "How in the world did you get here so fast?"

He crooks a finger at me. "Come with me, and perhaps I'll share my secret. And I'll give you the special Declan Wilde tour." He smiles in that easy, irresistible way I've come to both love and hate. "When I say 'come,' I mean the dirty version of that word."

When he offers me his hand, I accept it without hesitation. Yes, I crave all the dirty things this man gives me.

Chapter Fourteen

Declan

The Mediterranean sun is just beginning to set, lighting the sky on fire with shades of gold and red. The air seems infused with ancient mysteries, as if I might catch them in midair. What rot. When did I become a poetic moron? I watch while Sabrina's eyes grow larger and she takes in the grandeur of the Parthenon and the Acropolis as a whole. We both admire the massive marble columns. Her expression reminds me of a child in a candy store, and I do my best to stifle the laugh that wants to emerge from my lips. Who knew ruins could be so invigorating? I've seen quite a few before, but this is Bree's first time.

I seize her hand, tugging her toward one of the massive columns. Her slender fingers feel warm and delicate in mine, and for a moment, I wonder if she'll pull away. But she doesn't. As we approach one of the corner columns, I lean against it and cross my arms over my chest. Sabrina stands in front of me, her hair a tousled mess, her cheeks flushed from the climb up the Acropolis hill. She is breathing hard, but there's a spark in her green eyes that makes my cock begin to rouse.

"So, are you a history buff now?" I ask. "I thought you would be more interested in romance films and bad reality TV."

One corner of her mouth ticks upward. She crosses her arms in a defiant mimic of my pose. "I have depths you haven't even begun to plumb. Besides, this is research."

"Research, eh?" I let my gaze linger on her for a moment longer than necessary. "For what? A new insurance policy on ancient artifacts?"

Her lips press into a thin line, and for a second, I think she might be genuinely annoyed. Then she shrugs, and the tension breaks like a popped balloon. "I'm an insurance underwriter. That means I don't sell people insurance, I assess the risk of giving someone coverage. I take my responsibilities seriously and triple check all my calculations to make sure they're accurate. But a playboy like you probably doesn't know the meaning of the word responsibility."

I guide her away from the Parthenon, heading lower down the slope of the Acropolis toward another monument I think she'll enjoy. "I'm not immune to responsibility, you know. But I do believe it's often overrated. As for adventure…I'm ready and willing to take on that risk anytime, anywhere."

"You know I'm willing too. I've never had this much fun—ever."

I slip an arm around her shoulders as we walk. "We haven't even gotten to the most exciting bits yet."

Bree gazes at the ruins that surround us, seeming awed by the grandeur. She halts and gazes up at me. "You definitely know how to show a girl a good time."

"Just wait. I have more magic tricks up my sleeve."

"I have no doubts you do."

She may act as if she doesn't care about me, but I can read her like an open book. The sort with naughty pictures in it. Yes, it's possible I am an arrogant sod.

"Well then, Miss Remington, shall I perform a trick for you?" I gesture toward the winding path that leads down from the Parthenon. "I know a little taverna nearby. Best *souvlaki* in Athens. What do you say we grab a bite to eat and see where the evening takes us?"

"That's not magic."

"Oh, you'll change your mind about that once you've seen the taverna."

Sabrina's eyes lit up at the mention of food, and I can practically see her mouth watering now. "Lead the way. I'm starving after all this historical exploration."

Though I'm desperate to make love to this woman again, I won't do it right here. I have another location in mind. Before I found Sabrina on the Acropolis hill, I had done a bit of research on my mobile. I had visited Athens once before, but I hadn't bothered to learn the layout of the Acropolis. By the time I began my march up the hill, I had become somewhat of an expert on the various monuments I would find here. That information gave me a fantastic idea.

I offer her my arm. "Let's go to a different location inside the Acropolis complex."

"Sure, let's go."

As we leave the Parthenon, I escort Sabrina down the path known as the Sacred Way, which will lead us to our ultimate destination. The quickly fading sun casts long shadows across the ancient stones of the monuments that lie scattered within the Acropolis complex. I find myself stealing glances at Sabrina as we stroll hand in hand.

She notices me looking and raises her brows. "See something you like?"

I chuckle, not bothering to hide my appreciation. "Just admiring the view. It isn't every day that I get to escort a stunning woman through one of the world's most beautiful cities."

"Flattery will get you nowhere, Mr. Wilde."

"On the contrary," I retort with a smirk, "I find flattery gets me everywhere, especially with you." I pause, drawing her closer as we approach our destination. "And I do mean *everywhere*."

Sabrina's lips tick up at one corner. "I'm a divorcee, Your Knightliness. All your smooth talk flies right past me."

"Does it? Then how do you explain your behavior in the Beaufort Bar?" I slide my hand down to her arse and give it a squeeze, making her suck in a sharp breath. "See? I can push your buttons with such ease."

"Are you planning to stand here all night fondling my ass?"

"No, I mean to caress your bottom in various locations."

I clasp Bree's hand, guiding her toward our destination. We come to a stop in front of a structure much smaller than the Parthenon. This temple features elegant columns that are quite reminiscent of that structure. I can see well enough in the deepening twilight to steer Sabrina toward a particular column. Her lips fall open as she examines the surroundings.

"This is the Propylaia," I explain, gesturing to the damaged edifice before us. "It's a monumental gateway that separates the secular and religious quarters of the Acropolis."

Sabrina turns to me, seeming rather impressed. "You really know your stuff, don't you? I hadn't pegged you for an ancient history buff."

"I'm a man of many talents, pet." I wink, enjoying the way her cheeks flush at my suggestive tone. "I intend to demonstrate those talents tonight."

"Really? I assumed your talents were limited to looking pretty and making sarcastic comments."

I lay a hand over my heart in mock offense. "You wound me, darling. I'll have you know I'm gifted in many disciplines. Ancient history happens to be one of my more...academic pursuits."

She aims her curious gaze at me. "And what other pursuits might you have, Mr. Wilde?"

"Don't be coy, Bree. You know full well what my private hobbies involve."

"Tap the brakes, Casanova. I'm not that easy to seduce."

"Pretend that's true if you like. But who said anything about seduction?" I graze my thumb across her bottom lip. "I was merely suggesting we explore the Propylaia."

As we approach the massive gateway, I tip my head back to admire the monumental nature of the structure. After a moment, I glance round to make certain no one else is in the vicinity. Bree seems enchanted by the structure, but I wait until the last stragglers have finally exited the area, and we are alone, before I make my play.

Sabrina rises onto her tiptoes, peering deeply into my eyes. "Guess you wanted a private viewing of the Propuh-whatsit."

I pull her tightly against me as my cock begins to swell. The feel of her body against mine always does that to me. "No, darling, I intend to fuck you."

"You don't mean in this exact spot."

"That's precisely what I mean." I pull her skirt up little by little until I can feel her cream dribbling onto my fingers. I can't resist sucking in a long draft of her heady scent.

Sabrina's eyes flare wide, a mix of shock and excitement flashing across her face. "Declan, we can't possibly...Not here. This is an ancient monument, a revered piece of world history."

I grin at her scandalized tone. "That's what makes it exciting, love. Think of it as paying homage to the ancient Greeks. They were quite fond of a good shag, you know. And I swear we shall not deface even one centimeter of this column."

She glances around nervously, hugging herself. "But what if someone sees us? We've screwed outdoors, but never inside a sacred monument. What if security guards stumble onto us in the throes?"

"That's half the thrill, isn't it?" I murmur, my hands sliding up her sides. "But don't worry, I've been watching. The place is deserted."

Bree hesitates briefly, then a playful glint flickers in her eyes. "Well, when in Rome...or Athens, I suppose."

She is adorable when she reverts to her good-girl persona.

I flick my fingernail across her clit, and her eyes flash wide. "Precisely, darling. When in Athens..."

I press Sabrina against the cool marble of the column, my hands roaming her body with increasing urgency. When I nip at her earlobe, she moans with all the decadence of a courtesan.

"Declan," she breathes, her tits rising and falling heavily. "We really shouldn't...I kind of feel like I'd be breaking sacred laws or something."

Her protests fade as I capture her lips in a searing kiss. I can feel her resolve crumbling, her body melting against mine. My hands slide down to her thighs, hitching up her dress.

"Tell me to stop," I challenge, my voice husky. "Tell me you don't want this."

"Don't you dare stop." She grasps me by the collar of my shirt. Her lips collide with mine, urgent and demanding.

I waste no time as I drag my hands up her thighs and simultaneously plunge my tongue into her mouth. Sabrina whimpers, rocking her hips forward into my burgeoning erection.

"Impatient, are we?" I murmur, nipping at her lower lip.

"Shut up and fuck me already," she hisses.

I chuckle. "Whatever the lady wishes."

In one swift motion, I hoist her up and spin around, pinning her against the column. Sabrina wraps her legs around my waist, her dress bunching up at her hips. I hunt about in my trousers until I find a condom, then hurriedly roll it on. As I push her knickers aside, I tease her with my fingers until she's squirming against me. The ribbed condom must make her even randier than usual.

"Declan, please," she whimpers, her nails digging into my shoulders. "Stop teasing."

I smirk, enjoying her desperation. "Patience, darling. Good things come to those who wait."

But I can't resist her for long. With a low groan, I free myself from my trousers and push into her welcoming heat so swiftly and deeply that we both gasp. Her head falls backward against the column as I begin a frantic pace of pummeling her body. Her head thrashes. Her fingers clutch my head, and her nails dig into my flesh. I don't give a damn, despite the pain.

"Fuck," I hiss, freezing for a moment to savor the sensations. "You feel incredible."

Sabrina rolls her hips impatiently. "Move, Declan. Now."

I oblige, setting a steady rhythm that has her moaning softly with each thrust. The risk of discovery adds an extra thrill, and I have to remind myself to keep quiet.

"Shh, love," I murmur against her neck. "Don't want to alert the guards, do we?"

Bree bites her lip, stifling a moan as I hit a particularly sensitive spot. Her fingers dig into my shoulders, urging me on. The ancient marble column is cool against my palms as I brace myself, driving deeper into Sabrina's welcoming heat. The contrast of the cold stone and her warm skin is intoxicating. I can feel her pulse racing and see the flush spreading across her chest.

"Oh, Declan," she pants, her voice barely above a whisper. "This is...oh shit..."

I relish the way she falls apart in my arms, but we aren't done yet. "Enjoying our little history lesson, are we?"

Sabrina's response is cut off when I slam into her so deeply and thoroughly that she throws her head back, her mouth open in a silent cry of ecstasy. I capture her lips in a searing kiss that muffles her moans as I continue to thrust into her, our bodies moving in perfect synchronization. The risk of discovery only heightens our passion, every sound amplified in the ancient stillness surrounding us.

I trail kisses down her neck, tasting the salt on her skin. "You're close, aren't you? I can feel it."

"Yes," she shouts. "God, yes. Don't stop."

I increase my pace, angling my hips to hit that spot I know makes her see stars. Her body clenches around me, and I can feel she's about to come thanks to the way her inner muscles pulsate. The feeling drives me mad.

"Come for me, love, do it now." My voice has grown so harsh that I hardly recognize it.

Sabrina's body freezes, her legs tightening around my waist as she finally reaches her peak. I capture her cry of release with my mouth, kissing her deeply as she shudders against me. The feel of her inner muscles pulsing around me pushes me over the edge, and I follow her into ecstasy with a muffled groan. Then I punch into her twice more, groaning and sagging against her as I unleash everything I have. For a moment, we stay locked together, breathing heavily as we come down from our shared high. The ancient stones of the Propylaia stand silent witness to our indiscretion.

"Well," Sabrina says shyly, "that was certainly one way to appreciate history."

I chuckle, carefully setting Bree down on her shaky legs. "Indeed. I'd say we've paid proper homage to Aphrodite herself."

Sabrina smooths down her dress, a flush still coloring her cheeks, glancing around nervously. Her voice is almost a whisper. "I can't believe we just did that."

I grin, tucking myself back into my trousers. "Believe it, darling. That was one for the history books."

Sabrina smacks my arm lightly, but I can see the sparkle in her eyes. "You're incorrigible."

"And you love it," I retort, pulling her in for a quick kiss.

As we straighten our clothes and attempt to look presentable, I hear the distant sound of voices. Sabrina's eyes widen in panic.

"Relax," I murmur, taking her hand. "Act natural. We're just two tourists admiring the architecture who forgot when the Acropolis closes in the evening."

Once we've reassembled our clothing, we dash out of the Propylaia, not even caring if someone saw or heard our passionate encounter.

Fuck propriety. This woman has awakened me in ways I can't even describe, and it feels incredible.

Chapter Fifteen

Sabrina

As we rush through the city of Athens, clinging to each other's hands, we both can't stop grinning. I giggle too, which is not like me at all. Declan Wilde has shown me the kind of passion and excitement I had never dreamed of experiencing before I met him. Yeah, his last name is entirely appropriate. Declan is the wildest man I've ever met. I can't believe we had sex inside a half-demolished ancient building, up against a huge marble column.

Losing my mind feels surprisingly good.

Until I hear shouts behind us, emanating from the Acropolis. Declan releases my hand so he can spin around and look behind us. I don't notice he's fallen behind until I finally glance backward. He's just caught up to me again.

"Bree," Declan calls out, his voice husky with laughter and exertion. "I think we've lost them!"

"Lost who?" I glance over my shoulder, half wondering if an angry mob of archaeologists chasing us with trowels and brushes. But the winding cobblestone street behind us is empty, save for a stray cat watching us with judgmental eyes.

"The security guards," Declan announces, just as he reclaims my hand. "I think we lost them, though I can't be certain that an entire army isn't tracking us."

"Oh my god," I wheeze, slowing to a stop and doubling over. "I can't believe we just did that. I'm pretty sure we committed, like, seven different crimes against history."

Declan's hands find my waist, and he pulls me upright against his chest. "Only seven? I'd say we're slacking off, love."

I smack his chest again, but I can't help the laughter that bubbles up from my throat. "You're incorrigible, Declan Wilde."

That roguish grin always makes my knees weak. "And you love it, Sabrina Remington."

I'm about to issue a scathing retort when a nearby church bell chimes, reminding me of our precarious situation. I glance around nervously. "We should probably keep moving."

Declan nods, his expression turning serious for a moment. "Right you are. I know just the place. Remember that taverna I mentioned?"

"Ooh, yes, food. That sounds incredible. Our workout in the Propylaea burned off all my energy. I'm starved."

He reclaims my hand, leading me through a maze of narrow streets. The adrenaline is still coursing through my veins, making everything feel heightened and surreal—in the best way. We pass colorful doorways and balconies overflowing with flowers, the scent of jasmine mixing with the salt air and the faint aroma of grilled meat. As we turn a corner, I catch sight of a small, unassuming taverna tucked away in a quiet alley.

Declan pulls me inside, and we're immediately enveloped in the warm, inviting atmosphere. The walls are adorned with old photographs and rustic decorations, and the air is thick with the scent of garlic and roasting lamb.

"Ah, Declan!" A boisterous voice booms from behind the bar. An older man with a salt-and-pepper mustache waves us over. "Back so soon?"

"Nikos, my friend." Declan greets him with a hearty handshake and half hug. "We're in need of sustenance and perhaps a bit of...discretion."

"Ah, I see," Nikos says with a knowing wink. "The usual table in the back, then?"

Declan nods gratefully, and Nikos ushers us to a cozy corner booth partially hidden behind a wooden partition. As we slide into our seats, I marvel at how easily Declan seems to charm everyone he meets. It's like he has friends in every corner of the world.

I raise an eyebrow at him once we're settled. "So, the 'usual' table, huh? Just how often do you bring women here after defiling ancient monuments?"

Declan's eyes bulge in mock offense. "I'll have you know, Miss Remington, that you are the first and only woman I've ever brought here after such illicit activities." He curls a lock of my hair around his finger as he nuzzles my cheek. "Though I must admit, you're making me wish I'd started this tradition much sooner."

Clearing my throat, I reach for the menu to hide my flustered expression. I try to play it cool, refusing to let him see how intensely he affects me. But yeah, my resolve lasts about five seconds. That's when Declan clasps my hand, lifting it to his lips, and feathers them delicately over my skin.

Fortunately, Nikos appears with two glasses of ouzo and a knowing smile. "For the lovebirds," he says with a wink. "Now, what can I get you to eat?"

We order a feast of Greek delicacies—*dolmades, spanakopita, moussaka*, and more. As we wait for our food, sipping our ouzo, I'm struck by how surreal this all feels. Just a week ago, I was drowning in paperwork at my mind-numbing insurance job in Asheville, North Carolina, and now I'm on the run from Greek security guards with a devastatingly handsome Brit. Life has a funny way of surprising you.

"Penny for your thoughts?" Declan asks, his fingers tracing lazy circles on the back of my hand.

I take a sip of ouzo, savoring the anise flavor. "Just thinking about how crazy this all is. A week ago, I was living the most boring life imaginable. And now…" I gesture vaguely at our surroundings.

"Do you regret it? Coming with me, I mean."

I consider his question for a moment. Do I regret throwing caution to the wind and jetting off to Europe to play naughty games with a man I barely know? Do I regret the heart pounding excitement, the breathtaking scenery, the body-shattering climaxes? I peer into Declan eyes and feel my heart skip a beat, the answer suddenly clear.

"Not for a second," I reply softly, surprising myself with my honesty. "These past few days have been…incredible. Terrifying at times, but incredible."

Declan grins with a radiance that's dazzling. He leans across the table, his lips just inches from mine. "I'm glad to hear it, because I've got plans for us, Bree. Big plans."

"Oh, really?" I arch an eyebrow, trying to ignore the way my pulse quickens from his proximity. "And what might those be?"

"For starters, I was thinking we could hop on my friend's yacht tomorrow and sail to Santorini. I know a little cove there—"

"Uh-uh-uh," I chastise, wagging a finger at him. "We agreed to a chase, not a lazy getaway in the Mediterranean."

That devilish amusement twinkles in his eyes again. "Ah, but who says we can't have both, love? A bit of leisure between the thrills?"

I lean back, crossing my arms. "I thought you were supposed to be this big, bad adventurer. Don't tell me you're going soft on me already."

"Never, darling. But even the most daring adventurers need a moment to recover their breath." He slides his hand onto my thigh, caressing my flesh with his fingertips. "Besides, I have some ideas for that yacht that are anything but soft."

Declan is sneaky, but he won't distract me with silky promises, not this time. "That's not how this game is supposed to go. *You* chase *me*."

He slumps against his chair. "As you wish."

"I won't make it easy for you to find me this time."

"But how do you mean to foil me?"

"You'll see." My bladder thinks now is a good time for a bathroom break. So, I decide to use that to my advantage in this game of one-ups-manship with Declan. "Will you excuse me? I need to use the restroom. Please tell me this place has one."

"Naturally. It's directly opposite the doorway."

"Thank you."

I slink into the restroom and relieve myself, but that wasn't my only reason for sneaking in here. I get my phone and tap out a message to Diana Hahn. She seems the most likely to have the right connections to get this done for me. Her response comes quickly and provides exactly what I need. I follow her instructions, then thank her for the assist.

After sprucing myself up a bit, I return to Declan and our table. "How badly did you miss me?"

"Desperately."

I shiver at the tickly sensation of his breath on my ear but force myself to stay focused. "Well, you're about to miss me a whole lot more, Sir Declan."

His eyebrows shoot up. "Oh? And why is that?"

I lean in, mirroring his posture, my lips almost brushing his ear. "Because in about thirty seconds, I'm going to disappear."

"You've become a magician?"

"Nope. I told you the truth. I'm about to vanish from your sight."

Declan pulls back, his brows wrinkling slightly. "Is that a challenge, love?"

"It's a promise," I say, just as Nikos appears with our first round of dishes.

The taverna owner sets down plates of steaming *dolmades* and *spanakopita*, the aroma making my mouth water. But I can't indulge, not yet. I stand up abruptly, making Declan start.

"Enjoy your meal," I say with a wink. "I'll be seeing you... eventually."

With that, I turn on my heel and dash out of the taverna, my heart pounding with exhilaration. I hear Declan's surprised shout behind me, but I don't look back as I weave through the narrow streets of Athens, my feet carrying me swiftly over the worn cobblestones.

The dark alley casts long shadows onto the street ahead of me as I navigate the maze-like alleys, relying on the directions Diana sent me. Left, right, another right, then straight for two blocks. I can hear Declan's footsteps behind me, his deep voice calling my name, but I don't slow down.

Finally, I spot what I'm looking for—a yellow taxi. Once I flag the driver down, I climb inside. Diana had warned me about Athens cabbies and how they sometimes try to scam tourists by claiming they provided extra services, like music playing during the trip. Diana told me never to pay more than the actual fare, excepting the tip. I'm so lucky to have a friend who knows the ins and outs of traveling in Greece. Diana has been there twenty-two times.

Wow. That's a lot of traveling.

The driver twists around in his seat to smile graciously at me. "Where may I take you, miss?"

"The airport, please."

His smile mutates into a wide grin. "You are American, eh? Let me turn the radio on for you to enjoy local music."

"I appreciate the offer, but I'd rather ride in silence and enjoy the view."

"Are you sure? I could—"

"Thank you, but no."

He sighs, then faces forward again. As the car rolls down the street, I glance back, half expecting to see Declan's tall figure chasing after me. But the narrow alleyway behind us is empty. I settle back into the seat, my heart still racing from the thrill of the escape and the chase to come.

The driver weaves through the bustling Athens traffic, and I watch as the ancient city blurs past my window. Part of me wonders if I've gone too far, if this game of cat and mouse is pushing things to the limit and beyond. But then I remember the mischievous glint in Declan's eyes, the way he thrives on challenges, and I know this is exactly the kind of adventure he craves.

One thing I've learned lately? I crave adventure too.

As we approach the airport, I pull out my phone to alert the pilots that I'm on my way. Diana's connections have come through once again, and I'll be heading somewhere farther north once I reach the jet. The driver stops along the curb where passengers enter the terminal. As I hand him some euros, including a nice tip, he grins at me.

"I am Isaak, by the way. And if you wish to have more Greek experiences, I can drive you to all the best towns and villages that tourists love to visit—"

"Thanks a lot, Isaak. But I have an itinerary all set."

I smile and wave at him as I jog toward the terminal entrance. Traveling by private jet is fantastic. No need to wade through security, and one of Diana's pilots is waiting for me to guide me back outside to the plane. Soon, we're in the air, headed to my next destination.

As the jet climbs into the sky, I peer out the window, my mind conjuring images of Declan clinging to the wing. I just stifle a laugh at that thought. He may be wild, but even Sir Declan has his limits.

"Can I get you anything, Ms. Remington?" The onboard chef's voice pulls me from my reverie.

"Just some water, please," I reply, settling back into the plush leather seat. As he walks away, I pull out my phone and send a quick text to Tabitha.

Hey sis, hope the wedding plans are going well. Don't worry, I'm still planning to make it back in time. Just having a bit of fun first.

I hesitate before hitting send, wondering if I should mention Declan. But no, that would lead to too many questions I'm not ready to answer. I press send and tuck my phone away, letting out a contented sigh as I gaze out the window at the clouds drifting by.

The chef returns with my water and a small plate of Greek pastries. He smiles and says, "Compliments of the chef."

I'm an American on a British jet with British pilots, yet I'm eating Greek food. How strange—and wonderful at the same time.

I thank the chef and nibble on a flaky baklava, savoring the sweetness of honey and nuts. While I eat, my mind wanders back to Declan. I wonder how long it took him to realize I was truly gone, and how he reacted when he found out I'd slipped away. Part of me feels a twinge of guilt for leaving him behind, but a larger part thrills at the chase.

I pull out my phone again and open my email, finding the itinerary I'd crafted during the drive to the Athens airport. My next stop is Budapest, another place I've always wanted to visit. I smile to myself, imagining Declan's face when he finds me in that ancient and mysterious locale. I suppose it's not mysterious to the residents. But for me, this is like stepping into another dimension.

While I nibble on the pastry some more, I can't help fantasizing about where and how Declan might track me down this time. He can't track me with his phone anymore. Two things I'm certain of are that he will catch me eventually, and we'll have scorching sex afterward.

I'm already getting turned on just thinking about that.

Chapter Sixteen

Declan

I would never have expected an insurance under-writer to be such a bloody genius at covering her tracks. Sabrina is the cleverest woman I've ever met. She has led me on a merry chase, and I can't wait for the next destination in our European journey.

But I can't track her mobile anymore. So…how in the world will I know where she's gone?

I spent the night at a hotel in Athens, half hoping Bree might skulk into my room in the dead of night and snuggle up to me, nude and aroused. No such luck. In the morning, I took a ride in every taxi I could find in the city, asking every driver if they'd seen a strawberry blonde beauty with emerald eyes and a sweetly artful smile.

Yes, I admit I'm ruddy awful at playing detective.

So, I return to Nikos' restaurant in the hopes he might have some insight. When I tell him that, he laughs heartily.

"Ah, Declan, you are a babe in the woods, aren't you?" He pats my arm and chuckles again. "You didn't need to waste thousands of euros on taxis. The fair Sabrina must have gone to the airport. You said the two of you are playing a game and you are chasing her across Europe."

Maybe I shouldn't have divulged that secret to Nikos. But I'm truly flummoxed. Besides, he won't tell anyone else. Nikos insists on giving me a free lunch, and I can't say no to the best food in Greece. Now that I've satisfied my stomach, I hail one last taxi to reach the airport. It bustles with activity as I scan the departure boards. My gaze flicks from one destination to another. Where would Bree go next? Paris? Rome? Barcelona? She could be anywhere by now.

I run a hand through my hair, my frustration mounting. This game of cat and mouse is exhilarating, but bloody exhausting. Just as I'm about to give up and book a random flight, hoping for a stroke of luck, I note a whiff of a familiar scent. Vanilla and jasmine. Bree's perfume.

My head snaps around, searching for a glimpse of strawberry blonde hair. Nothing. But then I spot it—a small, folded piece of paper tucked into the frame of a nearby departure screen. With my heart racing, I unfold the scrap of paper.

I'm impressed, Your Knightliness. You've made it this far. But can you keep up? I hope you packed a warm jacket. Meet me where the lángos and gulyás are always hot, and if you're lucky, there will be some somlói galuska too. Don't be late, or I might just have to find a strapping young férfi to keep me company. Catch me if you can.

Yes, I will catch her. And once I'm with her again, I'll be so fucking randy that I might just shag her in the middle of the street. Sabrina is the only woman who could ever convince me to do something so reckless. But since the moment I met her, I've wanted nothing else, only her.

I head out to the tarmac and trot up the stairs to my jet. No one else is here. I prefer to fly myself wherever I might want to go. Sabrina probably has palatial accommodations on a billionaire's jet. My jet isn't anywhere near as large as I imagine Diana Hahn's plane must be. But it does well enough for me.

Once I'm in the air, I turn on the autopilot so I can try to decipher Sabrina's cryptic message. The fact that no one in the airport noticed her note seems odd, to say the least. But then, most people aren't particularly aware of their surroundings. All I need do is search for the non-English words she mentioned—*lángos, gulyás, somlói galuska, férfi*. A quick online translation proves I need to fly deeper into Europe.

To Hungary, and more precisely, to Budapest.

All right, perhaps she didn't mention that city in her note. But she seems to be enjoying a whirlwind tour of famous capital cities, beginning in London, then down to Athens, and finally Budapest. It makes sense. To me, at least.

Four of the five Hungarian words she mentioned are types of food. But the fifth…No *férfi* is going to make time with my girl. If a Hungarian bloke tries to steal her away from me, I'll bash his skull.

As I land in Budapest, the crisp autumn air nips at my cheeks. She suggested I should bring a warm jacket, and so I did. Now I find myself imagining Bree's face when I surprise her. The metropolis unfolds before me, a tapestry of Gothic and Art Nouveau architecture, the Danube River snaking through its heart.

I make my way to the bustling Great Market Hall, figuring it's as good a place as any to start my search. The aroma of paprika and freshly baked pastries fills the air, and I find myself salivating despite my mission.

As I weave through the crowd, my eyes dart from stall to stall, searching for a glimpse of strawberry blonde hair. Suddenly, I spot a familiar messy bun bobbing through the throng. My heart races as I push forward, determined not to lose her.

"Bree!" I call out, my voice lost in the cacophony of the market.

I quicken my pace, dodging shoppers and vendors, my eyes locked on that tantalizing glimpse of strawberry blonde hair. Finally, I break through the crowd and reach out, my hand grasping her shoulder.

"Gotcha," I say triumphantly, spinning her around.

But instead of Bree's mischievous green eyes, I'm met with the startled gaze of a middle-aged Hungarian woman.

"*Bocsánat,*" I mutter, backing away swiftly.

Blimey. I've made a right fool of myself. I can almost hear Bree's laughter echoing in my head. She'd be in stitches if she could see me now, chasing random women through a foreign market.

Dejected, I make my way to a nearby food stall. Might as well try some of this *lángos* Bree mentioned. I order one of those and learn it's deep-fried dough topped with sour cream and cheese. I sink my teeth into the pastry, savoring the comforting flavors. As I chew, I ponder my next move. Where would Bree go in this sprawling city?

Just then, I feel a tap on my shoulder. I turn, expecting another vendor trying to sell me something, but instead, I find myself staring into a pair of familiar emerald eyes.

"Took you long enough, Your Knightliness. I was beginning to think you'd given up."

I nearly choke on my *lángos.* "Bloody hell, Bree. How long have you been watching me make a fool of myself?"

She laughs, the sound like music to my ears. "Long enough to thoroughly enjoy the show. That poor woman you accosted…I thought she was going to wallop you with her shopping bag."

I grin and shake my head, enchanted by Bree's infectious laughter, and soon I'm chuckling along with her.

"Well, I'm glad I could provide such quality entertainment," I say, wiping a bit of sour cream from the corner of my mouth. "Care to join me for a *lángos*? I hear they're quite good here."

"Oh, I've already had my fill. But I wouldn't say no to some *somlói galuska* for dessert. That is, if you aren't too full."

I wave my arm in an imperious gesture. "Lead the way, love. I am never too full to enjoy a luscious Hungarian delicacy. Though nothing is as sumptuous as the taste of your cream."

She grabs my hand and drags me through the crowded market. We weave between stalls, the scents of paprika and freshly baked bread filling the air. I'm acutely aware of her small, warm hand in mine, her fingers intertwined with my own.

"So, tell me," I say as we navigate the bustling aisles, "how did you manage to stay hidden all this time? I thought I had caught you back in Athens."

Bree glances over her shoulder and winks. "A magician never reveals her secrets. But let's just say I have a few tricks up my sleeve that even you can't predict."

I smile at her playful evasion. "I'm beginning to think you missed your calling as a secret agent, love. MI6 would be lucky to have you."

She laughs, the sound sending a shiver down my spine. "And give up the thrilling world of insurance underwriting? Never."

We emerge from the market into the crisp Hungarian air, the sun casting a golden glow over Budapest's stunning architecture. Bree leads me down a winding cobblestone street, her hand still firmly clasped in mine.

"So, where are we off to now?" I ask, trying to ignore the way my heart races at her touch.

"Patience, Sir Declan," Bree teases, tugging me along. "You'll see soon enough."

We wind our way through the charming streets of Budapest, passing ornate buildings and quaint cafes. I'm content to let her lead, drinking in the sight of her bouncing strawberry blonde curls and the sway of her hips.

Finally, we arrive at a small, unassuming pastry shop tucked away on a quiet side street. The aroma of sugar and cinnamon wafts out as Bree pushes open the door, a tiny bell tinkling above us.

"*Szia!*" she calls out cheerfully to the elderly woman behind the counter.

I raise an eyebrow, impressed by her command of Hungarian pleasantries.

"Two *somlói galuska, kérem,*" Bree orders confidently.

While the woman behind the counter fills Bree's order, I whisper to her, "You're fluent in Hungarian?"

Her laugh becomes a splutter. "No, silly. I used an online translation thingy to learn how to say hello and how to pronounce the Hungarian phrases I needed to order the dumplings."

As we settle into a cozy corner table, my lips tick upward at Bree's effortless charm. She's managed to navigate three European capitals with the ease of a seasoned traveler, always one step ahead of me.

"So, tell me," I lean in, my voice low and teasing, "how long have you been planning this little escapade?"

Bree's eyes dance with mischief as she takes a delicate bite of her dessert. "A girl's got to have some secrets. Let's just say I've had a lot of time to daydream during those long, boring days of underwriting."

"You're full of surprises, aren't you?"

"You have no idea," she winks, licking a spot of chocolate from her lip in a way that makes my pulse quicken. "But I think you're figuring it out pretty quickly."

I lean in closer, my voice dropping to a low murmur. "Oh, I intend to do much more than that, love."

"Is that so? And here I thought you were just after my *somlói galuska.*"

"Well, I must admit, it is delicious," I say, taking another bite of the rich chocolate sponge cake. "But I'm far more interested in tasting something else entirely."

Bree's eyebrows arch. "My, my, Sir Declan. Are you propositioning me in the middle of a quaint Hungarian pastry shop? How scandalous."

I lean in closer, my voice a low rumble. "Darling, I'd proposition you on the steps of Parliament if I thought it would get me anywhere."

She laughs, the sound musical and sweet like the tinkling of bells. "Well, aren't you the charmer? But I'm afraid you'll have to try a bit harder than that."

"Is that a challenge?" I ask, my eyes locked on hers.

"Maybe," she teases, taking another bite of her dessert. "But then again, maybe I just enjoy watching you squirm."

I tap her chin. "You're a cheeky chit, do you know that?"

"I've been called worse. Now, are you going to finish that?" She eyes my half-eaten *somlói galuska* hungrily.

"Greedy little thing, aren't you?" I tease, but I push the plate toward her anyway. As she digs in with gusto, I find myself captivated by the way her lips close around the spoon and the soft hum of pleasure she makes as she savors each bite.

I clear my throat. "So, what's next on this whirlwind tour of yours? Paris? Rome? Or perhaps somewhere a bit more... exotic?"

Bree licks the last bit of chocolate from her spoon, her eyes never leaving mine. "That depends on you. Wouldn't you like to explore Budapest a little more before I shake you off again?"

"That's an excellent idea. I predict we'll be shagging very soon and in a thoroughly inappropriate location."

Her cheeks dimple. "My, my, aren't we presumptuous? What makes you so sure I'll let you lasso me this time? Maybe I want to explore Budapest on my own."

"No, pet, that's not the point of this exercise." I reach under the table to caress her thigh, making her suck in a sharp breath. "Because, my sweet, the thrill is in the chase, but the real excitement comes when you finally allow yourself to be caught."

"Is that so? And what if I decide to keep running this time?"

"Then I'll keep chasing," I reply without hesitation. "Across every continent if I have to. You're worth the pursuit, Sabrina."

For a moment, I see a flicker of vulnerability in her eyes, a crack in her carefully constructed facade. But it's gone in an instant, replaced by her usual mischievous sparkle.

"Well then, Sir Declan," she purrs, leaning in so close I can feel her breath on my lips, "catch me if you can."

With that, she's up and out of her seat, darting toward the door of the pastry shop. I'm momentarily stunned by her sudden movement, but I quickly recover, tossing some forints on the table before chasing after her. Yes, I even thought to get some Hungarian money when I landed in this country.

The cool Budapest air hits my face as I burst out onto the cobblestone street. I spot a glimpse of her strawberry blonde hair whipping around a corner and take off in pursuit. My heart races, partly from the exertion and partly from the thrill of the chase.

We weave through the narrow streets, dodging tourists and locals alike. Bree is quick and agile, darting between people with ease. But I'm no slouch either, my long legs shrinking the distance between us.

"Come on, Your Knightliness!" she calls over her shoulder, laughter in her voice. "I thought you said you'd chase me across continents!"

"Just you wait, love," I shout back, grinning despite my labored breathing. "I'm just getting warmed up!"

We race past ornate buildings and bustling cafes while Bree leads me on a merry chase through winding alleyways and across busy squares. I'm so focused on keeping her in sight that I barely register the stunning architecture around us.

Finally, we burst out onto a wide promenade along the Danube River. Sabrina slows her pace, her chest heaving, her smile lopsided. I close the distance between us, my own lungs burning from the exertion.

She turns to face me with a triumphant grin. "Looks like you managed to keep up after all."

I stumble to a halt mere inches from her, close enough to see the flecks of gold in her emerald eyes. "Did you ever doubt I would?"

Chapter Seventeen

Sabrina

I don't even try to stifle my laughter. "Maybe for a moment there I wondered if you'd turn tail and run for the nearest pub. You aren't as spry as you used to be, old man."

"Old man?" He scoffs, feigning offense. "I'm only three years older than you."

Before I realize what he intends to do, Declan wraps an arm around my waist and pulls me flush against his muscular body. I gawk at him, unable to speak even one syllable. I always feel that way when he crushes his firm body to mine. The heat of his body awakens mine as my chest rises and falls rapidly. He always does this to me.

His voice has become a silken whisper that stimulates me in every way imaginable. "What was that you said about being caught, Bree?"

My lips part slightly as my gaze flickers between his entrancing eyes and his nibble-worthy lips. For a moment, I think he might kiss me right here on the promenade. But then that roguish glint ignites in his eyes again.

"This time, darling, I might be waiting for you instead of the other way round."

"It's doubtful. I had to slow down to make sure you could find me. Otherwise, you might've traipsed down the wrong street."

With a swift movement, I slip out of his grasp and shuffle backward. "Tell you what. If you can find me before sunset, I'll let you claim your prize. But if not..." I let my voice trail off as I back away from him even more. "I guess you'll just have to keep chasing me across Europe, won't you?"

"You drive a hard bargain, Sabrina. But I accept your challenge."

"Maybe I'll even widen the net to take this chase onto other continents."

The suggestive quirk of his lips unleashes liquid fire deep inside my sex, and I'm suddenly breathing harder. Declan always has that effect on me. But when I whirl around, blowing him a kiss over my shoulder, he doesn't even try to follow me. Not yet. As I disappear into the crowd along the Danube promenade, I glance back at Declan—only to find him gone.

What is that sly, shameless Brit up to now?

I weave through the bustling crowd, my mind whirling with thoughts of what he'll do if he reaches our destination first. Just imagining how our game will unfold sends an electric charge down my spine. Declan might think he's a genius, but I've got a few tricks up my sleeve.

As I duck into a nearby café, the aroma of fresh pastries and coffee envelops me. Through the window, I scan the promenade, searching for any sign of Declan. But I don't see him. Might he be hot on my trail right now? He's good, I'll give him that. And he's totally committed to our game, just like I am.

Slipping out the back door, I find myself in a narrow alley. Perfect for losing a tail. I need to get to the airport, but I wouldn't mind a steamy interlude before we part ways again. So, I move out onto the street, slowing my pace, and allowing Declan to catch up—if he can. Then I notice an outdoor market up ahead and jog over there. Can't make it too easy for Declan to find me.

I'm browsing the offerings when a familiar scent wafts past me—a blend of spicy cologne and something uniquely Declan. My pulse quickens, but I force myself to remain casual, pretending to examine a display of colorful scarves.

"There you are, Bree." His deep, alluring voice shivers through me like a sultry breeze. "If you want to be surreptitious, my sweet, best cover up all that luscious strawberry blonde hair."

I spin around, pretending to be startled, though I doubt he buys my act. "Well, well, Sir Declan. Looks as if someone's navigation skills have improved."

"Perhaps." He leans against a display of fruits and vegetables, picking up a tomato to examine it. "Did you ever think that I might know you better than you know yourself, pet?"

"Now you're my therapist, hey?" I fold my arms over my chest, fighting the urge to close the gap between us. "I thought I was being so unpredictable. How did you find me?"

"Oh, you're unpredictable all right. But that's what makes this game so enticing."

His fingers brush my arm, sending sparks of electricity through my body. I bite my lip, trying to maintain my composure. "Well, Mr. Wilde, it seems you've found me before sunset. I suppose that means you've won your prize."

"And what a prize it is," he murmurs, his gaze roaming over my face, lingering on my lips.

I sashay up to him, using all my willpower not to rip his clothes off right here in the market. "But the question is, what are you going to do with me?"

In one swift motion, Declan pulls me behind a nearby stall, shielding us from prying eyes. His strong arms cage me against the wall, and I feel my heart racing. "How about a quick fuck before we part ways again?"

I gasp and clasp my hands to my breast, feigning shock. "Declan, we're in public."

His eyes darken with desire, and he leans in closer, his lips brushing my ear. "That's never stopped us before, love."

A shiver runs down my spine as memories of our past encounters flash through my mind. The thrill of almost getting caught, the rush of adrenaline...It's intoxicating.

"You're incorrigible," I whisper, but I can't keep the smile from my voice.

"Only for you, Bree," he murmurs, his hands sliding down to my ass.

I bite my lip, torn between wanting to give in to the temptation and the nagging voice of reason in my head. What we did back in the Propylaia had been the most incredible thing ever, but there wasn't anyone else around. Not sure if I'm ready for screwing Declan on a bustling street. "As tempting as that sounds, I have someplace to be. Remember?"

Declan groans, his forehead resting against mine. "You're killing me, Sabrina."

I can't resist running my fingers through his dark brown hair. "Oh, come on. You know you love the chase."

"That I do," he admits, pulling back slightly to look into my eyes. "But one of these days, I'm going to catch you for good."

For a moment, I let myself imagine what that might be like—no more running, no more games. Just Declan and me, together. But then reality crashes back in, and I push the thought away.

"We'll see about that," I tease, trying to lighten the mood. "For now, I'd like to know how you've been able to find me so quickly now that you don't have a tracker on my phone."

He studies me for a moment, his expression unreadable. "I'll tell you when we reach the next destination."

"But you won't know where to find me."

Declan smiles and shakes his head. "Oh ye of so little faith. Answers will come later."

I narrow my gaze on him, my curiosity piqued. "You're up to something, Your Knightliness. And I intend to find out what it is."

His lips curl into a sizzling smile. "I look forward to you trying, darling."

Before he has time to react, I'm ducking under his arm to step away, putting some distance between us before I lose all self-control. "Well, as fun as this has been, I really do need to get going. My flight won't wait for me."

He can't know that I'm flying private, on Diana's jet. Can he? Maybe he's good buddies with the billionaire, and that's how he tracked me down. The pilots might have given my flight plans to Diana. But I doubt that.

Declan's eyes follow me, and he seems both confused and aroused by my actions. "Where might you be jetting off to this time, Bree? You could at least give me a hint."

I tap my chin, pretending to consider his request. "Hmm, I don't know. Maybe I'll spin a globe and see where my finger lands. Or maybe I'll just follow the wind and see where it takes me."

"You're not going to make this easy for me, are you?"

"Why should I? The sex will be even better if you have to work to track me down. Time to put those detective skills of yours to good use."

"I fully intend to." He licks his lips, his gaze flitting to my bosom before he aims those baby blues directly at me. "And when I find you again, Sabrina Remington, there will be no escape."

"That's quite a promise. Now let's see if you can follow through."

I turn and disappear into the crowd, my heart pounding. As I weave through the throngs of people, I search for the familiar face of a certain Brit. I wonder if Declan will come up behind me, armed with his patented sexy sarcasm. But he's nowhere in sight.

I flag down a taxi and hop in, giving the driver directions to the airport in my best attempt at Hungarian. Okay, yeah, that means I speak very slowly in English until the driver gets annoyed when I wave a picture of the airport at him. As we pull away from the curb, I allow myself a small smile of triumph. I may have won this round, but I know Declan won't give up easily.

At the airport, I breeze through security and make my way to the gate. Just as I'm about to board Diana's jet, my phone buzzes with a text. It's Declan.

Safe travels, fair Sabrina. I'll see you soon.

Damn. How does he always manage to get the last word? It's impressive.

As I settle into my seat on the jet, I replay our encounter in my mind. The way Declan's arms felt around me, the intensity in his eyes, the promise of what could have been if I'd let it happen...I shake my head, trying to clear my thoughts. This game we're playing is dangerous, and not just because of the globe-trotting pursuit.

The jet takes off, and I watch Budapest shrink beneath us. Part of me wonders if Declan is down there somewhere, plotting his next move. Deep down, I hope he is.

"Still heading for Paris, Miss Remington?" the co-pilot asks.

I jump a little since I hadn't even noticed when he approached my seat. His question makes me stop and think for a moment. Where do I want to go? Though I had planned to head to Paris next, now I'm not so sure. Declan's always been good at predicting my moves, and I don't want to make it too easy for him.

Then an idea strikes me like a baseball to the head. "You know what? Let's shake things up a bit. How about we head to Marrakesh instead?"

The co-pilot nods, a hint of amusement in his eyes. "Very good, Miss Remington. I'll inform the captain."

As he walks away, I settle back into my seat, feeling quite pleased with myself. Marrakesh should throw Declan off my trail for a while. The vibrant colors, the bustling souks, the exotic scents—it's the perfect place to lose myself. And if Declan does manage to find me there...Well, I can think of worse places for our next encounter.

I pull out my phone, tempted to send Declan a cryptic message, but I resist. The less information he has, the more fun this will be. Instead, I shoot a quick text to my sister.

Change of plans. Heading to Marrakesh instead of Paris. Don't tell anyone!

Tabby's reply comes almost instantly. *Ooh, mysterious! Have fun and stay safe. Love you.*

I smile, grateful for my sister's unwavering support. As much as I love my globe-trotting game with Declan, I feel a twinge of guilt. Tabby's wedding is coming up soon, and here I am, gallivanting across the world with a man I can't seem to commit to.

What?! I jerk upright in my seat, suddenly struck by a cold panic. Commit to Declan? I barely know the man. He's yummy and incredible in bed, but I cannot ever marry anyone. Never again. But why did that thought slam into my mind? It doesn't mean anything.

The jet levels off, and I order a glass of champagne to calm my nerves. As I sip the bubbly liquid, I let my mind wander back to Declan. Those delicious muscles, that devilish smirk, the way his strong hands felt on my body...

I shake my head, desperately trying to dispel the images. This is exactly why I need to put some distance between us. Declan Wilde is dangerous—not just because of his ability to knock me off kilter, but also because of the way he can so easily talk me into doing crazy, amazing things. And the way he makes me feel as if I could actually trust a man again. Like I could fall...

No. I can't go there. Not after what happened with Peter.

I drain my champagne glass and signal for another. As the co-pilot refills it, I pull out my laptop, determined to distract myself with work. There are always insurance policies to review, risk assessments to complete. Boring, safe, predictable work—exactly what I need right now.

But as I stare at the screen, the words blur together. My mind keeps drifting back to Declan, to the way his eyes lit up when he found me in the market. The thrill of our cat and mouse game pulses through me, making it impossible to focus on actuarial tables and policy exclusions.

With a frustrated sigh, I snap my laptop shut. Who am I kidding? There's no way I can concentrate on work right now, not with the memory of Declan's touch still burning on my skin.

I gaze out the window at the endless expanse of sky as we soar over eastern Europe, my thoughts a jumbled mess. Part of me wonders if I'm making a mistake, running away to Marrakesh instead of letting things play out with Declan. But another part, the part that still bears the scars from my failed marriage, reminds me why I can't let myself get too close.

As the jet soars over the Mediterranean, I try to focus on the excitement of exploring Marrakesh. The vibrant colors, exotic scents, and bustling souks—medieval marketplaces that I'd love to check out—will be a welcome distraction. Plus, I've always wanted to stay in one of those luxurious riads in the old medina. Okay, maybe I read some articles online and used an online translation thingy to learn just enough Arabic to get by. But even as I picture myself sipping mint tea on a rooftop terrace, Declan's face keeps popping into my mind. That tousled dark hair, those luscious lips...

"Get it together, Sabrina," I mutter to myself, earning a curious glance from the co-pilot.

I flash him an apologetic smile and decide to get some sleep. Maybe a nap will help clear my head. As I recline my seat, I imagine what Declan might be doing right now. Is he still in Budapest, trying to figure out where I am?

When I wake up, the plane has already begun its descent into Marrakesh. Blinking away the last remnants of sleep, I peer out the window at the sprawling city below, a patchwork of terracotta rooftops and winding alleyways. The late afternoon sun bathes everything in a golden glow, and I feel a flutter of excitement in my chest.

As we touch down, I gather my belongings and thank the crew. The blast of toasty air that hits me as I step off the plane is a stark contrast to the cool air conditioning of the jet. I take a deep breath, inhaling the desert air.

My phone buzzes as I make my way through the airport. It's a text from Declan.

Enjoying the City of Lights, darling? Or have you given me the slip again?

I smile with no small measure of self-satisfaction, imagining his frustration at guessing wrong. But he isn't totally off base. I had intended to visit Paris next and only changed my mind once I reached the Budapest airport. While I'm exiting the jet, a sudden, wild thought rushes through my mind unbidden.

Declan, please catch me.

Chapter Eighteen

Declan

Sabrina absconded again, but I'm getting accustomed to that. We did agree that I would chase her. But she didn't provide any clues this time to help me figure out where she might be jetting off to next. Though I haven't known Sabrina for long, I feel as if I understand her well enough to make an educated guess about her destination.

How will I do that? It's simple. I have a secret weapon Sabrina doesn't know about yet.

So, I race to the Budapest airport and head out onto the tarmac. But I bypass my jet. I would recognize Diana Hahn's jet if I saw it, having taken a ride in it once so I could get to Milan on time to head a fundraiser there.

As I scan the area, I spot Diana's plane. Unfortunately, it's taxiing down the runway. I can't possibly catch up to it or stop the jet from taking off. Time to employ my secret weapon—namely, becoming a nosy arse.

I rush back inside the airport and track down the first employee I can find. He doesn't know where Diana's jet is going, but he points me to a flight attendant who is dating Diana's jet captain. She tells me the plane is heading for Marrakesh.

Yes, all right, I lied slightly to get that information. I told the flight attendant my girlfriend and I had a minor argument and she flew away without me to make a point. I'm to join her in Marrakesh. Well, that's at least partly true.

Now that I have my destination, I climb into my jet and head for a locale I have never visited before. Marrakesh sounds quite romantic.

As my jet soars over the Mediterranean, I grin at the thought of surprising Sabrina in Morocco. My heart beats faster, my pulse pounding in my ears, as I imagine how incredible the sex will be this time. Even better than the other times, I'd wager. The thrill of the chase is intoxicating, and I find myself more invested in this game than I'd care to admit.

As I approach Marrakesh Menara Airport, the air traffic controller informs me that we're next in line for touchdown. I peer out the window while I wait, taking in the ochre-hued buildings and palm trees swaying in the distance. When I finally hop down the steps to exit the jet, I'm hit by a wave of sultry warmth that oddly reminds me of Sabrina. I scan the area, wondering if she'll magically appear to greet me with a teasing smile. But of course, it won't be that easy.

I hail a taxi and head straight for the medina, figuring it's the perfect place for Sabrina to hide out and revel in the sensory overload of colors, scents, and sounds. The driver weaves through narrow, winding streets, and I find myself leaning forward, eyes darting from side to side, searching for a glimpse of strawberry blonde hair or the sound of that infectious laugh.

As we near the heart of the medina, I spot a flash of familiar freckles disappearing into a spice shop. My heart races as I practically throw some dirhams at the driver and leap out of the cab. I weave through the bustling crowd, dodging donkey carts and groups of tourists, my eyes locked on the shop's entrance.

I burst through the beaded curtain, my senses immediately assaulted by the pungent aroma of cumin, saffron, and a dozen other spices I can't name. The shopkeeper eyes me curiously as I scan the dim interior, searching for Sabrina. My eyes finally land on a shapely figure examining jars of spices in the back corner. As if sensing my presence, she turns, and those sparkling green eyes meet mine.

"Took you long enough, Your Knightliness," Sabrina quips, a playful smirk dancing on her lips. "I was beginning to think you'd given up on our little game."

I cluck my tongue, erasing the distance between us with a few long strides. "Give up? Darling, you should know by now that I never back down from a challenge."

She raises an eyebrow, her fingers toying with a jar of bright red paprika. "Oh? And what makes you think I'm a challenge worth pursuing?"

I lean in close, my voice dropping to a low murmur. "Because, Bree, you're the most intoxicating spice in this entire shop."

Her cheeks flush, matching the paprika in her hands, but she recovers quickly. "Smooth talker. But it'll take more than pretty words to win this game."

I chuckle, reaching past her to pluck a jar of cinnamon from the shelf. "Then how about we raise the stakes? Dinner tonight, my treat. If you can guess which spice I use in the main course, you win. If not..."

I trail off, letting the implication hang in the air.

Sabrina's brows lift as her lips curve into a playful smile. "And what do I win, exactly?"

"Whatever your heart desires, darling," I reply, deepening my voice to a seductive register. I know that drives her mad.

Sabrina's eyes widen for a moment, betraying her interest, but she quickly composes herself. "Careful what you offer, Declan. My desires might be more than you can handle."

I move in closer, my lips tickling her earlobe. "Try me."

She shivers slightly, then steps back with a coy smile. "All right, you're on. But don't think I'll go easy on you just because you tracked me down in this labyrinth."

"When will you learn that I never take anything for granted?" I offer her my arm. "Shall we explore this magical place before our culinary duel?"

Sabrina hesitates for a moment, then links her arm through mine. "Lead the way, Mr. Wilde. But remember, this doesn't mean you've won anything yet."

We step out into the bustling streets of the medina, the late afternoon sun casting a golden glow over the terracotta buildings. As we weave through the narrow alleyways, I notice how perfectly Sabrina fits into this vibrant, chaotic landscape. Her eyes dance with excitement as she takes in the colorful textiles hanging from shop fronts and the enticing aromas wafting from food stalls.

"You know," she says, tugging me toward a display of intricate silver jewelry, "I half expected you to give up after Budapest. Most men would have."

I chuckle, watching while she admires a delicate bracelet. "I'm not most men, darling. And you're certainly not most women. Besides, you had never gone on a true man hunt until you met me."

"What makes you think I haven't?"

"Any other blokes you tried on for size couldn't possibly have understood your needs and desires." I shuffle a bit closer. "Why else would you have let me fuck you with my hand in the Beaufort Bar? Or let me take you to my suite for a night of uninhibited shagging? You are one of a kind, just like me."

She glances up at me, a hint of vulnerability in her eyes. "Is that why you're chasing me across continents? Because I'm not like other women?"

I pause, choosing my words carefully. "I'm chasing you because you are Sabrina, the man hunter. Unpredictable, brilliant, maddening Sabrina. And I can't seem to get enough."

A flash of something—surprise? pleasure?—crosses her face before she masks it with a casual smile. "Well, don't get too attached, Sir Declan. This is just a game, remember?"

"Is it?" I murmur, reaching out to tuck a stray lock of hair behind her ear.

She shivers at my touch but doesn't pull away. "Of course it is. What else could it be?"

I don't answer, instead letting my gaze linger on her lips. The air between us crackles with tension, and for a moment, I think she might close the distance between us. But then she clears her throat and steps back.

"So, about that dinner," Sabrina says, her voice a touch breathier than usual. "Where exactly are you planning to wow me with culinary delights?"

I grin, glad for the slight reprieve from the intensity of the moment. "Ah, that would be telling, wouldn't it? Let's just say I have connections in interesting places."

She rolls her eyes, but I can see the curiosity sparkling in them. "Of course you do. Is there anywhere in the world where Declan Wilde doesn't have a friend with a favor to cash in?"

"Probably not," I admit with a wink. "It's part of my charm."

We continue our stroll through the medina, bantering back and forth as we explore the labyrinthine streets. As the sun begins to set, painting the sky in brilliant oranges and pinks, I guide Sabrina toward a hidden doorway tucked away in a quiet corner of the medina. She raises an eyebrow as I knock in a distinctive pattern that sounds almost musical.

Her brows knit together. "Secret knocks now? You really are going all out to impress me."

I wink at her. "Oh, love, you haven't seen anything yet."

The door swings open, revealing a dimly lit passageway. I place my hand on the small of Sabrina's back, guiding her inside. As we walk, the narrow corridor opens up into a breathtaking courtyard. Lush greenery surrounds us, and the gentle sound of trickling water fills the air. Lanterns hang from the trees, casting a warm, intimate glow over the space. Sabrina's eyes widen as she takes in the romantic scene.

"Declan, this is...wow."

I stand up taller, my chin held high, all because of her compliment. "Only the best for you, pet."

An elegantly set table for two sits in the center of the courtyard, surrounded by flickering candles. As we approach, a waiter appears as if by magic, pulling out Sabrina's chair.

"Your Highness," I tease, gesturing for her to sit.

She tries to play it cool but can't hide her smile as she takes her seat. "You're ridiculous."

I settle across from her, my eyes never leaving her face. "Ridiculously charming, you mean."

"Jury's still out on that one," she quips, but there's a softness in her gaze that makes my heart skip.

The waiter returns with a bottle of champagne, popping the cork with a flourish. As he pours the bubbling liquid into our flutes, I raise mine in a toast.

"To the thrill of the chase," I say, my eyes locked on Sabrina's.

She clinks her glass against mine. "And to the sweet satisfaction of being caught...maybe."

We sip our champagne, the tension between us palpable. The waiter discreetly places the first course before us—a delicate salad of fresh figs, arugula, and goat cheese.

"So," Sabrina says, spearing a fig with her fork, "are you going to give me any hints about this mystery spice I'm supposed to guess?"

I shake my head, clucking my tongue. "Now where's the fun in that? You'll just have to pay close attention to every bite."

"Challenge accepted, Mr. Wilde."

As we make our way through the courses, I watch Sabrina's face intently, searching for any hint that she's identified the secret spice. She savors each bite with exquisite attention, her brow furrowing in concentration. It's adorable, really, how seriously she's taking this little game.

While the waiter clears our plates, I rove my gaze over her body ever so slowly. "You look positively edible when you're deep in thought like that."

"Careful. Flattery will get you nowhere."

"Oh, I beg to differ," I murmur, reaching under the table to caress her thigh. "I think flattery has gotten me quite far already, wouldn't you say?"

Sabrina's eyes widen, but she quickly recovers, lifting her chin defiantly. "Don't get cocky. I haven't forgotten our little wager."

"Ah yes, the mysterious spice," I say, signaling to the waiter. "Are you ready for the grand reveal?"

She nods vigorously and rubs her hands together like a child about to unwrap her birthday gifts. The waiter appears with two covered dishes, placing them before us with a flourish.

"Ladies first," I gesture, watching intently as Sabrina lifts the silver dome.

The rich aroma of lamb tagine wafts up, filling the air with an intoxicating blend of spices. Sabrina closes her eyes, inhaling deeply. When she opens them again, there's a glimmer of triumph in those emerald eyes. She takes a bite, savoring it slowly, her expression one of intense concentration. I find myself holding my breath, waiting for her verdict.

"Well, darling?" I prompt, unable to contain my curiosity any longer. "Care to hazard a guess?"

She sets down her fork, a slow smile spreading across her face. "Oh, Declan. Did you really think you could stump me with something as simple as *ras el hanout*?"

I can't stop myself from laughing. I'm impressed and chagrined in equal parts. "I should have known better than to underestimate you. How did you figure it out so quickly?"

Sabrina leans forward, her voice dropping to a conspiratorial whisper. "Let's just say I have a few culinary tricks up my sleeve. A girl's got to have some secrets. But truthfully, I looked it up on my phone under the table while you were contemplating your chicken tagine."

I throw my head back and laugh, genuinely delighted by her cunning. "Oh, Bree, you never cease to amaze me. I should have known you'd find a way to outsmart me."

She grins, raising her champagne flute in a mock toast. "What can I say? I play to win."

"That you do," I concede, clinking my glass against hers. "So, my clever girl, what prize shall you claim for your victory?"

Sabrina's eyes sparkle with mischief as she sets down her glass. "Hmm, let me think..." She taps her chin thoughtfully, drawing out the moment. "I believe you said 'whatever my heart desires,' didn't you?"

I nod, suddenly feeling a bit nervous about what she might request. "I did indeed. And I'm a man of my word."

She leans toward me, her lips grazing my ear. "I want you, Declan. Tonight. In a hotel that has all the Moroccan charm that Marrakesh has to offer. I want—No, I demand that you treat me to the spiciest night I've ever experienced, complete with multiple orgasms and moves I've never seen before. Think you can handle that?"

I feel a jolt of electricity shoot through me at her words, my pulse quickening, my voice rougher from the hunger she inspires in me. "I thought you'd never ask. I know just the place."

With a discreet nod to our waiter, I stand and offer Sabrina my hand. She takes it, her fingers intertwining with mine. We weave through the maze-like streets of the *medina*, the anticipation building with each step.

Finally, we arrive at a small, unassuming door set into an intricately tiled wall. I knock, and it swings open to reveal a hidden oasis. The *riad* is breathtaking—a central courtyard with a bubbling fountain, surrounded by arched doorways that lead to luxurious rooms.

I lead Sabrina to the most opulent suite in the most incredible hotel in Marrakesh. As we enter the palatial accommodations, Her eyes widen, taking in the sumptuous decor. Rich jewel-toned fabrics drape the walls, and intricate lanterns cast a warm, intimate glow. The enormous bed is piled high with plush pillows, looking impossibly inviting.

"Well, Your Knightliness," Sabrina purrs, trailing her fingers along my chest. "You certainly know how to set the stage."

I capture her wandering hand, bringing it to my lips. "Oh, my sweet, you can't possibly imagine what I have in mind for you."

With a swift movement, I pull her flush against me, one hand tangling in her hair as I claim her mouth in a searing kiss. She responds instantly, her body melting into mine as she parts her lips, inviting me to go deeper.

I break away, trailing kisses down her neck as I slowly back her toward the bed. "Now, fair Sabrina, it's time to unleash our naughtiest, most secret desires, and we won't stop until dawn breaks. No running away this time. You belong to me tonight."

Chapter Nineteen

Sabrina

Whew, somebody get me a fan. Declan Wilde burned me up just from the way his voice sounded when he swore we would unleash our naughtiest desires. And when he vowed we won't stop until dawn breaks, I nearly fainted. No joke. I have never fainted in my entire life, but I seriously could do that tonight. I knew Declan was a sex god, but tonight he's like a human hot pepper—the kind that's so hot it could melt your brain.

No running away this time, fair Sabrina. You belong to me tonight.

Okay, I can admit I got a little spooked when he said that. But I want him so badly I can't think straight, and nothing will stop me from being with him tonight.

Tomorrow…who knows.

I take a deep breath, trying to calm my racing heart, but it's no use. Declan's eyes are locked on mine, blazing with an intensity that makes my knees weak. He takes a step closer, and I can feel the heat radiating off his body.

"Nervous, love?" he murmurs, his words dripping with lust.

I manage a shaky laugh. "Me? Nervous? Please. I eat nervous for breakfast."

His lips quirk up in that infuriatingly cocky smirk. "Is that so? Well, I hope you saved room for dessert."

Before I can come up with a witty retort, his hand is on my waist, pulling me flush against him. His other hand cups my cheek, his thumb brushing softly across my skin. "Last chance to run, Bree."

I swallow hard, my heart pounding so loudly I'm sure he can hear it. "I'm done running, at least for tonight. I want this. I want you."

Before I can take another breath, he crushes his lips to mine. The kiss is everything I've been fantasizing about and more—passionate, demanding, and exhilarating. My hands find their way to his hair, fingers tangling in those lush, dark locks as I pull him closer.

Declan groans into my mouth, the sound as decadent as the man himself. His hands roam my body, leaving trails of fire in their wake. When we finally break apart, both gasping for air, I feel dizzy with the need to take him inside me.

"Bloody hell, Sabrina," he pants, resting his forehead against mine. "You're going to be the death of me."

"Well, if you're going down, I'm coming with you."

Declan lifts me off my feet, my legs instinctively wrapping around his waist. "You most certainly are coming with me—over and over."

He starts walking us toward the bedroom, suckling my earlobe and fondling my breast at the same time. This man has impressive skills.

"Think you can handle me?" I ask, while I grow slicker and hotter by the second.

Declan's answering chuckle vibrates against my skin, though he doesn't respond to my question. As we cross the threshold into the bedroom, I gaze deeply into his eyes, amazed by how effortlessly he carries me, his muscles flexing beneath my fingertips. "I intend to explore every inch of you, fair Sabrina. And yes, I can handle you. Just wait and see."

My heart skips a beat at his words, and I tighten my grip on him. Before I can formulate a witty comeback, Declan lowers me onto the bed, his body hovering over mine for a brief moment before he settles on top of me. The weight of him, the heat of his skin, the intensity of his gaze—it's all overwhelming in the best possible way. I reach up, tracing the strong line of his jaw with my fingertips.

His hands explore my body with a delicious urgency, leaving goosebumps in their wake. I arch into his touch, desperate for more. When his fingers find the zipper of my dress, I hold my breath in anticipation.

"May I?" he asks, his voice an erotic growl.

I nod, not trusting myself to speak. Slowly, torturously, he unzips my dress with sure, strong fingers. As he pulls my dress down inch by inch, I struggle for breath, so aroused that it's almost painful. My panties are damp, and my nipples have pearled. When Declan pulls my undies down in a leisurely manner, I want to shout at him to hurry the hell up. But I won't. I love this delicious torture. As Declan peels my bra away, I shiver—partly from the cool air hitting my skin, but mostly from the way his eyes devour every inch of me. His gaze is so intense, so hungry, I feel like I might combust on the spot.

"Bloody hell," he breathes. "I love your body, Bree. You're even more beautiful and sensual than a Greek statue of Aphrodite."

Before I can come up with a clever retort, his lips are on mine again, and coherent thought becomes a distant memory. His kisses trail down my neck, across my collarbone, leaving a tingling path in his wake. When he reaches my breasts, I gasp. His tongue swirls around my nipple, teasing and tasting, while his hand kneads my other breast. The dual sensation sends sparks of pleasure shooting through my body.

"Declan," I moan, arching into his touch. "Please..."

He lifts his head. "Please what, love? Tell me what you want."

I bite my lip, suddenly shy despite our current position. But the hunger in his gaze emboldens me. "I want you. All of you. Now. Buried inside me so deep it almost hurts."

A wicked grin spreads across his face. "Your wish is my command."

In one fluid motion, he sheds his shirt, revealing that gloriously muscled chest I've been dying to run my hands over. I reach out, tracing the defined lines of his abs, reveling in the way his muscles flex and stiffen under my touch. Declan's breath hitches, and I feel a surge of feminine pride at the effect I have on him.

"Like what you see?" he teases, his voice husky.

"Mmm, very much," I purr, running my nails lightly down his chest. "But I think you're still a bit overdressed for the occasion, don't you?"

"We can't have that, can we?"

In a few quick movements, Declan stands and sheds his remaining clothes. My whole body grows warm and liquid as I take in the full sight of him. He honestly is the most magnificent man I've ever seen, all lean muscle and golden skin. My gaze travels lower, and I lick my lips in anticipation.

Declan skims his gaze over my naked form, sprawled across the bed. "Time to ramp up the eroticism, love. All the way up as far as the scale will go."

In an instant, he's on me again, his hot skin pressed against mine from chest to thigh. I gasp at the contact, so sensitized from his touch that it's painful—in the best way. His mouth lands on that sensitive spot behind my ear as his hands roam my body.

"God, Bree," he murmurs against my skin. "You drive me absolutely mad."

I arch into him, desperate for more friction. "Then do something about it."

With a wicked grin, Declan slides down my body, peppering kisses along the way. When he reaches the apex of my thighs, he looks up at me with smoldering hunger in his eyes. "With pleasure."

The first swipe of his tongue against my most sensitive flesh sends shockwaves through my body. I gasp, my fingers tangling in his hair as he works his magic. Declan's talented mouth explores every inch of me, teasing and tasting until I'm a writhing mess beneath him.

"Declan," I moan, my hips bucking involuntarily. "Oh god, don't stop."

I feel him smile against me before he redoubles his efforts, his tongue circling my clit with expert precision. When he slides two fingers inside me, curling them just so, I nearly come undone right then and there.

"That's it, love. Let go for me."

His words, combined with the exquisite sensations he's creating, push me over the edge. I shout his name as waves of pleasure crash over me, my body arching off the bed. Declan doesn't let up, working me through my orgasm until I'm trembling and oversensitive.

When I finally come down from my high, I open my eyes to find Declan hovering over me, a self-satisfied smirk on his face.

"Enjoying yourself, darling?" he purrs, and his cocky expression makes me want to pounce on him.

I manage a breathless laugh. "You could say that. But I think it's my turn to return the favor."

Before he can react, I flip us over, straddling his hips. The look of surprise on his face quickly morphs into one of hunger as I scrape my fingernails down his chest.

I bite my lip, letting it slide free little by little. "My, my, what do we have here?"

Declan grips my waist, his fingers digging into my skin as he groans. Slowly, torturously, I kiss my way down his body, savoring every dip and curve of his muscled form. When I reach his impressive erection, I look up at him through my lashes, relishing the way his eyes darken with anticipation.

"Sabrina, you don't have to—"

I silence him with a long, languid lick from base to tip. His words dissolve into a guttural moan that makes my clit pulse and my inner muscles tighten. Encouraged, I take him into my mouth, reveling in the way I can feel the tip of his dick nudging the back of my throat.

"Bloody hell," Declan gasps, his fingers clenching the sheets and his teeth locked. Harsh sounds emerge from him.

I hum in satisfaction, the vibrations making Declan's hips buck involuntarily. His reactions spur me on, and I lose myself in the taste and feel of him. I alternate between long, slow licks and quick, teasing flicks of my tongue, delighting in the way his breathing grows more ragged with each passing moment.

"Christ, Bree," he groans. "Your mouth is fucking incredible."

I look up at him through my lashes, never breaking my rhythm. The sight of him—head thrown back, muscles taut with tension—sends a fresh wave of arousal coursing through me. I redouble my efforts, taking him deeper, using every trick I know to drive him wild.

Just when I think he's close to the edge, Declan's hands tangle in my hair, gently pulling me off him. I make a noise of protest, but the look in his eyes silences me.

"As much as I adore your talented mouth," he growls, pulling me up his body, "I need to be inside you. Now."

He flips us over, pinning me beneath him again. I gasp at the abrupt shift, my body thrumming with anticipation. Declan's eyes lock onto mine as he positions his cock at my entrance. Damn, he's big. But I can't wait to feel all that manliness filling me up.

"Last chance to back out, love," he murmurs, his voice strained with the effort of holding back.

I wrap my legs around his waist, pulling him closer. "Not a chance in hell of that happening. I want you. All of you."

With a groan that sounds almost painful, Declan pushes inside me slowly, inch by delicious inch. I gasp at the stretch and fullness, my body adjusting to accommodate him. When he's fully sheathed inside me, we both pause to savor the intense connection for a moment. I can no longer form words, overwhelmed by the sensation of him filling me so completely. When he starts to move, setting a languid, torturous rhythm that has me arching beneath him, I beg him to go deeper. His strokes are powerful and purposeful, hitting all the right spots with each thrust.

"Faster," I plead, my nails raking down his back. "Harder, please, harder."

His expression becomes pinched, and his lips flatten while his nostrils flare with every exhalation. "As you wish, love."

The words emerged as a growl that turns me on even more.

His pace quickens, his hips lunging forward and back, forward and back, with a newfound urgency. The room echoes with the sounds of our passion—breathless moans, fervent whispers, the wet sucking of our bodies colliding, the slapping of skin against skin. I match him thrust for thrust, move for move. I drag him down for a searing kiss, our tongues tangling and our bodies moving in concert as if we've become one. When we finally break apart, gasping for air, I can feel the familiar tension building low in my belly.

"Declan," I pant, "I'm close. So close."

He shifts slightly, changing the angle of his thrusts. Suddenly, I feel like the tether that's been holding me to the earth is about to snap, and I'll fly out into the universe the second I come like a comet streaking through the solar system.

"That's it, Bree," he murmurs, his voice strained. "Let go for me. I want to feel you come undone."

His words, combined with the exquisite friction of his body against mine, push me over the edge. I cry out his name as waves of pleasure crash over me, my body arching off the bed. Declan doesn't let up, his thrusts becoming more erratic as he strives for his own release.

"Sabrina…" He buries his face in my neck. "Bloody hell, you feel amazing."

I can feel him trembling above me, so close to the edge. As I run my hands down his back, my nails lightly scraping his skin, I whisper, "Come for me, Declan. I want to feel you lose control."

With a guttural shout, Declan finds his release, his hips jerking against mine as he empties himself inside me. As we lay tangled together, our bodies slick with sweat and our hearts still racing, I can't believe the intensity of what we just did. Declan's arms are wrapped around me in a loose embrace, and his chest rises and falls rapidly against my chest. I've never felt so completely satiated, so utterly cherished.

Declan rests his forehead on mine. "That was…mind-altering, body-shattering sex."

"I suspect we just broke at least three laws of physics."

He hits me with a devasting smile. "Only three? I'd say we shattered at least a dozen, love."

I roll onto my side, into his waiting arms. As I drink in the sight of his tousled hair and flushed cheeks, I feel an odd warmth blossoming in my chest. "Is that a challenge? Because I'm pretty sure we could aim for a baker's dozen if we really put our minds to it."

"In that case…" He hoists himself up onto his straight arms, gazing down at me. "It's time for the naughtiest bits, darling."

Declan slides off the bed, kneeling to grab something from one of his bags. Then he jumps back onto the mattress, clenching several silk scarves in his hand. "Are you ready for this, Bree?"

I grin.

Chapter Twenty

Declan

Sabrina lies there, spread out on the bed, looking even more beautiful and sensual. She wants to try something different with me, something beyond the missionary position. What we've done so far has been extraordinary, but I have even more scandalous plans for her body. So, I toss the scarves onto the bed and climb onto the mattress, crawling forward until I'm on all fours with her body beneath me.

"How do you feel about bondage, Bree?"

"Never tried it. But I'd love to experiment with you in any way you want."

I grin wickedly, my heart racing at her eager response. "Oh, darling, you can't imagine what you're in for. But you will enjoy it, I promise."

Though I've never done this before, I have no trouble performing my task. I take one of the silk scarves and gently wrap it around her wrist, securing it to the bedpost. Then I repeat the process with her other wrist, my fingers lingering on her soft, creamy skin. Sabrina's tits jiggle, thanks to her heavy breathing. She keeps her gaze on me the entire time.

"I'll need time to recover from that orgasm before I can go again," I tell her. "But in the meantime, I'll play with you—with your delicious body."

She nibbles on her bottom lip in a leisurely fashion that makes my cock twitch.

"Too tight?" I ask.

She tugs at her bonds experimentally and shakes her head. "Perfect."

I trail my fingers down her arms, across her collarbone, and over the swell of her breasts. She arches into my touch, a soft moan whispering from her lips.

"Now, love, I'm going to worship every inch of you until you can barely stand the intensity of the pleasure I'm giving you."

I begin with her neck, planting feather-light kisses along the delicate curve. Sabrina tilts her head, offering more of herself to me. I accept the invitation gladly, nipping and sucking at the sensitive skin just below her ear. Her breathy gasps urge me on, and my hands roam freely over her body, tracing the dips and swells of her curves. I cup her breasts, rolling her nipples between my fingers until they're taut peaks. Sabrina writhes beneath me, tugging at her restraints.

"Declan," she whimpers, "please."

"Patience, Bree. It will be worth the wait."

I trail kisses down her breastbone, pausing to lavish attention on each breast, relishing the flavor of her skin and the feel of nipple in my mouth. I swirl my tongue around one peak, then the other, before I take each into my mouth to devour them one by one. Sabrina's back arches off the bed, a low moan spilling her lips.

She arches her back, exposing the delicious column of her throat. "Oh, shit, Declan. You're driving me crazy, and I love it."

I smirk against her skin, continuing my slow, relentless path down her body. My fingers trace the curve of her waist, the flare of her hips. I pepper kisses across her flat stomach, dipping my tongue into her navel so I can dip my tongue inside. Bree squirms beneath me, her legs parting instinctively. I settle between them, loving the feel of her thighs cradling me. I can smell her arousal, and it takes every ounce of my self-control not to dive in immediately. Instead, I tease her mercilessly, placing soft kisses along her inner thighs, inching closer to where she wants me most but never quite reaching it.

"Declan, please," Sabrina whimpers, her hips lifting off the bed in search of contact.

I chuckle, making her shiver from the vibrations against her sensitive skin. "All in good time, love. I did say I was going to worship every inch of you, didn't I?"

Onward I march, moving lower and lower with my decadent exploration of her body. I caress her legs as I work my way back up her body until I've reached her breasts again, lavishing attention on each nipple until she's writhing beneath me, her breath coming in short, desperate pants.

"You are exquisite, darling. I could spend hours doing nothing more than exploring every curve, every freckle, every millimeter of your body."

Sabrina lets out a breathy laugh that quickly turns into a moan as I nip at the sensitive spot beneath her ear. "Hours? You might kill me."

She does have a point. And so, I rise to my knees and grasp her hips. Then I shift my body, positioning myself between her legs once more. This time, I don't tease. I dive in, my tongue finding her most sensitive spot with practiced ease. Sabrina cries out, her back arching off the bed as much as her restraints will allow.

"Oh god, Declan!" she shouts. "Make me come now!"

I give her what she wants, alternating between long, languid licks and quick flicks of my tongue as I consume her clit. She writhes beneath me like a wild mare, her hips bucking against my face as she barrels toward the climax she so desperately needs. The silk scarves strain as she tugs at her them, desperate for something to hold onto.

"Declan, I'm so close. Don't stop, please don't stop."

I redouble my efforts, thrusting two fingers inside her as I continue to work her with my tongue. She's so wet, so responsive to my every touch, and the flavor of her is more decadent than any dessert. I curl my fingers to find the one spot inside her that will make her eyes roll back in her head. Sabrina's moans grow louder, more desperate. Her thighs begin to tremble, and I know she's teetering on the edge. I suckle her nub ruthlessly until that rope finally breaks, and she comes.

Bree lies there in a heap of sexy flesh, thoroughly satisfied and dazed from the power of her orgasm. "Can we do that again?"

"Yes, but I have a different idea this time." I reach for a few more scarves. "I'm going to tie you to the foot of the bed too, but only if you're comfortable with that. I'd also love to blindfold you."

"I'd like to try that."

I grab the additional scarves, my fingers working quickly to secure her ankles to the foot of the bed. Sabrina's breath hitches as I spread her legs wider, leaving her completely exposed to my gaze.

"Last chance to back out," I warn, holding up the blindfold.

"Don't you dare stop now."

I secure the silk over her eyes and tie it securely behind her head. "Remember, if it gets too much, just say the word and I'll stop."

"Less talking, more touching," she demands, arching her back invitingly.

"You need to learn a lesson in patience, darling."

I begin by barely ghosting my fingertips over her skin, tracing feather-light patterns across her arms, her stomach, her thighs. Without her sight, Sabrina's other senses are heightened. She shivers at each touch, her skin breaking out in goosebumps.

She tugs at her restraints.

"Shh," I soothe, leaning down to brush my lips against her ear. "Trust me."

I resume my feather-light touches, occasionally replacing fingers with lips or tongue. While she moans in a manner that makes my cock jerk, I flick my tongue over the curve of her breast, the dip of her waist, the arch of her foot. She writhes beneath me, desperate for more substantial contact. My cock has gone hard in record time, and a drop of liquid glistens on the crown, all because this woman drives me insane with the need to possess and consume her.

"Please," she gasps. "I need more."

"All in good time, love," I assure her. "I'm going to make you feel things you've never felt before."

I trail my fingers down her body once more, this time with more pressure. Sabrina arches into my touch, a low moan escaping her lips. I cup her tits, kneading them gently before rolling her nipples between my fingers. She gasps, tugging at her restraints.

"Declan, I need—"

"What, love?"

"Please...I need...you inside me. I love this, but I can't take much more."

"Tell me explicitly what you want. I need to hear it."

Sabrina sinks her teeth into her bottom hard enough to turn the skin white. "I want your cock inside me, Declan. I want you to fuck me until I can't remember my own name. Do it now, please."

Her words fire a bolt of desire straight through me. I growl low in my throat, positioning myself between her legs. "Anything for you, my sweet."

I enter her in one swift, hard motion, both of us groaning at the sensation. Sabrina's back arches off the bed as much as her restraints allow, her mouth falling open in a silent cry of ecstasy.

"God, you feel incredible," I huff, beginning to move within her. "So tight, so wet for me."

I set a punishing pace, driven by the sounds of Sabrina's moans and the sight of her thrashing beneath me. Her ankles strain against the scarves. I grasp her hips, angling them upward to hit that spot inside her that always flings her over the edge.

"Oh god, Declan!" she screams. "Don't stop!"

I increase my pace, pistoning into her mercilessly while the bed bounces. The room fills with the sounds of our passion—skin smacking against skin, hoarse cries, and whispered curses. I can feel her tightening around me, her inner walls pulsating as she approaches her peak. I reach down between us, my fingers finding her most sensitive spot, and rub tight circles that match the rhythm of my thrusts.

"Come for me, Bree, come *right now.*"

I pull out, grasping my cock in one hand while I mercilessly rub her clit. Sabrina screams again, shattering beneath me, her back bowing up off the bed. Her body finally goes limp as a tidal wave of pleasure crashes over her. The sight of her coming undone, coupled with the incredible sensation of her clenching around me, hurtles me over the edge too. With a roar, I throw my head back, shouting hoarsely while I pump my cock again and again. I follow her into ecstasy, my hips jerking erratically as I empty myself onto her belly.

We both remain still briefly, struggling to catch our breath as we come down from our shared high. I collapse beside Sabrina, my pulse racing. Gradually, my heart rate slows as sweat dribbles down my temples. With trembling hands, I reach up to remove her blindfold, then gently untie her wrists and ankles.

"Are you all right, Bree?"

She nuzzles my chest, her body still quivering slightly. When she speaks, her voice is soft and a bit hoarse. "I'm more than all right, Declan. That was...unbelievable. Mind-blowing. Earth-shattering. I think I had an out-of-body experience, reeling through the entire universe."

I chuckle, pressing a kiss to her forehead. "I'm glad you enjoyed it. You were absolutely amazing."

We lie here in comfortable silence for a few moments, basking in the afterglow. I run my fingers through Sabrina's tousled hair, marveling at how soft it is.

After a while, Sabrina clears her throat. "So, is this how all British men treat their lovers, or am I special?"

I can't help but laugh. Even after mind-blowing sex, she's still quick with the witty remarks. It's one of the things I adore about her. "Oh, you are definitely special, fair Sabrina." I roll onto my side, tracing delicate circles on her belly with my fingers. "Care for some food now?"

"Mm, yes. Something sweet and savory."

I press a kiss to her temple. "How about some of those chocolate-covered strawberries we picked up earlier? And maybe some of that fancy cheese?"

Her whole face lights up. "Oh, yes, please."

I reluctantly disentangle myself from her warm embrace and pad naked across the room to the mini fridge. I can feel her eyes on me as I bend to retrieve our snacks, and I can't resist giving her a little show, flexing my muscles just a bit more than necessary. When I wriggle my arse, she cat calls me.

No, I don't mind that at all.

We do indeed devour the strawberries and cheese, then we tease each other with sarcasm as we often do. I want to ask if our days of me chasing her are over now, but I worry she might panic if I suggest I'd like to date her, much less take her home with me to meet my family. She sort of met Julian, but that was a brief encounter.

Will she panic? I don't know, but I have to try.

As we lounge on the bed, savoring the last of the strawberries, I steal glances at Sabrina. The way her eyes crinkle when she laughs, the gentle curve of her lips as she smiles—it all makes my heart race in a way I've never experienced before.

"What?" she asks, noticing me staring.

I cough, using that as an excuse until I can find the right words. "I was just thinking...about us."

She hunches her shoulders, lowering her head. When she speaks, her tone is hesitant. "In what way were you thinking about...us? If you want more bondage fun, I'd love to tie you up this time."

"And I would love that too, but..." I take a deep breath and plunge into the cold waters. "I was wondering if...well, if our days of me pursuing you are over now."

Her head jerks up, and I can see her body tense. Bloody hell, I've spooked her. Sabrina's eyes dart away from mine, and her fingers fidget with the edge of the sheet. The playful atmosphere from moments ago evaporates, replaced by a palpable tension.

"Declan, I..." she begins, then trails off.

I reach out, gently clasping her hand. "Hey, it's all right. We don't have to label anything if you're not ready."

"Um, it's not that I don't want to. It's just...I've been hurt before, Declan. Badly. You know that. And the thought of opening myself up to that again terrifies me."

I grasp her chin, urging her to look at me. "I get it, love, believe me. I've been hurt before too. But can I tell you something?"

Sabrina nods hesitantly.

"I'm scared too," I admit softly. "The way you make me feel...it's unlike anything I've ever experienced. And that's bloody frightening."

Her head pops up, and her eyes go wide.. "Really? You're scared too?"

I run a hand through my hair. "I'm absolutely petrified. But you know what? I think it's worth it. *You* are worth it, Bree."

She's quiet for a moment, her gaze searching mine. Then, little by little, a smile spreads across her face. "You know, for a sarcastic British jackass, you can be pretty sweet sometimes."

I grin, relief washing over me. "Don't spread that rumor, please. I have an atrocious reputation to uphold."

Bree draws her knees up to her chest and finally looks at me. "Maybe part of me does want more than hit and run sex with you, but I…I can't do that. Not yet."

"How much more time do you need?"

She shrugs. "It hasn't even been a week yet."

"I understand." But yes, my heart just fell to the floor and lies bleeding at my feet. How can I feel so deeply for her? We've only just met. But I already know she's the one for me. "Let's have a shower together and curl up in bed."

She smiles, her eyes twinkling. "Yes, please."

By the time Sabrina falls asleep, I've concocted a plan to win her heart—for real, and forever. It's risky. She might run away and never come back. But I must try.

So, I gather my belongings and skulk out of the hotel. But I do write Bree a note, handwritten, and leave it on the nightstand where she'll see it. The note consists of seven words.

It's your turn to chase me, darling.

Chapter Twenty-One

Sabrina

I wake up to an empty bed, the sheets cool beside me. Confusion clouds my mind as I blink away the remnants of sleep. Where's Declan? Stretching, I sit up and scan the room. His clothes are gone, his bags no longer sit by the door. A knot forms in my stomach as realization dawns. He's left me.

Then my gaze lands on a folded piece of paper on the nightstand. Why are my hands trembling? *Sheesh.* It's not like I'm in love with Declan. Am I? Of course not. The paper crinkles when I reach for it, thanks to my unsteady fingers, as I unfold the note to reveal Declan's elegant scrawl.

It's your turn to chase me, darling.

Conflicting emotions cascade over me—frustration, confusion, and a spark of excitement I can't quite squelch. That sneaky snake. I can almost hear his deep, accented voice speaking those words and see the mischievous glint in his blue eyes.

I flop back onto the bed, groaning into the pillow. Naturally, he'd pull a stunt like this. Just when I thought I had him figured out, he goes and throws me another curveball. Classic Declan. But I've got a few tricks of my own that he's never seen. So, I sit up and lift my chin. If he thinks I'll run after him, he's mistaken.

"Okay, Your Knightliness," I declare, swinging my legs off the bed. "You want a chase? I'll give you a damn chase."

But I am not doing this to get him back. No way. It's not like I…care about him. Only Declan would do an obnoxious thing like this.

I grab my phone, firing off a quick text to my sister. *Sorry, Tabby. Slight change of plans. Might be a teensy bit late to the opening festivities, but I won't miss your wedding. Cross my heart.*

As I toss my phone onto the bed and dash to the bathroom, my mind is already plotting my next move. While brushing my teeth, I glimpse my reflection in the mirror—hair a mess, eyes faintly red, dark circles under them too. Despite my appearance, I grin around my toothbrush which makes foam dribble down my chin. This is insane. I'm about to embark on a wild goose chase across who-knows-where, all because of a man I've known for less than a week. A man who drives me batty. A Brit who makes my heart race and my knees go weak, but still.

I splash water on my face and start throwing clothes into my suitcase while I mutter to myself. "Focus, Bree. Where would he go first?"

No frigging idea.

Within an hour, I'm walking out of the suite. The desk clerk flags me down to tell me that Declan had paid the whole bill for our steamy night in Marrakesh. He also asked the clerk to give me a note. As I'm rushing to hail a taxi, I read his words.

Come fly with me, Sabrina.

Huh? I don't get it. Is he saying I should fly somewhere and chase him to…wherever? Or does he mean that he will join me on Diana's get? The whole point of the cat and mouse game has been to conclude each search with us being together in a beautiful city somewhere in the world.

Come fly with me, he said.

Okay, I'm rushing straight to the airport.

I can't find a car quickly enough, so I dash through Marrakesh's bustling streets as I weave through the crowd. My heart races, not just from the exertion but from the thrill of the chase. Declan's words echo in my mind once again, and I experience a sense of exhilaration like none I've felt before in my entire life. I'm flying high without an airplane, that's how excited I am to find him and kiss him and tell him…I don't know what.

Finally, I flag down a taxi. Breathing hard, I leap into the car and ask to go to the airport. Luckily, the driver speaks English.

Once I reach the airport, I scan the departure boards. My eyes flick from one destination to another. Where might Declan go? I close my eyes, trying to channel his thoughts, letting all the chatter of the terminal fade away. What would an adventure-seeking, thrill-loving Brit do next?

Like a flash, it hits me. *Fly,* he'd said twice. I'd assumed he meant that as a metaphor, but I wonder…Could he have meant it literally? Worth a shot. So, I sprint to the nearest information desk.

"Excuse me," I pant, "do you have any flight schools nearby? Or, I don't know, places where you can book scenic flights? Anything like that?"

The woman behind the desk gives me a bemused look. A name tag identifies her as Lajin. "There's a small airfield about thirty minutes from here. They offer scenic flights over the Atlas Mountains."

"No, I think I'd better stay here until I find my…um, boyfriend." Wow did that sound weird when I said it. "I doubt he'd leave the area without me."

Lajin puckers her lips, seeming to consider my problem. "We do have a private flight that's scheduled to take off soon. Perhaps they would take you on as a passenger."

"Perfect!" I exclaim, already turning away. "Thank you!"

I'm halfway to the exit when I realize I have no idea how to get to wherever I'm going. Spinning on my heels, I rush back to the desk. "Sorry to bother you again, Lajin. How exactly do I get to that airplane?"

She waves toward an attractive man. "Abad! Come here, we have a passenger in need."

The man obeys, jogging over to us. "How may I assist you, Lajin?"

His tone of voice suggests he's got the hots for her. She seems a touch flustered by him but remains professional. "Abad, could you please escort this lovely woman to the tarmac? She needs to board a jet. I believe you know the one. It will be taking off soon, and I'm certain the pilot won't mind taking on a passenger."

"I'm happy to help." He offers me his arm. "Allow me to assist you…"

"Sabrina."

He nods crisply.

I let Abad guide me through a maze of corridors. As we approach a small private hangar, I get a glimpse of a sleek aircraft waiting on the tarmac. A tingle races over my skin as I spot a familiar figure leaning against the plane's fuselage, arms crossed, a cocky grin plastered on his face.

Declan.

Abad discreetly returns to the terminal.

"Took you long enough, Sabrina," Declan calls out. "I was beginning to think you'd given up on the chase already."

I squint at him, torn between the desire to kiss him senseless and the urge to smack that smug look off his face. "You are such an ass, Declan Wilde."

"Am I? You had much more complimentary things to say about me last night." He taps a finger on his chin. "Let me see if I remember the exact words. 'Oh, Declan, you rock.' Yes, you said that. And there was—"

"Ugh, I don't need the instant replay," I huff, marching toward him. "Do you have any idea how worried I was?"

His grin softens into something more tender as I approach him. "Please forgive me, pet. I didn't mean to cause you anxiety. I simply wanted to surprise you."

I halt just short of him, crossing my arms. "Well, mission accomplished. I'm surprised. And annoyed. And..." I trail off, unable to find the right words to express the whirlwind of emotions I'm experiencing.

Declan reaches out, tucking a stray strand of hair behind my ear. "And what? You didn't finish your thought."

I throw my arms up, then let them flop back down again. "And exhilarated. Happy now? I can't believe I'm about to get on a private jet with a man I barely know."

He pulls me into his arms. "Oh, I'd say you know me quite intimately by now, Bree. But there's much more to discover. For both of us."

I shiver at his words, desire pooling in my belly. But I force myself to step back, fixing him with a stern look. "Hold on, mister. You don't get to just whisk me away without an explanation. Where are we going?"

Declan's eyes twinkle with mischief. "That, my darling, is part of the adventure. Don't you trust me?"

I snort. "About as far as I can throw you."

He clutches his chest in mock hurt. "You wound me, Sabrina. After all we've been through? But I don't believe you, pet. Our intimacy last night proved you're lying now."

"Oh, please. All we've been through is a week of incredible orgasms and questionable decision-making," I retort, even as my lips twitch with the effort of suppressing a smile.

"Ah, but what a week it's been."

I can't argue with that. My body tingles at the memory of our passionate encounters. But I'm not ready to let him off the hook just yet.

"Fine," I concede, poking him in the chest. "But I have conditions. One, you tell me where we're going. Two, we make it back in time for my sister's wedding. And three..." I pause, searching for a third demand.

Declan raises an eyebrow, amusement dancing in his eyes. "And three?"

I blurt out the first thing that comes to mind. "And three, you teach me how to fly this thing."

He tips his head to the side as a slow, sinful gring spreads across his face. "Deal."

Declan claims my hand, leading me toward the sleek aircraft. It isn't as large as I would have expected, but it's quite elegant. "Your flying lessons begin now, Miss Remington."

My heart races as we approach the plane. It's smaller than I expected, gleaming white against the tarmac with splashes of bright red here and there. Declan helps me up the steps, his hand on the small of my back.

Inside, the cabin is luxurious, all soft leather and polished wood. But Declan doesn't pause, guiding me straight to the cockpit.

"Alright, darling," he says, settling into the pilot's seat. "First rule of flying—always check your instruments."

I slide into the co-pilot's seat, overwhelmed by the array of dials, switches, and screens before me. Declan's voice is low and steady as he walks me through the pre-flight checklist, his hands moving confidently over the controls. I try to focus on his words, but I'm distracted by the way his muscles flex under his shirt and the intensity of his focus as he explains each step.

"Are you listening, Sabrina?" he asks, a hint of amusement in his voice.

I blink, realizing I've been staring at his lips. "Yes, of course. Checking instruments. Very important."

He chuckles, patting my thigh. "You know, if you wanted to stare at me, you could have just asked."

I roll my eyes, pushing his hand away playfully. "Just fly the plane, Captain Wilde."

As we roll down the runway, I feel a mix of excitement and nerves bubbling up inside me. The engines roar to life, and suddenly we're hurtling down the tarmac at ever increasing speed. I instinctively reach for Declan's hand but then realize that might distract him. I don't want our plane to crash because I'm feeling him up. As the plane lifts off the ground, he gives me a reassuring smile.

"Breathe, love," he tells me, his gaze fixed on the sky ahead as we climb higher.

I force myself to take a deep breath, my grip on his hand loosening slightly. As the ground falls away beneath us, a sense of wonder replaces my initial anxiety. The sprawling city of Marrakesh shrinks into a patchwork of terracotta and sand, the Atlas Mountains rising majestically in the distance.

"It's beautiful," I breathe, unable to tear my eyes away from the scenery.

Declan glances at me, a soft smile playing on his lips. "Not as beautiful as you."

"You don't need to romance me anymore. I'm already yours." I can't believe I said that, but I meant it. As I relax in my seat, I allow myself to enjoy the high-altitude scenery. "So, are you going to tell me where we're headed now?"

Declan squeezes my thigh gently. "Patience, darling. All will be revealed in due time."

I huff, but secretly, I'm thrilled by the mystery. As we soar higher, I can no longer see the bustling city we left behind us, and I feel a sense of freedom I've never experienced before.

"All right, co-pilot," Declan says, interrupting my thoughts. "Ready for your first lesson?"

I sit up straighter, trying to look more confident than I feel. "Ready as I'll ever be."

He guides my hands to the yoke, his touch awakening my body. The softness of his voice doesn't help me focus either. Everything about him gets me horny, but I try to pay attention to his commands.

"Gently now," he murmurs, his hands covering mine on the controls. "Feel how she responds to the slightest movement."

I follow his directions and feel the jet shift tack minutely under my guidance. Being in control of a massive machine gives me both a heady sensation of power and the scary feeling I might send us plummeting to the ground with one false move.

"That's it, love," Declan encourages, his voice low and intimate in my ear. "You're a natural."

I grin, a rush of confidence flowing through me. "Maybe I missed my calling. Sabrina Remington, man hunter, has become Sabrina Remington, ace pilot."

Declan chuckles, the sound vibrating through me. "I'd fly anywhere with you, darling."

The moment feels charged, intimate in a way that goes beyond physical attraction. I turn my head slightly, meeting Declan's intense gaze. For a moment, we're suspended in time as if the rest of the world no longer exists, and we are the only two people in the universe. He sets the autopilot so he can lean in to cup my face in both hands. The moment his mouth meets mine, my eyes flutter shut. When he slips his tongue between my lips, I sag against him and moan.

The kiss lasts only for a moment. But it felt like forever. And the longer we gaze into each other's eyes, the more I realize I need to tell him the truth.

"We haven't been together for very long," I say, "and I know I've been skittish about getting tangled up in another serious relationship. But I now know I want to be with you forever. Is that too crazy for you? Am I too crazy for you?"

"No, love, it isn't barmy at all." He lays his hands over mine. "I've known I want to be with you for the rest of my life since the night we met. I couldn't admit it to myself at first."

The time has come, and I don't even flinch at what I need to say next. "The chase is over. You've got me. I'm yours, Declan, body and soul."

"You've owned my heart, my soul, and my body since that night at the Savoy when I took you to my suite."

My heart soars higher than the jet we're flying on. I press my forehead against his, loving the way our breaths mingle. "So, what now?"

Declan's hands slide down to my waist, and he lifts me onto his lap. The yoke is behind me now, but he doesn't seem perturbed by that fact. "Now, my darling Sabrina, we embark on the greatest adventure of all."

"And what's that?" I ask, my fingers tracing the strong line of his jaw.

His eyes sparkle with mischief and something deeper, something heady and sweet and as irresistible as the man himself. "Life, Bree. We live it together, to the fullest."

The joy bubbling up inside me is almost overwhelming. "That sounds suspiciously like a proposal, Sir Declan."

His lips gradually slide into that heart-stopping, knee-weakening grin that first drew me to him. "And if it was?"

Every hair on my body lifts and stiffens, but it's not from fear. I've never felt safer in my entire life than I do with Declan. "Then my answer would be yes. A thousand times, yes."

Declan's face lights up, his smile so bright it could outshine the sun. He pulls me into a kiss that's tender and passionate all at once, filled with promise and hope for our future together.

When we finally separate, both breathless and giddy, laughter bubbles out of me. "I can't believe this is happening. We're engaged, and I don't even know where we're flying to."

Declan smirks and winks. "Well, future Mrs. Wilde, allow me to enlighten you." He gestures to the horizon, where I can just make out the shimmering blue of the Mediterranean. "We're headed to Japan."

Chapter Twenty-Two

Declan

Japan?" Sabrina's eyes bulge, and she's almost gaping. Then she shakes her head, rather violently. "Declan, that's halfway around the world. What about Tabby's wedding? I can't miss that. As much as I love bouncing around the world with you, I need to be there for my sister."

"Relax, you won't miss anything. I'll make certain of that."

She gnaws on her bottom lip. "Well, if you're absolutely sure…"

"I promise you will be on time to your sister's nuptials." Since I still have the autopilot on, I pull Bree onto my lap so I can wrap my arms around her. "I have a mate who lives in Nikko. It's a beautiful, romantic destination. We'll need to make stops along the way to refuel, but even that long a trip won't take more than a day or so. Don't worry, love. We'll be back in plenty of time. I've got it all planned out."

She shakes her head, laughing despite herself. "You know, most people just go out for dinner when they get engaged."

"Ah, but we're not most people, are we?" I give her a quick kiss, then pat her arse. "Now, you need to return to your seat, please."

She climbs back onto her seat. "I trust you, Declan. You'll get me home in plenty of time."

"Thank you for the vote of confidence." I turn my attention back to the controls. "I thought you wanted an adventure, anyway."

"Yes, I do want that. But we can't tell anyone about our engagement yet." She bites her lip. "I wouldn't want to steal Tabitha's thunder. She deserves to be the center of attention."

"We will keep it a secret, for now." I lift my brows. "Does that mean I can't even buy you a ring yet?"

"Hmm, I'll need to think about that." As the reality of our impromptu engagement sinks in, a giddy excitement bubbles up inside me. "So, tell me about this friend of yours. And please tell me we're not staying in some kind of luxury resort that costs ten thousand dollars. I've had plenty of that, but I'd love something more low-key this time."

"Whatever you want, I shall provide." I chuckle at Bree's request. "Low-key, eh? I think I can manage that. My mate Inada Ren operates a traditional *ryokan*—it's a type of Japanese inn—that's just outside the city of Nikko. Think sliding paper doors, futons on *tatami* mats, and hot spring baths under the stars."

Bree's expression lights up. "Hot springs? Now that sounds like my kind of adventure."

"I thought you might approve," I say, unable to keep the smugness from my voice. "And don't worry about the ring. We'll find something perfect when the time is right. For now, let's just enjoy the journey."

As we soar over the vast expanse of the Pacific, I replay my time with Declan in mind and can't believe how fast things have changed. Just a few weeks ago, I was a restless soul, drifting from one adventure to the next. Now, with Bree by my side, every moment feels like a new discovery.

"So, tell me more about this *ryokan*," Bree says. "I've never stayed in one before."

I grin, picturing the serene beauty of Nikko. "It's nestled in the mountains, surrounded by ancient cedar trees and babbling brooks. The rooms are simple but elegant—all natural materials and clean lines. The *onsen*, the hot spring baths, are the real draw. There's nothing quite like soaking in mineral-rich waters while gazing up at the stars."

"Okay, it does sound magical. But...do we have to wear those kimono things? I'm not sure I can pull off that look."

"They're called *yukata*, actually. And yes, they're traditional, but don't worry—you'll look stunning in anything."

Bree rolls her eyes, but I note the hint of a blush on her cheeks. "Oh, Declan, you are the consummate sweet talker. But seriously, I'm going to need some serious guidance on Japanese etiquette. I don't want to offend anyone."

"That's what you've got me for, love," I say, reaching over to give her hand a squeeze. "Though I have to warn you, my Japanese is a bit rusty."

"Oh, fantastic," Bree laughs. "We'll be the clueless couple stumbling around, butchering the language and probably using the wrong chopsticks or something."

"Probably," I agree with a grin. "But that's half the fun, isn't it? Besides, Ren speaks excellent English. He'll keep us from making complete fools of ourselves."

"I thought his name was Inada."

"Sorry, pet, I should have explained. Japanese names are flipped round from the English-language perspective. His first name is Ren, and his surname is Inada."

Bree leans back in her seat, a dreamy look in her eyes. "I can't believe we're really doing this. Flying halfway around the world on a whim, staying in a traditional Japanese inn...it's like something out of a movie."

"Well, if it's a movie, I'd say we're the stars," I tease, giving her a wink. "Though I hope it's not one of those lost-in-translation comedies where everything goes wrong."

She snorts, shaking her head. "With our luck? It just might be. But you know what? I don't even care. As long as I'm with you, I'm up for anything."

While we soar through the sky, taking the requisite stops to refuel and find sustenance, we also share more of our pasts with each other. We're already engaged, yet we have so much to learn. I know the most important things about Bree, though. She is beautiful, clever, sexy as hell, and adventurous. Sabrina Remington is the perfect woman for me. How I got lucky enough to bump into her at the Savoy, I'll never know. But I'm deeply grateful to whatever power gifted me with this strawberry blonde angel.

"How long will our trip take?" Sabrina asks.

"Well, love, the flight itself will take about fourteen hours, give or take," I reply, checking our flight plan. "We're traveling faster than an airliner. So, even with our stops for fuel and rest, we're looking at about a day and a half of total travel time. We'll touch down in Tokyo first, then take a scenic train ride to Nikko."

Bree's eyebrows shoot up. "A day and a half? That's not as bad as I thought. I was picturing us island-hopping across the Pacific for weeks."

I flash her a cocky grin. "Don't worry. I've done longer hauls than this. Besides, I've got the best co-pilot in the world to keep me alert."

She raises an eyebrow. "Co-pilot? I thought I was just eye candy."

"Oh, you're that too," I tease, earning a playful swat on the arm. "But seriously, if you're interested, I could show you some of the basics. It might come in handy someday."

Bree's face lights up with excitement. "Really? I'd love that."

Our journey becomes an even more exciting adventure than our mutual chasing of each other. Over the next day and a half, we explore lesser known locales that even I haven't explored yet. Bree loves every minute of it, and I love it too—because she's with me.

When we finally touch down in Tokyo, I swear I can feel the bustling energy of the capital city buzzing around us. Bree's eyes are wide with wonder, taking in the neon lights and towering skyscrapers. We navigate the crowded streets, hand in hand, behaving like any tourists might. But we aren't mere tourists. We are international adventurers.

"Um, sweetie, I think I just ordered us something with tentacles," Bree giggles, pointing at a picture on the vending machine screen.

I peer over her shoulder, chuckling. "Actually, darling, that's...Well, I'm not entirely sure what it is. Shall we find out?"

Her radiant smile could light up the entire city. "Absolutely. When in Rome, right?"

I abruptly realize what she said a moment ago. "Did you just call me 'sweetie'?"

"Yep. Do you mind?"

I kiss her cheek. "Not at all. You can call me 'sweetie' anytime."

We spend the night in a capsule hotel, marveling at the tiny, pod-like rooms and high-tech amenities. Bree can barely contain her excitement as we squeeze into our adjacent capsules. It isn't my favorite way to sleep, but Sabrina insisted on having a pod experience.

"This is insane," she whispers loudly, poking her head out to look at me. "I feel like I'm in some futuristic spaceship."

I grin back at her. "Welcome to Tokyo, love. Just wait until you see what Nikko has in store for us."

The next morning, we board a train to Nikko, watching the urban sprawl of Tokyo give way to lush green mountains and tranquil forests. Bree's face is pressed against the window, drinking in every detail of the passing landscape.

As we step off the train in Nikko, the air feels different—cleaner, crisper. The bustling energy of Tokyo is replaced by a serene calm that seems to emanate from the very earth itself.

"Oh, Declan," Bree breathes, taking in the picturesque scenery. "It's absolutely gorgeous here."

I squeeze her hand, feeling a sense of peace wash over me. "Wait until you see the *ryokan*. It's just up this path."

We make our way along a winding stone path, surrounded by towering cedar trees and the gentle sound of a nearby stream. As we round a bend, the *ryokan* comes into view—a beautiful traditional wooden building with a sloping tiled roof.

"Declan-san!" a voice calls out. A middle-aged Japanese man in a simple yukata approaches us, beaming. "Welcome, welcome!"

"Ren!" I grin, clasping his hand warmly. "It's been too long, mate. This is Sabrina, my fiancée."

Bree's eyes widen slightly at the word "fiancée," but she quickly recovers, offering Ren a warm smile and a slight bow. "It's a pleasure to meet you, Ren-san. Thank you for having us."

Ren's eyes twinkle as he returns the bow. "The pleasure is all mine, Sabrina-san. Any friend of Declan's is welcome here. Please, come inside and make yourselves comfortable."

As we follow Ren into the *ryokan*, I can feel Bree's excitement radiating off her. The interior is just as beautiful as I remember—all polished wood and soft tatami mats, with sliding paper doors separating the spaces.

"This is incredible," Bree whispers, her eyes darting around to take in every detail.

Ren shows us to our room, a spacious area overlooking a serene garden. As he slides open the *shoji* doors, Bree gasps in delight.

"It's even more beautiful than I imagined," she proclaims, stepping inside. The room is minimalist yet elegant, with a low table, cushions, and a small alcove adorned with a simple flower arrangement and a calligraphy scroll.

Ren smiles warmly. "I'm pleased you like it. The *onsen* is just down the path outside. Please, enjoy your stay. Dinner will be served in two hours."

After he leaves, Bree turns to me, her green eyes sparkling. "Declan, this is...I don't even have the words to describe it. Thank you for bringing me here."

I pull her close, reveling in the scent of her hair. "Anything for you, love. Now, what do you say we check out those hot springs?"

"Yes, please. I thought you'd never ask."

We change into the provided yukata, Bree giggling as she struggles with the unfamiliar garment. The simple robe accentuates her sensual body.

"How do I look?" she asks, giving a little twirl.

"Absolutely ravishing," I reply, pulling her in for a quick kiss. "Though I must say, I prefer you without any clothes at all."

She swats my arm playfully. "Behave yourself, Mr. Wilde. We're in a respectable establishment."

We make our way down the stone path to the onsen, the cool evening air nipping at our skin. The sound of bubbling water grows louder as we approach.

"Now, remember," I whisper to Bree, "we have to wash thoroughly before entering the bath. And no splashing or loud noises—it's meant to be a peaceful experience."

Bree nods solemnly, but there's a glimmer of excitement in her eyes. We part ways at the entrance, heading to the separate men's and women's changing areas.

A few minutes later, I'm easing myself into the steaming water, feeling the tension melt from my muscles. The outdoor bath is surrounded by smooth rocks and lush greenery, with a breathtaking view of the starry sky above.

I hear a small splash and turn to see Bree entering the water, her pale skin flushed from the heat. She lets out a contented sigh as she sinks deeper into the bath, her strawberry blonde hair piled messily atop her head.

"This is heavenly," she murmurs, her eyes closed in bliss. "I could stay here forever."

"Careful, darling. You might turn into a prune if you do."

She cracks one eye open, a smirk playing on her lips. "Would you still love me if I was all wrinkly?"

"Always," I reply, pulling her onto my lap. The water splashes gently around us as I trail kisses along her neck. "Though I must say, I prefer you soft and smooth."

We spend four days in Nikko, and Bree loves getting to know Ren and learning about Japanese traditions. But then it's time for us to move on. I can sense that Sabrina wants to head home, but I ask her to be sure.

"Yeah, I'm ready to go home. And by 'home' I mean your place in London."

"Would you like to meet my family?"

She boosts herself up on her tiptoes to kiss my cheek. "Of course I would. And you'll meet my family when they descend on England for the big wedding."

"Can't wait for that." I pull her close and kiss her forehead. "I was thinking we could take a more southerly route to go home. That would let you see more exotic places."

Bree grins. "That sounds perfect."

As we board the jet, she clasps my hand firmly. "So, where to next, Captain Wilde?"

Her enthusiasm captivates me. "Well, I thought we might make a pit stop in Bali. Beautiful beaches, lush jungles, and some of the best surfing in the world. What do you say?"

"Bali?" She squeals, bouncing on her toes. "I've always wanted to go there! But wait, can we really fit that in before Tabby's wedding?"

I chuckle, guiding her to her seat. "Trust me, love. We've got plenty of time. I promised to get you back for the wedding, didn't I?"

As we take off, leaving the serene beauty of Japan behind, I'm surprised by how different this flight feels compared to when we first set out. The excitement is still there, but there's a new sense of comfort and belonging between us.

"So, tell me about Bali," Bree says, settling into her seat. "What should I expect?"

I let my lips relax into a serene smile, picturing the paradise that awaits us. "Imagine pristine beaches with crystal clear water, lush green rice terraces, and ancient temples hidden in misty jungles. It's a place where you can lounge on the sand all day or dive into adventure at a moment's notice."

"It sounds amazing. But what about the surfing you mentioned? I've never tried it before."

"Ah, you're in for a treat then," I say, reaching over to tuck a stray strand of hair behind her ear. "Bali has some of the best waves for beginners. I know a quiet little beach where we can get you started. By the time we leave, you'll be riding waves like a pro."

Bree raises an eyebrow skeptically. "I don't know about that. I'm not exactly famous for my grace and balance."

"Nonsense," I chuckle. "You're graceful as a gazelle. Besides, half the fun is falling off the board and getting back up again."

She wags her eyebrows. "Well, if nothing else, at least you'll get to see me in a bikini."

"Now that's something I'm very much looking forward to."

The next day, we're on our way.

Chapter Twenty-Three

Sabrina

As we fly over the Pacific Ocean, heading for the Indian Ocean, I can't hide my excitement. It feels like a palpable, undeniable force. Just like me, as Declan quips. I pepper him with questions about Bali, eager to learn everything I can before we arrive in paradise.

"Will we stay in one of those thatched-roof bungalows? Oh! Can we visit a monkey forest? I've heard there are sacred temples everywhere. Will we get to see those too?"

Declan laughs, delighted by my enthusiasm. "Slow down, love. We'll have time for all of that and more. I know a fantastic little villa right on the beach in Canggu. It's quieter than the touristy areas, but still close enough to explore everything."

My eyes must be bulging now. That's how excited I am. "A villa? On the beach? Declan, that sounds incredible."

"Only the best for my fiancée," he says with a wink.

I think I might be blushing. Only Declan Wilde could ever turn me back into a teenager with a crush on the hunkiest guy in school.

He leans in close, his breath tickling my ear as he whispers, "And wait until you see the private pool. It's perfect for skinny dipping under the stars."

"Declan Wilde, are you trying to seduce me at high altitude?"

His deep chuckle reverberates through me. "Darling, I'm always trying to seduce you. It's part of my charm."

I playfully swat his arm, but I can't deny the heat blooming in my cheeks. "You're incorrigible."

"And you love it," he quips, capturing my hand and pressing a kiss to my knuckles.

As we begin our descent into Bali, the lush landscape unfolds beneath us. Emerald rice paddies, pristine beaches, and volcanic peaks paint a breathtaking panorama. My heart races with anticipation as we touch down on the runway.

The moment we step off the plane, the warm, fragrant air envelops us like a lover's embrace. I inhale deeply, savoring the exotic scents of this magical island.

"Welcome to paradise," Declan murmurs, his arm sliding around my waist.

We breeze through customs thanks to Declan's charm. He works his magic on everyone we encounter. Before I know it, we're being whisked away in a sleek black car, the windows rolled down to let in the balmy breeze.

As we wind our way through narrow streets lined with ornate temples and swaying palms, I can't stop grinning. It all feels like a dream—the kind you never want to wake up from.

"You look happy," Declan observes.

"I'm ecstatic." I clutch his hand as a giddy excitement rushes through me. "Can't believe we're really here."

The car turns onto a secluded road, and suddenly we're pulling up to a stunning villa nestled among lush tropical gardens. My jaw drops as I take in the thatched roof, the intricately carved wooden doors, and the glimpse of sparkling blue beyond.

"Declan, this is...wow," I say, fumbling for words.

He grins, clearly pleased by my reaction. "Wait until you see the inside."

As if on cue, a smiling Balinese woman appears, greeting us with folded hands and a gentle *"Selamat datang."*

Declan responds in flawless Indonesian, because of course he does. Is there anything this man can't do?

"How do you know so many languages?" I ask. "My linguistic skills never went further than high school Spanish."

"I've traveled to many places around the world as part of my philanthropic work. Native speakers helped me learn quickly." He smirks at me with an impish glint in his eyes. "I learn languages the fastest when a woman teaches me."

"I see. Why do I get the feeling you learn languages best when you're in bed with your teacher?"

He smiles with his lips sealed.

Oh, yeah, Declan Wilde definitely acquired his multilingual skills in the bedroom.

After one day in Bali, it's time for us to move on again.

I reluctantly follow Declan back to the car, my mind still reeling from our whirlwind tour of Bali. I steal one last glance at the stunning villa. "I can't believe we're leaving already. We barely got to enjoy the private pool."

He wraps an arm around my shoulders. "Don't worry, darling. Our next stop has an even better one."

"Oh? And where might that be?"

He taps my nose playfully. "I won't tell you, not yet. But I promise you'll love it."

As we settle into our seats in the cockpit of Declan's jet, I think back on how quickly my life has changed. Just a few weeks ago, I was a small-town girl with big ambitions that were never realized. Now, I'm jetting around the world with the most infuriating, irresistible man I've ever met.

With a roar of engines, we're airborne again, soaring over the sparkling Indian Ocean. As the lush green of Bali fades into the distance, I feel a twinge of sadness.

"I wish we could have stayed longer," I say, gazing out the window. "There's so much more I wanted to see."

Declan's hand finds mine, giving it a gentle squeeze. "We'll come back, love. I promise. But for now, our adventure is just beginning."

I rub my hands together. "So, where are we off to next, Your Knightliness?"

"Egypt."

I sit up straighter, my pulse accelerating. "As in, pyramids and sphinxes and mummies Egypt?"

Declan chuckles. "The very same, darling. Though I can't promise any mummies. They tend to stay tucked away in their tombs these days."

I can barely contain my excitement, bouncing in my seat like a child on Christmas morning. "Holy cow, Declan. I've always wanted to see the pyramids! And the Nile! And—"

"Slow down, love," he laughs, placing a steadying hand on my knee. "We'll have plenty of time to explore. I've arranged for a private tour of the pyramids and the Sphinx at sunset."

"A private tour? How did you manage that?"

Declan's lips quirk. "I have my ways."

"Naturally," I roll my eyes, but can't keep the smile off my face. "I'm engaged to Indiana Jones, aren't I? Is there anything you can't do?"

He roams his gaze over me, his attention landing on my breasts. "Well, there is one thing I haven't managed yet."

"Oh really? What's that?"

In one fluid motion, Declan unbuckles his seatbelt and stands, towering over me. "Getting you to join the mile-high club."

My throat constricts as he extends his hand, an invitation and a challenge in his eyes. For a moment, I hesitate. We're alone in the cockpit, though no one else is on board anyway, but still...The responsible part of my brain tries to protest, but Declan's smoldering gaze silences it instantly.

With a coy smile, I accept his hand. "Well, I suppose there's a first time for everything."

He pulls me to my feet, his strong arms encircling my waist. "That's my girl."

The world falls away as Declan's hands delicately massage my body, leaving trails of fire in their wake. I melt into him, all thoughts of propriety forgotten. His lips blaze a path down my neck, and I can't hold back a soft moan.

"Shh," he murmurs against my skin. "Wouldn't want to scandalize the autopilot, now would we?"

I giggle like a freaking schoolgirl, the sound turning into a gasp as his teeth graze my earlobe. My fingers tangle in his hair, and when he kisses me, it's the deepest, most possessive, tongue-thrusting liplock ever.

But I have to ask him a question. So, I peel my lips away from his. "Declan?"

He pulls back just enough to look into my eyes. "Yes, darling?"

"Are you sure this is safe?" I ask, even as my body arches into his touch.

His low chuckle sends shivers down my spine. "Trust me, love. I've got everything under control."

And with that, he sweeps me off my feet—literally—carrying me to the small bedroom at the back of the jet. As he lays me gently on the mattress, I love how perfectly I fit in his arms.

"Now, pet," he purrs, hovering over me with a predatory gleam in his eyes. "Where were we?"

Hours later, as we descend into Cairo, I'm still floating on cloud nine. As we step off the jet, the heat hits me like a wall. The air is dry and dusty, a stark contrast to the lush humidity of Bali. But there's an electric energy here that suffuses the air with ancient mysteries that seem to pulse through the very ground beneath our feet.

Declan rests his hand on my back, guiding me through the crowded airport. "Welcome to Egypt, Sabrina."

I can't wipe the grin off my face as we make our way to a waiting car. The driver greets us with a warm *"Ahlan wa sahlan,"* and Declan responds in flawless Arabic. Does that man know every language on earth?

As we wind through the chaotic streets of Cairo, my eyes are glued to the window. The city is a fascinating blend of old and new—gleaming skyscrapers rising next to crumbling buildings, ancient mosques nestled among modern shops. The streets are a cacophony of honking horns, shouting vendors, and the occasional bleat of a goat.

"It's so...alive," I breathe, unable to tear my gaze away from the vibrant scene outside.

Declan claims my hand. "Just wait until you see the pyramids, love. They'll take your breath away."

As if on cue, we round a corner and there they are—the Great Pyramid of Giza, rising majestically against the golden sky with the two smaller pyramids around it. My heart skips a beat at the sight.

"I've always wanted to see Egypt," I whisper, awestruck. "The pyramids are incredible."

Declan's eyes are on me, not the scenery. "You're incredible."

As we approach our hotel, a stunning oasis nestled near the pyramids, I can hardly contain my excitement. The lobby is a marvel of modern luxury with touches of ancient Egyptian decor—golden statues, hieroglyphic-adorned pillars, and a towering palm-fringed atrium.

"Your suite is ready, Sir Declan," the concierge says with a respectful nod.

Declan's arm slides around my waist as we follow the bellhop to the elevator. "I hope you don't mind sharing."

"I suppose I can tolerate your company for a few more days," I tease, leaning into his embrace.

The elevator doors slide open, revealing a private foyer leading to our digs. As we step inside, my jaw drops. The room is nothing short of palatial, with soaring ceilings, intricate mosaic tiles, and floor-to-ceiling windows offering a magical view of the pyramids.

"Declan, this is..." I trail off, at a loss for words.

He grins, clearly pleased by my reaction. "Only the best for you, darling."

I wander to the window, mesmerized by the sight of the ancient wonders bathed in the golden light of the setting sun. Declan's arms encircle me from behind, his chin resting on my shoulder.

After a sumptuous meal and a good night's sleep, we take a river boat trip down the Nile to visit more ancient monuments. The gentle lapping of the Nile against our felucca's wooden hull is hypnotic. I lean back against Declan's chest, savoring the warmth of the Egyptian sun on my skin and the cool breeze coming off the river.

I tilt my head up to gaze at him. "This is heaven."

His blue eyes crinkle at the corners as he smiles down at me. "I'm glad you're enjoying it, love."

Our traditional sailboat glides effortlessly down the Nile, the shoreline a patchwork of lush green fields and sandy banks. Palm trees sway in the breeze, and occasionally we spot a herd of water buffalo cooling off in the shallows.

"Look!" I exclaim, pointing to a flock of white ibises taking flight from a nearby marsh. "They're so graceful."

Our felucca captain, a weathered old man named Hassan, calls out to us in Arabic, pointing to something on the shore. Declan translates for me.

"He says we're approaching the Temple of Kom Ombo," Declan explains. "It's one of the most unique temples in Egypt, dedicated to two gods at once—Sobek the crocodile god, and Horus the falcon god."

As we draw closer, I gasp at the sight. The temple rises majestically from the riverbank, its golden sandstone columns gleaming in the sunlight. Two identical entrances face the Nile, a testament to its dual nature.

By the time we return to our hotel suite, we agree that we need to move on tomorrow. Declan suggests a stop in Spain, and I trust his judgment completely. The next morning, we head back to the airport.

As we settle into our seats on Declan's jet once again, I experience a mixture of excitement and wistfulness. Egypt was beyond amazing, but Spain promises its own unique charms.

"So, where exactly are we heading in Spain?" I ask, buckling my seatbelt.

"How do you feel about flamenco and *tapas*?"

"Seville?" I guess, my heart skipping a beat.

He clasps my hand and kisses it. "Got it in one, darling. I thought we could use a bit of passion and spice after all that ancient history."

The flight passes in a blur of stolen kisses and whispered promises. Before I know it, we're touching down in Seville, the warm Andalusian sun greeting us as we step off the plane. A driver awaits us on the tarmac and whisks us through the winding streets of Seville, past whitewashed buildings adorned with wrought-iron balconies and colorful tiles. The city is a vibrant tapestry of old and new, with modern shops nestled alongside ancient churches and palatial mansions.

As we pull up to our hotel, a stunning converted palace in the heart of the old town, I'm fascinated by the beauty of this place. Declan takes me to our suite which is, of course, ginormous and gorgeous. After a good night's sleep, the time has finally come.

We are flying straight to London.

Chapter Twenty-Four

Declan

We leave the hotel in the early hours of the morning. That had been Sabrina's idea. She wants to stop off in Spain for one last adventure as a tourist, and I can't refuse her anything she wants. I would do anything for her, even strap my naked body to the back of a crocodile if that would make her happy. That explains why we're now strolling down the cobblestone streets of Seville. Bree's eyes sparkle with excitement as she twirls, her sundress floating around her while her hair conceals most of her face.

"Wow, isn't it magical?" she gushes, grabbing my hand and pulling me toward a quaint café. "We simply must try the churros here. I've heard they're to die for."

"Careful there, love. At this rate, you'll have us eating our way through all of Spain before noon."

She shoots me a playful pout. "Are you saying you don't want to indulge in a little...sweetness with me?"

The way she emphasizes the word sweetness makes my cock wake up and begin to hunger for a different kind of treat. I pull her close, my lips brushing her ear. "Oh, I'll indulge in all the sweetness you're offering, darling. But let's start with those churros, shall we?"

Sabrina's enthusiastic laughter echoes down the street, drawing smiles from passersby. We settle at a small table outside the café, the morning sun warming our skin. As we wait for our order, I gaze at Bree's lovely face and the way she seems to glow in this light. The golden rays of the sun that ignite her strawberry blonde hair make me hunger to fist my hands in those locks as I drag her in for a scorching kiss.

"Why are you smiling?" she asks.

"Nothing," I reply with a smirk. "Just wondering how I got so lucky."

She pats my cheek. "Better save the smooth talk for when we're alone."

"Oh, I intend to do just that."

The arrival of our churros interrupts our flirtatious banter, and Sabrina's attention immediately shifts to the golden, sugar-dusted treats before us. She picks one up, dipping it generously in the thick chocolate sauce, and takes a bite. The moan that escapes her lips is downright sinful, and I have to shift in my seat to adjust myself because my trousers have suddenly grown tight. Sabrina notices, of course.

"Something wrong, Declan?" she asks innocently, licking a stray bit of chocolate from her thumb.

I lean in, my voice low. "You know exactly what you're doing, you cheeky minx."

She grins, unrepentant. "Me? I'm just enjoying my breakfast."

Two can play at this game. I pick up a churro, making a show of slowly dipping it in the chocolate. I bring it to my mouth, maintaining eye contact as I take a bite. A drop of chocolate escapes. I thrust my tongue, dragging it slowly across my bottom lip.

Sabrina catches her lip between her teeth as if she means to devour me instead of her chocolaty treat. "It's not fair to tease me that way."

I lean back, savoring both the dessert and her reaction. "All's fair in love and churros, darling."

She narrows her eyes playfully, accepting the challenge. "Well then, perhaps we should take this tasting...somewhere more private."

My body responds instantly to her suggestion, but I force myself to remain calm. "Afraid we can't do that, pet. Duty calls—and in this case 'duty' means we need to contend with our families."

Sabrina pouts again, but there's a glimmer in her eyes that tells me she's enjoying this game as much as I am. She sighs melodramatically. "If you insist. But you owe me for this torture."

"Gladly." I reach across the table to brush my thumb across her lower lip, wiping away a smudge of chocolate.

In that moment, as the bustling sounds of Seville fade into the background, I'm struck by how effortlessly we've fallen into this dance of desire and playful banter. It's as if we've known each other for years.

Sabrina fastens her hand around mine before I can pull it away, pressing a soft kiss to my palm. The gesture is so unexpectedly tender that it catches me off guard, sending a shudder of something deeper than lust through my chest.

I fold my palms around her hand. "We need to get to the airport. Our journey back to London wont' be long, less than two hours depending on the conditions."

"Okay, let's go. I'm so excited to meet all of your family."

I love her enthusiasm, but I feel a knot of anxiety tightening in my gut. "Are you now? Well, I hope you're ready for the Wilde clan in all their chaotic glory."

"I'm sure I can handle a little chaos. After all, I've managed to keep up with you so far, haven't I?"

"Touché," I concede, rising from our table and offering her my hand. "And I'm looking forward to meeting your family as well as all your mysterious friends."

"Mysterious?" she says with a slight laugh. "They're just good people, that's all."

We make our way through the winding streets, the scent of orange blossoms and freshly baked bread following us like a sweet memory. As we near the taxi stand, Sabrina suddenly stops, tugging me back.

"Wait," she says, her voice softer now. "Before we go...I just want to say thank you. For being you, for playing my crazy game, for taking me on so many wonderful adventures, for...everything."

The sincerity in her voice astounds me, and for a moment, I'm at a loss for words. It's a rare feat, rendering Declan Wilde speechless, but Sabrina seems to have a knack for it.

I pull her close, one hand cupping her face. "No need to thank me, love. If anything, I should be thanking you for turning my world upside down in the best possible way."

Her lips curve into a smile that's equal parts shy and seductive. "Well, I do excel at shaking things up."

"That you do," I murmur, unable to resist pressing a kiss to her forehead. "Now, let's hurry back to the jet before I change my mind and whisk you off to some remote island instead of taking you home with me."

Bree laughs. "As tempting as that sounds, I think we've had enough island adventures for now. Besides, I'm dying to see the look on your family's faces when they meet me."

We hail a taxi and settle in for the ride to the airport. As we weave through Seville's streets, Sabrina twines her fingers with my own. It's a small gesture, but it sends a warmth through my chest that has nothing to do with the Spanish sun. I ask if she'd like to check out the duty-free shop at the airport, but she assures me she just wants to get in the air.

Soon, we land at Gatwick airport and jump directly into another taxi. I had texted my brother Julian so he would know to expect Sabrina and myself at Wildewick Manor. I know he will have alerted the rest of the family.

As our car pulls up to the imposing gates of Wildewick Manor, I feel Sabrina tense beside me. Her usual effervescence seems to have dimmed, replaced by a nervous energy I've rarely seen from her.

"Don't worry," I say softly, giving her hand a reassuring squeeze. "They're going to love you. How could they not?"

She offers me a weak smile. "Easy for you to say, Mr. Charming British Accent. I'm just a divorced American girl with a penchant for trouble."

"Darling, if you think my family isn't intimately acquainted with trouble, you're in for quite a surprise."

The gates swing open, revealing the sprawling estate beyond. Sabrina's eyes widen as she takes in the manicured gardens and the grand Georgian mansion looming before us.

"Holy shit," she breathes, her green eyes wide as saucers. "You didn't tell me you lived in Downton Abbey."

I chuckle at her reaction. "It's not quite that grand, love. Though I'm sure my grandmother would be thrilled by the comparison."

As we pull up to the front entrance, I spot a familiar figure waiting on the steps. My brother Julian, looking every bit the proper English gentleman in his tailored suit, stands tall and proud. But there's a mischievous glint in his eye that betrays his polished exterior.

I give Sabrina's hand one last squeeze. "Ready to face the wolves, darling?"

She takes a deep breath, squaring her shoulders. "Bring it on, Sir Declan."

We climb out of the car, and Julian hops down the steps to meet us, his grin widening as looks at Sabrina.

"Well, well, well," Julian drawls. "So, this is the infamous Sabrina who's managed to tame our brother-in-chief."

I roll my eyes at my brother's theatrics. "Tame is hardly the word I'd use, Julian."

Sabrina, bless her, rises to the occasion beautifully. She extends her hand to my brother with a cheeky grin. "Pleasure to meet you. I prefer to think of it as 'expertly wrangled' rather than tamed."

Julian throws his head back and laughs, a rich, warm sound that seems to break the tension. My brother smiles at Sabrina, then winks at me. "Oh, I like her already. Welcome to Wildewick, darling. I hope you're ready for absolute chaos."

"I was born ready," Sabrina quips, her confidence seeming to grow by the second. "I grew up in a commune, after all. Chaos is my middle name."

Julian's eyebrows shoot up at that, but he seems impressed rather than shocked. "A commune, you say? Oh, I absolutely must hear more about that. Come on in, both of you. The rest of the family is dying to meet you, Sabrina."

As we follow Julian into the grand foyer, I am utterly amazed by how deftly Sabrina is handling herself. She's taking in the ornate surroundings with wide-eyed wonder, but there's no trace of intimidation in her expression or her posture.

"So, this is what you ran away from?" she whispers to me, a hint of teasing in her voice. "I'm starting to question your life choices."

I slip my arm around her shoulders, tugging her close. "Trust me, love, I've never made a better choice than the one that led me to you."

Sabrina's cheeks flush a delightful shade of pale pink, but before she can respond, we're interrupted by a whirlwind of excitement barreling down the grand staircase.

"Declan! You're finally here!" My sister Darcy practically launches herself at me, her arms wrapping around my neck in a tight hug. "And you must be Sabrina!"

She releases me and turns to embrace Bree with equal enthusiasm.

I watch, amused, as Sabrina's eyes widen in surprise before she returns the hug. "It's great to meet you, Darcy. The way Declan talks about you, I could tell I'd like you."

Darcy kisses Bree's cheek and commandeers my fiancée's hand, drawing Sabrina away from me. "Oh, we're going to be the best of friends, I can already tell. Come on, let me introduce you to the rest of the family."

I watch with a mixture of amusement and trepidation as my sister whisks Bree away, chattering a mile a minute as she often does. Darcy does seem more animated than usual, though, most likely due to her excitement over meeting Sabrina.

Julian sidles up beside me, an amused smirk playing on his lips, and speaks in a soft voice. "Well, dear brother, you've certainly outdone yourself this time. She's quite something."

I can't help the proud grin that spreads across my face. "That she is."

We follow the sound of laughter into the drawing room, where the rest of the family has gathered. My parents are there, along with our youngest brother, Leo, and our grandmother, the formidable Constance Wilde. As we enter the drawing room, I feel Sabrina's hand tighten around mine. The chatter dies down as all eyes turn to us. My mother, ever the gracious hostess, is the first to break the silence.

"Declan, darling!" she exclaims, gliding toward us with open arms. "And this must be the lovely Sabrina we've heard so much about."

"How have you heard anything about her? Sabrina and I have been on a whirlwind holiday—alone."

"Oh, don't be so grumpy," Bree says as she bumps her shoulder into my arm. "The grapevine grows like an invasive weed, you know." She steps forward to approach my mother, her smile bright but with a hint of nervousness. "It's wonderful to meet you, Mrs. Wilde. Thank you for having me."

"Oh, please call me Elizabeth," my mother insists, pulling Sabrina into a warm embrace. "We're so thrilled to finally meet you."

I can see Sabrina visibly relax at my mother's warm welcome. My father approaches next, his usually stern face softened by a genuine smile.

"Welcome to Wildewick, Sabrina," my father says, extending his hand. "I hope my son has been treating you well on your travels."

Bree accepts my father's hand. "Oh, he's been an absolute gentleman, Mr. Wilde. Well, most of the time, anyway."

Her cheeky response makes me chuckle. My father raises an eyebrow, clearly amused. "Please, call me Richard. And I'm glad to hear it. Though knowing Declan, I'm sure there's been plenty of adventure as well."

"You have no idea," Sabrina laughs, shooting me a look that makes my heart race.

Before I can respond, a sharp voice cuts through the room. "Well, are you going to introduce us properly, Declan, or shall we all just stand around making small talk all day?"

I turn to see my grandmother, Constance, eyeing Sabrina with keen interest. Despite her advanced years, her gaze is as sharp as ever, missing nothing.

"Of course, Gran," I say, guiding Bree toward her. "This is Sabrina Remington. Sabrina, this is my grandmother, Constance Wilde."

Bree extends her hand, her smile unwavering. "It's an honor to meet you, Constance."

My grandmother regards Sabrina for a long moment, her steely gaze softening ever so slightly. Then she takes Bree's hand. "American, I see. And quite vivacious, I'm sure. Only a strong, delightful woman could tame our Declan. Tell me, dear, what do you do?"

"I'm an insurance underwriter," Sabrina replies, her voice steady despite the intensity of my grandmother's gaze. "But

I'm also a bit of an adventure seeker in my free time. At least, I have been since I met Declan."

Constance's eyebrows rise slightly. "How interesting. And how exactly did you come to meet our Declan?"

I start to interject, but Sabrina beats me to it. "Well, it's quite the story, actually. It involves a stolen yacht, a case of mistaken identity, and a rather daring escape from some very determined art thieves."

My jaw drops. Art thieves? What on earth is Bree talking about?

The room falls silent for a moment.

But then Sabrina winks and grins. "Just kidding."

My grandmother lets out a hearty laugh, surprising us all. "Oh, I like you already, my dear. You must tell me all about your antics with my grandson over tea." She winks at Bree. "I enjoy a good fib now and then myself."

All my anxiety fades away. If Sabrina's won over my grandmother, the rest of the family will be a breeze.

My mother claps her hands to gain everyone's attention. "Well, now that the introductions are out of the way, why don't we all sit down for some tea and get to know Sabrina better?"

Chapter Twenty-Five

Sabrina

I love the Wildes. They've welcomed me into their family and made me feel like I belong here. Julian and his wife, Margaret, tell me how they met and fell in love, then share the story of their son Finn's birth, which is quite a tale.

I listen intently, sipping my tea and trying not to choke on my laughter as Julian recounts how Finn decided to make his grand entrance into the world during a charity polo match. Margaret, bless her heart, had insisted on attending despite being ready to pop. As Julian mimes swinging a mallet while simultaneously attempting to usher his wife into the car, I catch Declan's eye across the room. He's leaning against the doorframe, arms crossed, a hint of a smirk playing on his lips.

"And where were you during all this excitement, Declan?" I call out, unable to resist the urge to draw him into the conversation.

He pushes away from the wall, sauntering over here with all the grace of a panther on the prowl. "Oh, I was there, love. Someone had to keep Mum from throttling Dad for suggesting that Margaret 'hold it in for just one more chukker.' "

I snort into my teacup, nearly spilling the contents down my front. "Chukker? Sounds like a drinking game."

Declan's eyes sparkle with mischief as he plops down next to me on the sofa, his thigh brushing against mine. The contact sends a jolt through my body that I desperately try to ignore. "Ronald Wilde has never left a match early, so he couldn't understand Julian's refusal to keep going. I managed to pry Father away from Julian so he could rush to his wife's side."

Julian rolls his eyes good-naturedly. "I'll have you know I handled that situation with the utmost grace and composure."

Margaret lets out an unladylike snort. "Oh yes, darling. Nothing says 'grace and composure' quite like shouting 'My wife's having a baby, you wanker!' while frantically waving a polo mallet in the air at our father."

I burst into laughter, picturing the scene. "I'm sure it was quite the spectacle."

"Oh, it was," Declan chimes in. "The entire crowd thought it was part of some elaborate halftime show. There were cheers and whoops."

I turn to him, eyebrows raised. "And I suppose you just stood there looking devastatingly handsome and completely unruffled?"

His lips curl into a slow, dangerous smile. "Naturally. Someone had to maintain their composure."

A doorbell rings elsewhere in the house.

Constance Wilde abruptly leaps out of her chair. "Come, Sabrina, we have a wonderful surprise for you."

"You didn't need to do anything special."

"Nonsense." She seizes my arm, politely yet forcefully pulling me off the sofa. "Declan, dear, will you please escort Sabrina?"

Declan and I exchange bemused glances as Constance practically drags us out of the room. I love how easily his hand finds the small of my back, guiding me through the hallway with a gentle pressure that sends tingles up my spine.

"Any idea what this is about?" I whisper, leaning in close enough to get a whiff of his enticing cologne. It's woodsy and intoxicating, and I have to resist the urge to bury my face in his neck.

"Not a clue," he murmurs back, his breath tickling my ear. "But knowing Mum, it's bound to be...interesting."

We reach the foyer just as the butler opens the massive oak door, revealing familiar faces, and my jaw drops. "Tabitha?"

"Surprise!" my sister squeals, launching herself at me with all the grace of an excited teenager.

I stagger backward, nearly toppling over as Tabitha's enthusiasm threatens to bowl us both over. Declan's steady hand on my back keeps me upright, and I'm torn between gratitude for his support and acute awareness of his touch.

"Tabby?" I gasp, returning her embrace with equal fervor. "What on earth are you doing here?"

She pulls back, blinking in confusion. "Did you really think I'd let you have all the fun in jolly old England without me?"

Before I can respond, a deep, accented voice chimes in. "Don't forget about me, love. I'm not just the chauffeur, you know."

I peer around Tabitha to see her fiancé, Spencer, standing in the doorway while wearing a grin that could rival the Cheshire Cat's. His brown hair is tousled, and his blue eyes are focused on Tabby.

"Spencer!" I exclaim, breaking away from Tabitha to give him a quick hug. "I can't believe you're both here. We weren't expecting you until next week."

"We couldn't very well let you gallivant around London on your own, could we?" Spencer says, his accent somehow more pronounced than I remember. "Someone's got to keep you out of trouble."

I roll my eyes, but can't keep the grin off my face. "I'll have you know I'm perfectly capable of staying out of trouble on my own, thank you very much."

"Is that so?" Declan's voice is low and teasing in my ear, sending a shiver down my spine. "And here I thought you were actively seeking it out."

I turn to face him, ready with a snappy retort, but the words die on my lips as I realize my parents are standing just behind Tabby and Spence. My mouth goes dry as I take in the sight of my parents, standing there like they've just stepped out of a time machine.

Mom, with her flowing tie-dye dress and silver-streaked hair twisted into an elaborate braid, beams at me with all the brilliance of the sun. Dad, sporting a blend of hippie chic and academic professor style—complete with elbow patches on his tweed jacket—offers a sheepish wave.

My eyes narrow on them. "Why are you two dressed like that? You haven't worn hippie chic since I was ten years old."

Dad shrugs. "It was Tabby's idea. She thought it would be fun to show off our old hippie selves to your soon-to-be in-laws."

"In-laws!?" I virtually shriek.

The word "in-laws" echoes through the foyer, and I feel my face flush crimson. I shoot a panicked glance at Declan, who looks equally stunned, his blue eyes wide with surprise.

"Oh, sweetie-pie," my mother coos, pulling me into a quick hug. "We're just so thrilled you've found someone special. When Tabby told us about your whirlwind romance with this dashing Englishman, we simply had to come and meet him properly. You are engaged, after all."

Dad smirks and chucks my chin. "Relax, Bree. We're so damn happy that you've found your PC. That loser husband of yours didn't deserve you."

I feel the blood drain from my face as I whirl around to face Declan, who looks equally stunned. His gaze darts between me and my family. While my mouth gapes, Declan recovers first.

He flicks his gaze between Mom and Dad. "Ah, what gave you the idea that we're engaged?"

Julian inserts himself between my parents, setting a hand on their shoulders. "You underestimated the international grapevine, didn't you, Decky?"

"I don't understand."

"Ren sent Leo a text, asking when the wedding would be. He even offered to bring some Japanese food for the reception."

Declan's arm snakes around my waist, pulling me close against his side. "Well, darling, it seems our little secret's out."

Tabitha shrieks and claps. "Let's make it a double wedding!"

Spencer does a literal double take, and his eyes grow so wide that I think they might fall out of their sockets. "Double wedding? I don't see how we can pull that off in such a short."

"Let's all go inside and discuss the possibility." Tabby slides her arms around Spencer's waist and raises onto her tiptoes to whisper in his ear, "I know you can make it happen...for me."

Her suggestive tone makes it clear she plans on using sex to convince her fiancé.

I feel like I've stepped into some bizarre alternate reality where everything's gone topsy-turvy. My brain is scrambling to comprehend the chaos unfolding around me. A double wedding? Declan and I have only just gotten engaged. We weren't planning to tell anybody yet. Now, my sister has turned this into a twofer. My heart is pounding so hard I'm surprised it hasn't burst right out of my chest.

"Whoa, whoa, whoa," I finally manage to sputter, holding up my hands. "Let's pump the brakes here for a second. There's been a huge misunderstanding."

But my protests are drowned out by the excited chatter of my family and the Wildes as they usher us further into the house. Declan's arm remains firmly around my waist, and I'm torn between wanting to melt into his embrace and wishing I could elbow him in the ribs for playing along with this charade.

Declan clears his throat. "Sabrina, darling, I think we need to have a little chat. In private."

I nod my agreement, feeling dizzy from the whirlwind of events. Our families file into the drawing room, chattering excitedly about wedding plans. But Declan smoothly steers me away from the doors and straight toward a quiet alcove off to the side.

"Sit down, please," he says. "It seems that we're not only engaged, but also becoming parties to a double wedding."

I groan, burying my face in my hands. "I am so, so sorry about this. I have no idea how they got that ridiculous notion in their heads."

Declan gently pries my hands away from my face. "No need to apologize, love. Though I must say, if we're to be married, I would've liked to have been consulted."

I can't stop the nervous laugh that bubbles out of me. "Consulted? You mean you're actually considering this crazy idea?"

He scratches his chin. "Well, I must admit, the idea of being married to you isn't entirely unappealing."

My heart does a little flip-flop in my chest, but I force myself to stay focused. "Declan, be serious. We can't get married. Not now. We barely know each other."

"Do we?" He raises an eyebrow, his voice dropping to a low, intimate tone. "I'd say we know quite a bit about each other, Bree. For instance, I know how you take your tea—Earl Grey with a splash of milk, no sugar. Or how you scrunch up your nose when you're trying not to laugh at one of my jokes."

A blush creeps up my cheeks as Declan's words sink in. He's right. We do know each other better than I'd care to admit. But still, marriage? It's absurd.

"Okay, fine," I concede. "We're not complete strangers. But that doesn't mean we should get married on a whim just because our families have decided we should do it."

He tugs me against his side and places a soft kiss on my forehead. "Who says it has to be on a whim? We could have a long engagement. Very long. Years, even."

I snort at that. "And let our families plan this elaborate double wedding for years? That sounds like torture."

"Fair point. The alternative is that we…go along with it and see where this new adventure takes us. Just imagine our honeymoon in Tahiti…"

"That does sound sublime. But still—"

He holds my face with both hands, urging me to stare into his eyes. "This could be our wildest adventure yet. Why not jump in headfirst, like we did on the night we met? Let's see how the future unfolds. I love you with all my heart and soul, and no amount of waiting will change that. What do you say, Sabrina?"

I gaze deeply into Declan's eyes, my pulse accelerating by the second. His proposal is crazy, impulsive, and absolutely terrifying. It's also thrilling in a way I can't quite explain. For a moment, I let myself imagine it—waking up next to Declan every morning, building a life together, facing whatever challenges come our way as a team, having children.

"You're insane," I whisper, but there's no force behind the words. "This is completely bonkers."

"Perhaps. But isn't that what makes life interesting?"

Laughter snorts out of me, and I shake my head. "You're impossible."

"And yet, you love me anyway." He nuzzles my cheek. "Just say yes. You know you want to."

"God help me, I must be as insane as you are, but…" I grasp his face with both hands and kiss him passionately. "Yes, Declan, yes. I want a double wedding."

He sweeps me up in his arms and leaps off the bench, spinning us round and round while whooping. I laugh and whoop too, clinging to Declan, my heart soaring with a mixture of excitement and sheer terror until we finally come to a stop.

"You won't regret this, Bree."

"I better not," I tease, my fingers playing with the hair at the nape of his neck. "Otherwise, my hippie family will have to shoot you. We're all crack shots, you know. Or maybe Spencer's crazy friends will neutralize you."

Our families burst out of the drawing room, shouting various exclamations of joy. They clearly heard me shrieking and Declan whooping.

"Oh, sweetie!" my mother exclaims, rushing over to envelop us both in a suffocating hug. "We heard the commotion. Does this mean what I think it means?"

I exchange a glance with Declan, and he shrugs. I decide to torture them a little. "Well…"

Our families wait with rapt attention for our announcement.

I take a deep breath and say, "We're in. Double wedding it is."

The room erupts in more cheers and squeals of delight. Tabitha practically launches herself at me, nearly knocking me over in her enthusiasm. "Oh, Bree! This is going to be amazing!"

As our families swarm us, offering congratulations and already beginning to chatter about wedding plans, I feel a moment of panic. Declan must sense my unease because he pulls me close.

"Don't worry, Bree. We've got this."

His words, and the tickling of his breath on my skin, make the hairs on my arms lift. I lean into him, drawing strength from his solid presence.

"All right, All right!" Constance's voice rises above the excited chatter. "This calls for a celebration. Champagne for everyone!"

As if by magic, the butler appears with a tray of champagne flutes. The glasses and the bottles get passed around, and I find myself clinking glasses with my sister, her fiancé, my parents, and the entire Wilde clan.

"To the happy couples!" Julian toasts, raising his glass high.

"To love and adventure!" my mother chimes in, her eyes misty with happy tears.

As everyone sips and laughs, I smile at Declan over the rim of my glass. He winks at me with that familiar mischievous glint in his eye. The butterflies fluttering in my stomach prove to me I've made the right choice—with Declan and with our wedding plans—and I smile right back at him.

"So, when's the big day?" Darcy inquires, throwing an arm around Tabitha.

"As soon as we can arrange everything. Spencer and I already have the venue booked, though we'll need to move the date up."

Constance scrunches her brows. "How can you change the date so quickly? Wedding planners require—"

"Our friends are doing the planning," Tabby tells her. "And the venue will be Sommerleigh House."

"The home of Lord and Lady Sommerleigh? I know Hugh and his mother quite well. Rosalyn is a wonderful woman."

The double wedding is now officially on. And I can't wait.

Epilogue

Declan

The sun shines in a clear blue sky as we stand at the altar in front of the pastor, who recites the traditional wedding vows. Mother nature blessed us with perfect weather—sunshine and temperate conditions. The sunlight casts a warm glow over the lawn at Sommerleigh House, where the Parrish family has lived for generations. They graciously allowed us to have this double wedding here. It's the loveliest venue we could have hoped for.

Only six days have gone by since I proposed to Sabrina.

I can't help but steal glances at my beautiful bride, her strawberry blonde hair cascading in loose waves around her shoulders. Sabrina's green eyes sparkle with joy, and I'm struck once again by how lucky I am. My bride notices me watching her and throws me a playful wink. Her lips curve into that teasing smile I've grown to love.

Inada Ren made it to the wedding, and I can spy him in the second row. He waves and smiles. Roger the taxi driver and Daniel the desk clerk at the Savoy were invited as well. They both played a part, unwittingly, in making this day possible.

The pastor's words fade into the background as I recall the whirlwind of the past week. From our impromptu engagement in London to the mad dash to find the perfect dress for my bride, it's been a blur of excitement and anticipation. I hear my brother Leo chuckle behind me, no doubt amused by the moronic grin plastered across my face. But I can't bring myself to care. Not when I'm about to marry the woman who turned my world upside down in the best way imaginable.

The pastor's voice breaks through my reverie. "Declan Joseph Wilde, will you take Sabrina Bluebell Remington to be your wife? Will you love her, comfort her, honor and protect her, and forsaking all others, be faithful to her for as long as you both shall live?"

I lock eyes with Sabrina, my voice steady and sure. "I do."

The pastor turns to my bride. "Sabrina Bluebell Remington, will you take Declan Joseph Wilde to be your husband? Will you love him, comfort him, honor and protect him, and forsaking all others, be faithful to him for as long as you both shall live?"

Bree's eyes twinkle with mirth as she replies, "Well, I suppose I'm stuck with him now, aren't I?" A ripple of laughter runs through the gathered guests. She squeezes my hand and says, "I do. With all my heart."

As we exchange rings, I marvel at how perfectly they fit. Just like us. The pastor pronounces us husband and wife, having already married Tabitha and Spencer. I waste no time, crushing Sabrina to my chest and kissing her with all the passion and devotion she deserves. Her lips are soft and warm against mine, and I can feel her smile as we embrace.

The pastor smiles and declares, "I now pronounce you husbands and wives. Please welcome these two couples to their new lives—Tabitha and Spencer Halfenaked, and Sabrina and Declan Wilde!"

The cheers and applause from our friends and family fade into the background as I lose myself in this moment, unable to stop myself from claiming her lips again. When we finally break apart, Bree's cheeks are flushed, and her eyes are shimmering with happy tears.

"Well, Sir Declan, I think you might be stuck with me."

I grin, unable to contain my happiness. "Wouldn't have it any other way, Lady Wilde."

We turn to face our guests, hands clasped tightly together. Tabitha and Spencer look equally as radiant in their newlywed bliss. Tabitha gives Bree a tearful smile, and I'm struck by how similar yet different the two sisters are. Tabitha's elegance complements Spencer's quiet charm, while Bree's vivacity matches my own restless energy.

As we make our way down the aisle, showered with rose petals and well-wishes, I can't help but marvel at how quickly life can change. Just weeks ago, I was a lonely sod with a satisfying career yet an emptiness inside me that I never spoke of. Meeting Sabrina changed everything. I became an adventurer, bouncing from one far-flung locale to the next, chasing the most enchanting woman I'd ever met. Now I'm married to a woman who challenges me, excites me, and makes me want to be a better man.

The reception is a blur of toasts, laughter, and dancing. I twirl Bree around the dance floor, and her joyful spirit infects me too. Once we finally sit down to relax for a moment, my wife turns toward me.

"This is the best day of my life," she tells me. "I never thought I'd be the type to have a whirlwind romance and get married so quickly. But with you, it just feels right."

"I know exactly what you mean, love. It's the best day of my life too." A sense of deep satisfaction comes over me, and my eyes sting—with happiness. "Who would have thought a chance encounter at a posh hotel would lead to this?"

Bree laughs, the sound melodic and sweet. "Certainly not me. I was too busy trying to avoid you and your obnoxious charm."

"You loved my insufferable attitude from the start."

"That, and your persistence." She takes hold of my tie, running her fingers up and down the silk fabric. "But it was your ability to keep up with me on our little globe-trotting adventures that sealed the deal."

I glance round to make sure we're truly alone. Then I whisper into her ear. "Speaking of adventures, Lady Wilde, how do you feel about starting our next one tonight?"

Bree as she pulls back to meet my gaze, her eyes alight. "Why, Sir Declan, are you suggesting we make an early exit from our own wedding reception?"

I grin. "Of course I am. We do have a honeymoon to start. How does Patagonia sound?"

She toys with the hairs at my nape. "Mm, I like that idea."

"I've heard Torres del Paine National Park is a must-see."

The next morning, the four of us gather on a runway at Gatwick airport to depart for our respective honeymoons. Tabitha and Spencer are on their way to Scotland on Diana Hahn's jet. Apparently, Tabitha has always wanted to go to the land of kilts and single-malt Scotch. But I have different plans for my wife.

Once Tabitha and Spencer have boarded their jet and it's rolling down the runway, I carry Bree onto our jet. It used to be only mine. Now it belongs to both of us. We've just settled in with me in the pilot seat and Bree as my copilot.

"Where are you taking me, Declan?"

"To Patagonia, of course. I never renege on a promise." As I start up the engines, I glance at my wife. "Are you ready to see guanacos, Patagonian foxes, and stunning glaciers? We could also try out hands at gaucho life on an *estancia*. That means Patagonian cowboys and ranch houses."

She snuggles up to me as much as she can while strapped into her seat. "Ooh, that sounds fabulous. How soon will we get there?"

"Patience, my love," I say with a wink, my fingers dancing over the controls as I prepare for takeoff. "You'll find out soon enough. This will be a long flight, but it'll be worth it in the end. I have quite a few stops planned along the way including overnight stays. We could even check out Machu Picchu and anywhere else you'd like to visit."

She claps and literally jumps up and down—which is quite a feat considering that she's restrained by her seatbelt. My wife also throws in a whoop or two.

I chuckle, enchanted by her enthusiasm.

As we soar into the sky, leaving London behind, I can't help but steal glances at my new wife. The morning light streaming through the cockpit window makes the gold flecks in her green irises seem to glow.

"Where will we stop first," Bree asks. "Mexico? Panama?"

"I'm keeping our first destination a secret. Guess all you like, but I shall never tell."

With a dramatic sigh, she settles back into her seat. "Just remember, payback's a big hairy yak with bad breath."

I laugh, reaching over to squeeze her hand. "That's not the version I've heard, but yours is far more creative."

As we cruise at altitude, I can see Bree's eyes darting between the instruments and the vista outside the cockpit, her quick mind no doubt trying to piece together our destination. I've made sure to file a flight plan that's deliberately vague, wanting to preserve the surprise for as long as possible.

"You know," she muses, tapping her chin thoughtfully, "for someone who claims to be so adventurous, you're awfully fond of mysteries."

"Only when it comes to surprising my beautiful wife." I adore the way her cheeks flush every time I use the word wife. It's still new to us both, this shift in our relationship, but it feels bloody fantastic.

"Okay, Your Knightliness," Bree says, unbuckling her seatbelt so she can stand up. "If you won't tell me where we're going, I'll just have to find other ways to entertain myself."

She stretches languidly, her lithe form silhouetted against the morning sun. Her blouse has become almost transparent, and her nipples jut out as if they're inviting me to devour them.

I swallow hard, helpless to stop my eyes from tracing every curve of her body. "What did you have in mind, Lady Wilde?"

"Oh, I don't know." She stretches her arms high, exposing her navel. "Maybe I'll go explore the jet. See what kind of trouble I can get into."

"Sabrina," I warn, my voice low. "You're playing with fire."

"Good thing I like it hot, then."

My wife sashays toward the back of the jet, swaying her hips in a deliberate attempt to tease me until I give in and fuck her.

I groan, gripping the controls tighter as I try to focus on flying. But my mind keeps drifting to thoughts of Bree and what she might be up to in the cabin behind me. The autopilot is engaged, but I'm reluctant to leave my post. After all, I am the pilot.

A few minutes later, I hear the soft pad of bare feet approaching. Sabrina reappears, now wearing nothing but one of my dress shirts, the white fabric barely skimming the tops of her thighs.

"Mm, I'm getting warm all over," she purrs, perching on the edge of my seat, "I was thinking, since you won't tell me where we're going, maybe I can seduce the information out of you."

I inhale sharply, my eyes roving over Bree's long, bare legs and the pearls of her nipples that I can just see beneath the fabric. Those peaks have stiffened even more. My voice turns husky when I point out, "Darling, you're making it very difficult for me to fly this jet."

"That's the idea, Sir Declan." She leans over the back of my seat to brush her lips over my ear—and to give me a fantastic view of her bare tits. "Now, one more time, are you going to tell me where we're going, or do I need to up my game?"

I grip the controls tighter, torn between lust and responsibility. "Sabrina, darling, as much as I'd love to play this game with you right now, I really do need to focus on flying."

She feigns a pout, running a finger down my chest. "Spoilsport. Fine, I'll behave...for now."

With a sassy grin, she settles back into the co-pilot's seat, crossing her legs in a way that makes my cock twitch. I force my attention back to the controls and struggle to focus on our flight path. But Sabrina isn't done toying with me. She spreads her thighs just enough that I can glimpse the pink, slippery flesh of her folds.

My barely clothed wife gets a sneaky look on her face. "I could always just check the flight plan myself."

"Nice try, pet. But I've made sure it's not that easy to figure out."

She sinks back in her seat. "I do love a good puzzle."

For the next hour, Bree alternates between trying to guess our destination and attempting to distract me with increasingly creative methods. It's a delightful torture, and I find myself both dreading and eagerly anticipating our arrival. At least my wife put some clothes on. She halfway to giving me a heart attack.

Finally, as we begin our descent, I turn to my wife. "Ready to find out where we're going?"

Bree sits up straighter. "Yes! I've been dying to find out."

I grasp her wrist when she tries to lean over the console and get a peek at our itinerary. "Uh-uh-uh, Bree. Do I need to blindfold you?"

She covers her eyes with her hands. "Tell me when I can look."

As we make our final descent, I guide the plane toward our destination. The lush green landscape below comes into view, dotted with vibrant colors and sparkling water.

I pat her thigh. "All right, darling. You can look now."

Bree uncovers her eyes and gasps as she takes in the panorama. Crystal clear turquoise waters stretch out before us, fringed by pristine white sand beaches and lush tropical forests. In the distance, majestic mountains rise up, their peaks shrouded in mist.

"Declan," she breathes, her eyes wide with wonder. "Is this… are we in Bora Bora?"

I spread my arms wide and grin. "Welcome to French Polynesia, Lady Wilde. I thought we could use a bit of paradise for our honeymoon. After that, we'll make our way to South America. You can choose the flight plan for that leg of our holiday."

We touch down on the small island runway, and I taxi into the hanger. Bree can barely contain her enthusiasm. The moment we come to a stop, she's unbuckling her restraints and bouncing in her seat like an excited child.

She flings her arms around me. "Oh, Declan, it's absolutely breathtaking! I can't believe you planned all this."

I reach over and take her hand, bringing it to my lips for a soft kiss. "Only the best for my bride. I wanted our honeymoon to be unforgettable."

"Come on, let's go," she urges, tugging at my arm. "I want to feel that sand between my toes."

I laughter and her enthusiasm are infectious. "Patience, Bree. We've got two whole weeks to explore every inch of this paradise."

The moment I open the door, Sabrina races down the stairs, and I rush to catch up with her. She leaps into my arms, her hair flying around her face. I can't resist ravishing her mouth with steamy kisses. As my wife drags me away from the jet, a wide smile stretches my lips and I feel something I never imagined I'd experience.

Happiness. Pure, unadulterated happiness.

And I'll have the rest of my life to enjoy it.

I hoist Bree up into my arms. "Let me carry you to our bungalow, darling. A knight should treat his bride like the treasure she is."

And our adventure has only just begun.

Love the

Hot Brits

series?

Visit
AnnaDurand.com

to subscribe to her newsletter for
updates on forthcoming books in this series
plus exclusive content!

Anna Durand is a bestselling, multi-award-winning author of contemporary and paranormal romance. Her books have earned bestseller status on every major retailer and wonderful reviews from readers around the world. But that's the boring spiel. Here are the really cool things you want to know about Anna!

Born on Lackland Air Force Base in Texas, Anna grew up moving here, there, and everywhere thanks to her dad's job as an instructor pilot. She's lived in Texas (twice), Mississippi, California (twice), Michigan (twice), and Alaska—and now Ohio.

As for her writing, Anna has always invented stories in her head, but she didn't write them down until her teen years. Those first awful books went into the trash can a few years later, though she learned a lot from those stories. Eventually, she would pen her first romance novel, the paranormal romance *Willpower*, and she's never looked back since.

To get exclusive content, join Anna's Facebook group, Anna's Romance Addicts, or sign up for her newsletter.

Visit AnnaDurand.com to sign up.